hours ⌐
librarie

16 S:
9 D

Mary Hobson was born in London in 1926. One of three children, she alone was sent to boarding school. She subsequently studied piano at the Royal Academy of Music, raised four children and cared for a severely disabled husband, before three of her four novels were published by Heinemann in the early 1980s. The fourth, *Promenade*, completed in 1984, has remained unpublished until now. In 1988, she started a Russian degree at London University, studying in Moscow as the USSR collapsed and completing her PhD at the age of 74.

Also by Mary Hobson

Fiction
This Place is a Madhouse

Oh Lily

Poor Tom

Poetry
Death and the Biker

Non-fiction
The Feast: An Autobiography

Translation
Aleksandr Griboedov's Woe from Wit:
A commentary and translation

Evgenii Onegin, Pushkin: A parallel text

Forthcoming translation
Evgenii Onegin, Pushkin

After Onegin:
The Last Seven Years,
Poems and Letters of Aleksandr Segeevich Pushkin

Promenade

Mary Hobson

Thorpewood Publishing
2015

The moral right of Mary Hobson to be identified as the author
of this work has been asserted in accordance with
the Copyright Designs and Patents Act, 1988.

All rights reserved. No part of this publication may be reproduced
or transmitted in any form or by any means, electrical or mechanical,
including photocopy, recording, or any information storage and retrieval
system, without permission in writing from the publisher.

This book is a work of fiction. Names, characters, businesses,
organisations, places and events are either the product of the author's
imagination or are used fictitiously. Any resemblance to actual persons,
living or dead, events or locales is entirely coincidental.

Copyright © 2015 Mary Hobson
First published 2015 by Thorpewood Publishing
57 Thorpewood Avenue, London, SE26 4BY
thorpewoodpublishing@gmail.com

ISBN 9781910873001
eISBN 9781910873014

Cover design by WEEF
Cover photograph of Worthing seaside shelter © Elaine Purtell
and reproduced with her kind permission.

Printed in England and the United States by Lightning Source

Contents

Foreword

As soon as our dear friend Mary gave us *Promenade* to read we knew it had to be published. The story of a friendship between a resident of a nursing home, Bideawhile, and a pupil from a nearby boarding school, the novel is an intelligent, sparky delight. Like Mary Hobson's well-received earlier novels (*This Place is a Madhouse*, *Oh Lily* and *Poor Tom*), all published in the early 1980s. *Promenade* is immensely readable and characterised by unflinching examination of emotional truths, cool wit and brilliant dialogue. To our minds, it is reminiscent of the work of Iris Murdoch, Penelope Fitzgerald and Tessa Hadley. Like Penelope Fitzgerald, Mary came to novel-writing relatively late in life. Her first book was published when she was in her early fifties. Her next two followed in quick succession. All three garnered praise:

> There is comic realism here of a high order ... Mrs Hobson is a writer to be trusted ... she tells a deceptively simple tale with unstrained skill. (John Osborne, *The Evening Standard*, March 1981)

However, Mary's publisher then rejected *Promenade*: apparently worried that the subject of old age might be off-putting to readers at that time. We believe that today's readers are more willing to engage with such material – especially when it is as well written as *Promenade* – and that the relationship between the generations and society's attitude towards, and care of, the elderly have taken on a new urgency as areas of intellectual and artistic exploration in recent years.

Mary was not to be beaten by her publisher's rejection. By that time she had other fish to fry. During a stay in hospital one of her daughters had given her a copy of *War and Peace* in English to pass the time. She adored it so much that she determined to study Russian in order to read it in the original. This she did, going to university in the UK and then moving to Moscow for a while during the time the USSR was collapsing and completing her PhD at the age of 74. She went on to become an acclaimed translator of Pushkin, winning the Pushkin gold medal for translation. Just recently Mary has penned her autobiography - *The Feast*. Penned is the right verb. She writes in longhand; *The Feast* has been typed up by a neighbour who has suffered from agoraphobia for years and, through this project, has found a new energy and a firm friendship with Mary. Like many episodes in Mary's eventful life, their relationship is a story in itself.

As the autobiography details, Mary was hardly lying idle before her careers as a novelist and then translator took off. She served in the Women's Voluntary Service, stationed near Suez, and studied piano at the Royal Academy of Music as a young woman. She then married, raised four children and cared for a disabled husband (badly incapacitated by an illness early in their marriage) before turning to novels. Mary has suffered more than her fair share of emotional hardship. In addition to her husband's illness and the subsequent toll of care, her only son died in his thirties in a road accident, and her marriage finally ended in divorce. But Mary's resilience and spirit have seen her through all of these trials and her accomplishments over the past two decades are proof that it's never too late to embark on new adventures and strive for fulfilment and excellence. Mary's life story will be published in the coming months.

As even our bare-bones telling of her life makes clear, Mary is a fighter, an intellectual, an inspiration and a force of nature. She has overcome the barriers of her sex, her generation, her age and her family obligations to achieve her heart's desire. In so doing, she has enriched the lives of others through her artistic achievements – and enjoyed the mutual devotion and support of her three daughters. As soon as you meet Mary you know that you are in the presence of someone extraordinary. And then she tops it off by serving up delicious blinis, washed down with neat vodka.

We hope that you enjoy meeting Mary through *Promenade* and that this will be the beginning of a rewarding literary relationship with a remarkable woman.

Helen Shreeve and Rebecca Asher

Author's note

I owe a huge debt of gratitude to my good friends Rebecca Asher and Helen Shreeve. Thirty years ago Heinemann took my first two novels at once with options on the next two. I wrote the third one. They published it. I wrote *Promenade*. They rejected it. I tell myself that old age and isolation were not much discussed in the early eighties; the sales manager said 'I can't sell that'.

Heartbreak ensued. I stopped writing novels and life took a different direction. The book lay on my shelves at the bottom of a heap, as presented to my agents, A.M. Heath - all typed out on my little Olivetti.

About a year ago Helen read it. She passed it on to Rebecca. Since then they have both worked tirelessly to get it published. At some point I had had the book made fit to be sent about electronically, but it was in "read only" form. Rebecca retyped the whole novel.

I was 57 when I wrote *Promenade*. Now I am 88 as old as Nora, the oldest inhabitant of Bideawhile. Then I was imagining old age; now I am experiencing it. It's not so different. I still feel 57. Until I move.

I want to thank the two of them for the present joy I feel in the publication of my *Promenade*. Most of all I want to thank them for believing in it.

For Matthew, Emma, Sarah and Lucy

Chapter I

The ladies of Bideawhile were accustomed to thinking about death. For eighty years or more, day after day after day, they had thought about the next important thing that would happen to them. Death being now the next – the only – important thing that could happen to them, they thought about it. And they talked about it.

'What I can't stand is those cheap handles.'

The ladies, assembled for tea in the lounge, sat with their backs to the picture window and considered cheap handles. Children ran past on the cold pavement; a philodendron drooped in the heat; the budgie pecked at its cuttle fish.

'None of us can, dear. But you try asking for brass.' Mrs Annerley, unaware of offending, persisted. 'They're plastic, those silvery things. I'm sure they are. Painted plastic.'

'They wouldn't hold,' someone said.

Miss Shard ignored the irrelevance. 'You won't get brass.'

'You can get anything if you pay.' Mrs Annerley had been at Bideawhile for less than a month and was used to speaking her mind.

Several ladies turned to Miss Shard for guidance; could this be right? Miss Shard gripped her handbag.

'We'll be having tea soon.' Miss Kess had been the headmistress of a primary school until her retirement, twenty-six years ago. Her attempts at distraction, so effective with the intake class, were not always welcome.

'I'm perfectly aware of the time,' Miss Shard said. 'She brings it after Playschool.' She leaned back in her chair and looked through the square window at a man making a pot.

'Anyway,' Mrs Annerley said. 'My son'll see to all that.' He would certainly visit her this Sunday. After a month. "And no visits for the first month please, Mrs Annerley," the headmaster had told her. She could see Guy standing there, signalling his despair. Could remember wondering if perhaps, after all, the really good start in life for which they had saved so hard and so long could be less than an advantage. Silly really. She'd cried all the way home in the train and then he'd loved it there. Couldn't wait to get back after the holidays. "You can't wait to get away from me and Dad," she used to tell him. How they laughed.

'In the end he never got it.' Nora, alone of all the ladies, sat at the window, facing a wall of white net; she spoke out as though she meant to be heard but without turning her head.

Nothing united the ladies more surely than their dislike of Nora Gitting. Her habit of releasing random sentences from her interior monologue unnerved them. As Miss Kess had said, more than once, you never knew where you were with her. It was Miss Shard's opinion that they shouldn't be with her at all. 'That woman needs seeing to,' she said. Something more punitive than therapeutic, she seemed to suggest.

'What didn't he get, dear?' Mrs Annerley asked her.

Miss Shard sighed. 'I wouldn't pander to her. She'll only take advantage. Then we'll have "never got it" all evening.'

'Never got it,' Nora said.

Miss Shard turned her head to conceal raised eyebrows and a tight smile. Then she loosed it on Mrs Annerley. 'You remind me of Irene Crose, dear. She left it all to her son to do. Well. He was on holiday, wasn't' he? In Spain. Stayed there, too. Sent a wreath. Enormous thing it was. Waited till it was all over, comes home and helps himself to the lot.'

'He'd've had to pay in the end, surely?' Mrs Annerley said.

'Oh yes, he paid. The bare minimum. No tea, nothing like that. I'm glad she didn't see how it was done. Poor Rene. I'll never forget that funeral.'

'Not that he cared,' Nora said. 'Going like that.'

Only Mrs Annerley assumed this apparent hitting on the subject under discussion could be anything more than an amusing coincidence. She waited in silence to be told how he went.

'Never got a penny of it.'

'Goodness, can't somebody stop her?' Miss Shard said.

'I've put aside for it in the post office.' Miss Kess had attended the funeral of Mrs Crose.

'So did Irene Crose, Miss Shard assured her. 'Putting it in's all very fine. It's getting it out.'

'I've paid in for mine. Every week, regular as the clock. Right up till I stopped working. A hundred pounds I'll get. I've seen too much of it.' Mrs Shreeve, though deaf, had caught the word 'funeral'.

Miss Shard drew breath to explain the inadequacy of this sum, remembered that Mrs Shreeve's batteries had run out and saved her strength.

'No veneers for me,' Mrs Shreeve continued. 'Solid elm and a decent do. They can keep their grant.'

Miss Shard sniffed her pity as such ignorance.

'They might as well for all the good it is,' Mrs Annerley said. That Miss Shard wasn't being very nice to the poor old soul.

'Not that he cared,' Nora said.

It was more than Miss Shard could stand. 'What that woman's doing here is a mystery to me.'

'I expect she's got her pension like the rest of us,' Mrs Annerley said.

'Dr Stacey would never have allowed it.'

Miss Shard had been Dr Stacey's receptionist until she retired at sixty-five. She had defended his waiting room for nearly thirty years. The way they tried it on, she told the ladies. She stood between the doctor and his patients, a blue-rinsed Cerberus in a white coat, deflecting cut fingers to Casualty, terrorising medical certificates back to work, rendering the semi-articulate perfectly speechless, shaming the illiterate. And she had done it all for Dr Stacey. Had made herself disliked for him. Allowed him to hide in his office, preserve his image of harassed concern, pretended that for him as well as for them her word was law. 'I don't know how I'm going to manage without you,' he said when she left. He had introduced her to Bideawhile, where he visited each week, so that – as he felt bound to assure her – he could keep an eye on her. It had given her, at first, a special status, to which she still held tenaciously, though the doctor himself had long since died.

In medical matters her opinion was respected at least as much as that of Dr Walsh, the young woman who succeeded Dr Stacey. Sometimes more. Even Mrs Fransey, proprietress and matron of Bideawhile, consulted her. Diagnosis was her forte. A reputation based on some lucky guesses was finally established by one really inspired shot in the dark. In an attempt to prevent young Dr Walsh from moving her friend, Irene Crose, to the psychiatric ward of the local hospital she had written to Irene's son, telling him that she knew a thyroid deficiency when she saw one and urging him to demand tests. The test had proved her right. Irene took the tablets and improved amazingly. Useless for Dr Walsh to explain that those were the tests she had already discussed with the hospital, were in fact the reason for the suggested admission. That young girl would have had Irene Crose put away if it hadn't been for Miss Shard, the story went, and Miss Shard could not deny it.

'Dr Stacey wouldn't have allowed it. Not for a minute,' she said, pursuing the subject of Nora Gitting.

Mrs Annerley refused the bait. A month had taught her all she needed to know about Dr Stacey. She smiled in a friendly way and feigned deafness.

'Buried with ham, they used to say.' Mrs Shreeve laughed quietly to herself, still comforted by the prospect of solid elm.

'Haven't you got any batteries, dear?' Miss Shard shouted.

Mrs Shreeve looked surprised. 'Well. They can do everything nowadays, can't they? Not that I'd've expected hand made. But elm. Solid elm.'

A trolley rattled at the door of the lounge.

'Cave,' Miss Kess said. 'It's Mrs Fransey.'

'K.V?' Mrs Annerley turned to her for explanation. She seemed a sensible woman. There would be an explanation. Though she could understand why they smiled. There was something odd about Miss Kess. An unfinished look. More like a very old child than a woman. She reminded Mrs Annerley of the little green apricots that lay on the lawn after the June fall, wrinkled and rotting, old before they'd ever been properly young. She wondered if they would manage the apricot jam without her next year. Or perhaps they wouldn't bother.

'My children always used to say that. When they heard me coming. "Cave, it's the Kestrel!" I used to wear a necklace that jingled, specially.'

It seemed a thoughtful warning, more credible than the ferocious nickname. Mrs Annerley tried to imagine Miss Kess swooping in for the kill and smiled. 'I see. But who's coming?'

Mrs Fransey manoeuvred the tea trolley over the non-slip rug at the door and positioned it in the centre of the room.

'Doesn't like us talking about funerals.' Mis Kess leaned over

5

the arm of her chair and mouthed the words under cover of a song about jumping in puddles.

'Now ladies.' Mrs Fransey always referred to the residents of Bideawhile as ladies, regarding it, in most cases as a kindly exaggeration, part of her stock-in-trade. 'What have you all been talking about behind my back?' A need to know sharpened the laugh behind this habitual joke.

The ladies laughed with her. It was their part in the ritual. She was very good, Mrs Fransey. They were really very lucky to have her. 'We've been talking about which of us is going to run off with your handsome husband,' Miss Kess said. They laughed again, reassuring her. She was a good girl, Mrs Fransey. It was understood that some of them weren't so good.

'Now. While it's brewing.' Mrs Fransey took a notebook and pencil from the pocket of her nylon overall. 'Who's out for Sunday lunch?'

There was a moment's pause, while Miss Shard pretended to give the matter thought. 'Ah yes,' she said. 'That's right. My nephew's calling for me at eleven. No. I shan't be in, dear.' She was the only lady who called Mrs Fransey 'dear'. 'Not this Sunday.'

After Miss Shard's name had been entered in the book one or two other ladies were afraid that they too would be out. Just for Sunday lunch. Miss Kess's being invited to stay over-night in order to babysit for her niece's children caused comment, not all of it kind.

'That's nice for you, Miss Kess,' Mrs Fransey said. 'Can't they get their usual? Only I don't want you overdoing it. And I know how tiring children can be when they've got you to themselves.'

'So do I,' Miss Kess reminded her, as though they were sharing some splendid joke.

'O yes. Of course. Well.' Mrs Fransey raised her eyebrows.

Let us hope that you will not be tried beyond your strength they said, landing you back here in a right old state on Sunday afternoon in the middle of Bette Davis.

Nora stared, unmoving, through the picture window.

'Did Miss Gitting hear, do you think?' Mrs Annerley asked. They went on as though the poor woman wasn't there at all.

'Don't worry, Mrs Anerley. Ye have Miss Gitting with you always, as they say.' Mrs Fransey laughed and the ladies laughed with her.

Why do they do it? Mrs Annerley wondered.

They'd be home from school now. The children. Guy was quite right. They couldn't have gone on sharing a room for ever. This really was the only sensible arrangement. It didn't have much else to recommend it, but you had to hand it to him, it was sensible. Mrs Annerley sighed, we lost him to that school, she thought. It wasn't his fault. It was how we wanted him to be. The snobbery. Keeping in the background on speech-day like a pair of second class second raters. Fools, we were. Jim would never have let him do this. And this is the best. This is a place with a waiting list.

Mrs Shreeve, who had been searching her handbag for several minutes, suddenly emptied it into her lap. 'I had it this morning, I know I did,' she said. She began to drop pieces of paper to the floor, one by one. 'Because I made sure before I came down.'

'What is it dear,' Mrs Fransey said. 'What have you lost?' The old woman felt about in the empty pockets of her empty handbag. 'My Policy. It was in here this morning, I made sure before I came down.'

'You'd much better give it to me like everybody else.' She knelt at Mrs Shreeve's feet and made a neat pile of letters and Christmas cards. 'Look at this mess.' She held her face close to Mrs Shreeve's and exaggerated each mouth movement beyond all hope of lip reading. 'Aren't you a naughty girl? Giving me all this trouble.'

Mrs Shreeve looked at her, not understanding, and began to cry. Someone's taken it' she said. 'Someone's been in here and taken it.'

Miss Shard barely glanced at Nora Gitting but one or two ladies thought they took her meaning. They frowned and shook their heads, or expressed their disapproval in a noisy release of suction between the tongue and the top set. Miss Kess searched in her knitting bag for her post office book.

'Who could have taken it?' Mrs Fransey said. 'You'll be accusing me next.'

Everyone who could hear it laughed politely at this absurdity. Miss Shard smiled. 'I should look in her other bag,' she said. 'It's where she usually finds it.'

Mrs Fransey found the policy in the other bag and restored it to Mrs Shreeve. Several ladies looked a little ashamed, but no accusation had been made, an apology was out of the question. The suspicion lay between them, unresolved, irrational; it was only what you'd expect with that sort of person.

Nora still stared, not seeing, through the picture window. She was aware of the sound but not the sense. A sudden silence might have reached her but the words fell short. In any case, she had no time to waste on words. Someone had to remember it all. Her family was dead, her friends were dead, her enemies were dead. All her heroes had died, one by one, never knowing how she had worshipped them, how she could have loved them. More fool them, she thought. There was no one left who remembered her as a girl, as a young woman even; no one who found it easy to call her Nora. Miss Gitting, it was now. Mind you, Arthur had always called her Miss Gitting. Gone off and got himself killed and never called her anything else but Miss Gitting. Even that one time under the pier. Miss Gitting. He couldn't wait with the rest of them. Had to go off one of the first. Flower of England they called him afterwards. When they were dead. 'More of a weed,' Nora said, and sighed, remembering under the pier.

'What did you say, Miss Gitting?' Mrs Annerley asked.

Miss Shard breathed deeply and looked at the ceiling, expressing the view that there were some people who would never learn.

Nora lay in the dark and salty triangle where the beach sloped up to meet the pier on the promenade. She heard the slap and suck of the summer tide, felt her hand plunge into the orange stones, rolled smooth as a bowl of lentils set to soak, saw Arthur sitting hunched on his jacket, hugging his knees instead of her, starting at the sea. He seemed to care more about his broken pen than anything. He'd left it in his top pocket and she'd sat on it. Well. He'd offered her the jacket. Proper little Walter Raleigh. Now this. And all about a rotten pen.

'What are you being so mouldy about?' she asked him.

Arther looked over his shoulder. 'Do your blouse up. Someone might come.' He looked away again.

'Ha.'

'What do you mean, "Ha."?

Nora was silent.

'We can't do it here,' Arthur said.

'You couldn't do it anywhere.'

That was it. That did it. Off he went and got himself killed. Nora always referred to Arthur's death in this way. Other people's sons and lovers were killed. Arthur got himself killed. It was his own fault. He needn't have gone. Or not then, at any rate. 'No good looking at me,' she said angrily, defending herself.

'I'd have that tea, Miss Gitting,' Mrs Annerley advised her. 'It'll be stewed if you wait any longer.'

'I wouldn't bother, dear.' Miss Shard smiled. 'You'll get used to her after a bit. Well, I shouldn't think she'll be here that long. Mrs Fransey's going to have a word with Dr Walsh's friend.'

'Would that be the Almoner?' Mrs Annerley said. It had to work. There was no going back. It would only upset the children. And she could always sit in her room. Although she had found that Mrs Fransey didn't encourage it during the day. She didn't like her ladies to mope. 'Can't have you moping up there on your own, can we?' she would say. Moping was the very thing she feared. Moping led to thinking, and thinking to the realisation of loss; lost husbands, lost children, lost grandchildren. Except, in some cases, on Sundays. Worse, thinking led to the inescapable conclusion that they were waiting to die and might as well get on with it. Mrs Fransey had seen ladies mope themselves to death in a matter of weeks. It was why she thought television so wonderful for the elderly. She got the best, twenty-one inch colour, switched it on in the morning and turned it off at night. It fitted nicely into the old fireplace when the central heating was installed. They like something to sit round, she always said. And so much safer than coal! There really was nothing like it for taking them out of themselves.

Her assumption that the ladies, who had faced, between them, an impressive assortment of disasters, could no longer be safely left within themselves was better understood by the ladies than by Mrs Fransey. Mrs Fransey, they perceived, liked surfaces. Of wipe-clean plastic wherever possible. She liked things that looked like other things; teapots like cottages, nutcrackers like female thighs, brought out each Christmas to be smirked and tutted over, tea cosies like beehives and toilet roll holders like tea cosies. If an object could not be totally disguised it seldom went uncovered, a policy she applied equally to the less pleasant facts of life.

'Well now, are we all settled down for a nice quiet evening? Only I'll have my hubby after me if I don't go and see to his tea.' This was an easily recognisable cover; beneath it lay the truth of the matter, perfectly well understood by all the ladies, with the exception of Mrs Annerley and Nora. Jack Fransey was an empty looking man a few years younger than his wife; he did odd jobs about the house, waited at table in a white jacket, going handsomely about his life like a fighter pilot or a film star who chose not to use his talent, smiling a one-sided smile with the more mobile half of his face, a near miss of a man.

The married ladies laughed. Hadn't their men been difficult and demanding, just like Mrs Fransey's man? Why do we put up with it? they wondered. She was a good girl, Mrs Fransey, but a bit nervy.

'I wouldn't have thought Mr Fransey was the masterful sort,' Mrs Annerley said, laughing, when his wife could be supposed to have reached her kitchen. There was a moment's uncomfortable silence. This was a tactless infringement of the rules. Not playing the game.

'She doesn't have an easy time of it, I can tell you,' Miss Shard said, speaking for them all. Her supporters murmured their approval.

'I've nothing against him. He just seems a bit...' Mrs Annerley wished that she had never mentioned the wretched man.

'He's a perfectly normal young man,' Miss Kess said.

The possibility of his being otherwise had not occurred to Mrs Annerley till now. 'Oh I'm sure he is,' she said, re-running her month-long acquaintance with Mr Fransey, allowing the oddities to fall into place.

'And he's devoted to Mrs Fransey. Do anything for her.' Again the murmur of approval.

Mrs Annerley thought that she would finish her tea and then go to her room.

'At least I got him before they did,' Nora said. Her voice was harsh, defiant. She jumped up and ran from the room. Or would have done. Only they were holding her down, pressing the breath from her lungs, the strength from her muscles. She got to her feet, fighting all the way, and then fell back against her chair.

'Call Mrs Fransey. Quick dear. The bell.' Miss Shard directed Mrs Shreeve's attention towards the bell beside the fire-place, using her stick with the black rubber ferule. Mrs Fransey came running, followed by her husband. Together they lifted Nora into an upright position. Jack Fransey drew the curtains against the darkening street.

'You do see?' Miss Shard said quietly as Mrs Fransey passed her chair.

'I'll talk to Dr Walsh,' Mrs Fransey promised.

'Good afternoon ladies.' Mr Fransey smiled the lop-sided smile.

'Come and get your tea,' Mrs Fransey said. She took his arm and accompanied him from the room.

They sat in silence for a while and watched a fairy story in Polish. 'Irene Crose went like that,' Miss Shard said suddenly. 'One minute she was reading us a card from her son. The next, finish. Out like a light.' And that woman still sitting there, a misery to herself and everybody else. There's no justice, she thought.

A suitor failed to make the princess smile and was beheaded. 'I never think these foreign stories are quite suitable for children,' Miss Kess said. 'I do hope my niece's little girls aren't watching it.'

Nora stared through the drawn curtains, angry and sad at the waste of it all. How was I to know he'd go and get himself killed, she thought. It's no good blaming me.

Chapter II

The Mount was not a very successful school. Those girls who got themselves into university would have done so without its help, and they were rare enough to be worth a half-holiday apiece. The food was adequate, the accommodation spartan. 'We aim to give your daughters something that money can't buy,' Miss Byfield told prospective parents. This was true. Almost everything that money can't buy was valued very highly at the Mount. Manners, discipline, pulling together, anything that could be imparted to the girls without the expense of a specialist teacher. The staff, a migrant bunch who usually taught at the Mount for a term or two on their way to somewhere else were seldom employed as specialists. 'We all muck in,' was the way Miss Fernihough (Junior Games, English and Spanish) put it. She was the only permanency, a sort of acting unpaid vice-principal, the Mount's first head-girl, Miss Byfield's friend. By the time the younger teachers had got the hang of it and decided on the form their protest should take it was hardly worth bothering because they were leaving anyway at the end of the term. Mucking in flourished. Everything doubled as something else. The lab doubled as sewing room, its benches being ideally suited to cutting out. The smell of gas from unlit Bunsen burners, turned on in murderous fun, had made sewing unacceptable to generations of Mount girls. Novels, on the other hand, had acquired the status of forbidden fruit. The library doubled as sixth-form common room, a plan which excluded the younger girls, except on brief supervised visits, and rendered the dullest fiction desirable.

Most ingenious of all Miss Byfield's economies was the gymnasium. One end was a raised and curtained stage, the other a fishmonger's. Or at least it seemed to Margaret that it ought to have been a fishmonger's. It had a proper fishmonger's shop front and a pole with a hook for rolling it up. But on Sundays Harris arranged all the chairs to face the fishmonger's and the prefects opened up shop to disclose not fish, but an altar. The pleasure that this transformation gave Margaret, the knowledge of what lay concealed behind the weekday stacked chairs, springboards and vaulting horses was acute and private. She had watched it for the first time on the previous Sunday, her first at the Mount.

Two days at the Mount had shown her that she had lived till now in a simple dream. She had put on the new clothes, watched the new trunk being loaded into the guard's van, seen her mother a waving midget on the platform, and never guessed for one moment at the possibility of change. Soap burned her face, elastic bit into her chin, the rough train velvet rubbed the bare backs of her knees. None of it warned her. She sat in an exaltation of newness, travelling most hopefully. Her legs didn't reach the floor of the carriage; they dangled in metallic gusts of warm air as she rocked and shuddered to the pleasant motion.

By that first Sunday she had learned all about life. Useful stuff. Whom to avoid, when to lie, where to hide. The stage was a good place. It was from the stage, concealed by the black velvet curtains that smelt so bitterly of dust and dye, that she had first witnessed the transformation of the fishmonger's. Now she stood among the juniors and longed for chapel to be over. Morning service, taken by Mr Bury, a retired clergyman glad of a little untaxed extra, was making her forget that here at least she was safe.

The choir, trained by Miss Fernihough, accompanied on the harmonium by one of the migrants, was getting on with the psalm. Miss Fernihough had never fully understood the metrical system indicated in her psalter by accents and vertical lines. She attempted to make each verse the same length by a simple method of her own. The more words before the first accent, the more quickly they were to be sung. In the longer verses this encouraged some astonishing feats of diction; the choir would arrive at the accent in a breathless gabble, lean heavily on it while they waited for stragglers, then complete the verse at a brisk march.

After the singing Mr Bury gave his sermon, scholarly and unintelligible. The children watched the clock. Margaret listened to the buzz and thump of a bluebottle dashing itself against the window, followed it with envy out into the cold sunshine and turned again to the Table of Kindred and Affinity. Uncle Mike shalt not do it to Mum, Dad shalt not do it to Auntie Vi, Dad shalt not do it to my daughter. I shalt not let him if I have one, she thought. I should bloody well think not. Whatever it is. She wondered if it could really be what they said it was.

'We must strike out the "I",' Mr Bury was saying. 'The message of the cross is a striking out of the "I". Now, I hear you say. What could be harder than that?'

These benches, Margaret thought. The senior had proper chairs with places on the back for hymnbooks, but the juniors sat at the front on backless benches. Dad shalt not do it to Gran or me, and he can't do it to Gran's mum because she hasn't got one. There was only one hymn still unsung on the hymn board. Not one she knew, all about the blood of a lamb. Why did he look so good when secretly, inside, he was into all this blood and dead lambs stuff? She tried to guess what they would have for lunch. Last Sunday's had been really nice. Ah, but the

Sunday before that. The last before the Mount. Dressing up in the uniform to make them proud. I can't leave before I've grown out of it, Margaret thought. It cost two hundred pounds. She stretched her arms down beside her till her shoulders ached but the sleeves of her blazer still covered her knuckles.

Mr Bury finished his sermon. They were to remember what the Lord had suffered for them as they joined him in singing the final hymn, he said. Margaret stood with the rest and opened her hymn book. She wondered if Jesus could have stuck it at The Mount.

'Go on,' someone pushed at her. 'Get a move on.' She shuffled in line to the door. Above the sweet Victorian harmonies of the outgoing voluntary she could hear the Seniors, first to be freed, laughing and shouting in the corridor. She left Jesus where she had hidden him, behind the fishmonger's shop-front with a supply of biscuits and the left overs from break-milk, stopped dreaming and made her plan. There was half an hour before lunch. If she could get through the seniors unnoticed she could stay in the lavatory till the bell. The end one was the funniest. Harris hadn't painted it over yet. And there was no need to worry about lunch. Even Julie O'Connor couldn't do much at meal times. Meals and lessons, Margaret had learned, were the only certain safety. There had to be a teacher for meals and lessons. And chapel, of course. Apart from that, it was you against them.

She could see that it was not the same for all the new girls; some of them had made friends with each other and one very tall girl with real silk pyjamas had been going around with Julie O'Connor from the very first day. It's me, she thought. I'm different.

At ten, Margaret had known herself to be both beautiful and clever. Suddenly she was surrounded, all day long, by people who thought her neither. I don't care, she thought, caring deeply. To admit the desirability of any change would be treachery; their perception of her as different was in a half-understood way a criticism of every one she loved, and she would have no part in it. She clung to her difference and they disliked her for it. 'Look at the newbug,' they implored each other, 'look how she walks, how she eats, how she talks. How ever can her parents afford the fees? I bet they don't pay. I bet she comes here free. Here, newbug. Are you The Byfield's pet charity? I bet we've had jumble sales for you.'

Miss Fernihough, who took the junior walk on Sundays, felt sorry for her. 'She doesn't really fit, does she?' she told them in the staff room. 'And girls can be so cruel.'

'You seem to have got me again,' she said to Margaret, when no one chose the child as a partner. She usually let them walk three together at the back of the crocodile if she was taking an odd number of girls but it would surely be kinder not to insist.

Margaret stared up at her without speaking. What an unattractive child. Could she be really healthy? No colour in her cheeks at all, all skin and bone. Her lip was hitched up over a pair of large front teeth, her fine mousey hair did nothing to soften a bumpy forehead on which one or two blue threads wriggled about looking for cover. That mac'll see her into the sixth form, Miss Fernihough thought. She'll have worn it out before ever it fits her. 'Right,' she called to her juniors. 'Are we all ready?' No breaking ranks till we're actually on the Promenade.'

The Mount was situated in the residential hinterland of a small town on the south coast whose stony beach and mud coloured sand had preserved it, nearly undeveloped, for half a century. It had a pier and a promenade and a bandstand. A line of quiet hotels faced it out along the Parade. One or two closed each winter to be reopened, briefly, as fish restaurants, sale rooms or poodle parlours. The little side streets offered bed and breakfast, the sweetshops were hung with beach balls, buckets and plastic spades. But the real business of the town was with the elderly. On their behalf the council went in for roadside seats, attempted to vote down the amusement arcades in favour of clock-golf, sent meals, libraries, district nurses wheeling along the broad flat roads, resisted change.

The half a mile of road which lay between the Promenade and The Mount was quite as flat as the rest. Miss Byfield had named the school, bought with her father's money, after her father's home. She joked to parents about Parnassus, but personally she saw nothing incongruous in the name. The school and her headship of it raised her up, singled her out for special respect. Without it she would be down there like poor Fern, taking orders, getting old.

Miss Fernihough held Margaret's hand and strode off towards the sea. It was a fine September afternoon. Almost like summer. A mood of baseless optimism seized her. It was not too late. Things could still happen. 'Almost like summer, isn't it?' she called back to her juniors. The juniors waited until she had turned away from them. Then they writhed and clutched at each other, struggling to suppress their giggles. Not that they found her remark especially funny. Individually they respected, even feared Miss Fernihough; but as a group they were possessed. The giggles lay just below the surface, a badly packed explosive in an unstable condition. The most sensible remark could detonate them.

'Don't be silly dears,' Miss Fernihough said. She looked over her shoulder at her Juniors, still holding Margaret's hand. A smouldering fuse ran from one to another, touching off fresh explosions. Best to ignore it, she thought. 'Tell me about yourself, Margaret. Do you have brothers and sisters at home?'

'No.' The mention of home nearly defeated Margaret but she managed pretty well by keeping her mouth shut and holding her breath.

'Just Mummy and Daddy?'

'No.' There were three of them. Mummy, Daddy and Margaret.

'What about a Granny?' Miss Fernihough guessed. 'Perhaps she lives with you?'

'No.' Margaret could feel the woman's patience beginning to give. 'She lives down here. Very near. Just about in that next street. That's why they sent me here.' There had to be a reason.

'Isn't that nice?' Miss Fernihough said. 'Well. You are a dark horse. I didn't know you had a Granny living so near. Did you tell Miss Byfield about her? I expect your Mummy and Daddy did.'

'Oh no,' Margaret said quickly. 'They didn't want her to know because then Granny might come up and make a fuss. She's very old.' She stared at Miss Fernihough without blinking and dared her to find this explanation inadequate.

'Well. Goodness,' Miss Fernihough said. Odd child. You didn't know what to believe. She held onto Margaret's hand and led her along the red brick pavement in silence.

Julie O'Connor, first in the crocodile, clutched at her partner's hand, leaned forward, lifted her chin, and began to walk, step for step, in the manner of Miss Fernihough. Her partner, the tall girls with the silk pyjamas, caught on fast; she pulled her felt hat down over her eyes, shrugged her shoulders till her free hand disappeared into the sleeve of her raincoat and did a passable Margaret. A fresh wave of explosions shook the juniors. Margaret, who knew what was happening behind her as surely as if someone had projected the performance straight through her head onto a screen in front of her, tried unsuccessfully to

19

regain her hand. Miss Fernihough was determined to ignore them. She gripped the hand more securely and led them all across the Parade to the Promenade.

'There!' she said, letting go at last and turning to face the children. 'Isn't that lovely?' They shuffled restlessly about, unsurprised by the sea. 'All right. All right. I know you're longing to be off. Now. No leaving the Promenade and back at the bandstand in an hour. Anyone late back, no prom-time next Sunday. Understood?'

'Yes Miss Fernihough,' they said, and ran from her in twos and threes.

Margaret stood quite still and prayed for a miracle.

'Come along, dear, we'll have a little walk together,' Miss Fernihough said.

And it wasn't as if she'd asked for loaves and fishes or raising from the dead, Margaret thought. Just Miss Fernihough not saying that. She wondered if they could have got it right about miracles.

Nora Gitting was taking her Sunday walk. Sunday wander, more like, Miss Shard said. She supposed the woman was fit enough. But what good was it to her in that condition? It only made her more of a liability. Poor Mr Fransey was out till eight o'clock one night, looking for her. The police found her in the end. And where do you think she was? Sitting under the pier. No deck chair. Sitting on the stones, soaking wet and no idea of the time.

'No idea,' Mrs Fransey had said. 'And me out of my mind with worry.' She encouraged her ladies to take little walks along the front on a Sunday. To blow the cobwebs away. But eight o'clock. What could she have been thinking about?

Nora had been thinking about Arthur. She had waited, only half expecting him, all afternoon. It seemed that he ought to come, that this was where he had said. She thought that she had always waited in this place, listening to this sea, touching these stones. But she couldn't be sure. Couldn't be sure of anything now. Sometimes she thought that perhaps, after all, Arthur had had the best of it.

On the afternoon of Margaret's second Sunday walk she had been sitting in the old shelter for nearly an hour when Margaret and Miss Fernihough walked by. The shelter, cast iron in the Chinese manner, stood on the Promenade between the pier and the bandstand. Out of the wind it was warm enough.

'Shall we have a little sit down?' Miss Fernihough suggested. It really was a bit much. She had been looking forward to prom-time; she would be on duty for the rest of the day and she hadn't learned Monday's Spanish yet. The text-book was in her handbag.

'If you like,' Margaret said. It wasn't fair. The others had all gone off. She could hear them laughing, calling each other, staggering about as the stones, banked up by the high tide, gave way and sent them shrieking towards the sea. Julie O'Connor and the new girl had found something dead at the water's edge and were poking it with a stick. Why did she have to miss everything nice?

'This'll do.' Miss Fernihough led Margaret round to the seaside shelter and stood in front of Nora.

The shelter had an end-of-season look; its windows were opaque with dirt, its floor was littered with lolly sticks and can rings.

'Oh, Come along dear. This one's taken,' she said.

The sun fell on Nora's hands. They're like claws, Margaret thought. She stared, fascinated, at the swollen joints, the prominent veins, the odd brown patches like out-size freckles, the nails grown curved and ridged.

'Margaret! Come along dear. It's not kind,' Miss Fernihough hissed at her.

The old woman seemed to have more skin that she knew what to do with. She'd got it all pushed together like curtains. In the flatter parts of her face there were small holes and bumps, some black, some blue, filled – or crowned – with pink powder. She's probably a hundred, Margaret thought. She didn't much like the way Nora's lower lids hung down in a wet red curve. Or the wet filled cracks at each side of her mouth. Even her nose wasn't quite dry. Her life is leaking away, Margaret invented, trying to frighten herself. That's why she plugs up her ear. She knew about hearing aids but preferred this idea.

'I'm not telling you again Margaret.' Miss Fernihough spoke through her teeth.

Yes you are, Margaret thought. I wondered why they say that. A powerful longing to be one up on Miss Fernihough took hold of her. To amaze, to overrule, to overpower her. Above all, to get rid of her before the others came back.

'But Miss,' she said.

'Miss Fernihough.'

'Miss Fernihough, then.'

'Well?'

Margaret looked her in the eye. 'It's my Granny.'

Miss Fernihough took it like a man. 'What a lovely surprise!' she said. Her face expressed the opposite view.

Margaret took her hand away from Miss Fernihough, sat down next to Nora and smiled up at her. 'Isn't it?' she agreed.

Nora became aware of a pressure on her elbow. She looked amiably at the girl beside here, accepting her presence as no surprise at all.

You'd think she'd been expecting the child, Miss Fernihough thought. Perhaps she had. Margaret could have told her parents about the Sunday walk. But wouldn't you think they'd have more sense? she argued. As if the child hadn't enough problems. And Miss Byfield wasn't going to be pleased. Miss Fernihough meant, there had to be standards. She didn't need a second look to know that Nora fell short of Miss Byfield's.

'It's just that…..' Margaret watched her struggle to find the admissible objection and felt like a hero. She had won, she was on top. 'The only thing is….. the others may be a bit jealous.'

'What of?' Margaret said. She opened her eyes a little wider. Miss Fernihough braced herself to address Nora directly. 'I'm sure you understand,' she said. Nora continued to smile at Margaret.

'She's very deaf,' Margaret said.

'Does your Granny live far from here?'

'She lives ever so near. In the road behind the hotels. Behind the big white one. Can I just walk home with her?'

'Now…If I let you…will you promise to be back before the end of prom-time?'

'Yes Miss. Thank you Miss.'

'Miss Fernihough.'

'Sorry Miss. Miss Fernihough I mean.' Margaret put her arm through Nora's and attempted to hoist her to her feet. 'Come along Gran. I'll walk you home.'

It took a little time for Nora to grasp what was required of her. 'Deaf,' Margaret mouthed to Miss Fernihough over her shoulder, wrinkling her nose and shaking her head.

'Use the zebra crossing both ways,' Miss Fernihough said. Now that she had given the special permission she was sure that she should have withheld it. Nevertheless. It would give her a chance to do Monday's Spanish.

Nora and Margaret crossed the Parade and disappeared from Miss Fernihough's view. It didn't take as long as Margaret thought it would; Nora seemed to be better at walking than almost everything else. They took the road beside the Plage Hotel and turned at once to the left. The back of the hotel was a shock to Margaret. She was getting used to shocks, but this was nearly as bad as back-stage after the pantomime, a disillusion only recently displaced in her private scale of awfulness by the total disillusion of The Mount. The white façade, wide steps, revolving doors of mahogany and glass had not prepared her for dustbins and drainpipes, kitchen noises and kitchen smells. They hadn't even painted it white.

'Is that really the plague hotel?' she asked Nora. She looked fearfully at the overflowing dustbins.

Nora screwed up her eyes at Margaret until the tears in them threatened to run down her cheeks. 'You're never Betty's child,' she said.

'That's right. That's who I am. Betty's child,' Margaret said. 'You are glad to see me, aren't you?'

The houses which faced the dustbins and drainpipes were nearly all derelict. There was a little shop, boarded up; a tiling company, apparently functioning – not, at least, as neglected as the shop; a run of blind doors and windows sealed with corrugated iron. Where there might once have been railings a rough fence of stakes and twisted wire prevented the passer-by from falling into the basement areas. Only the tiling company had removed the stakes and covered the area at pavement level with a metal grating.

'I knew they'd never make a go of it,' Nora said.

'I'll walk you home if you like,' Margaret offered. 'You'd like that, wouldn't you? As I'm Betty's child.' She dragged at the old woman's arm. 'Come on, Gran. Let's go home.' A vision of what a Gran's home should be was obscuring the facts. The deception had been, at first, a means of annoying Miss

Fernihough, escaping from Miss Fernihough; now it began to generate its own excitement. 'Show me where you live,' she said more urgently. 'I've got to go in a minute. Show me.' Wooden chairs with heart-shaped backs out of Heidi, the lace table-cloth from Little Women, jam in a cut glass dish from a television commercial; these things would be there and she needed to see them.

'Too soft for business,' Nora said. She seemed to have forgotten about Margaret.

'Who was?' Why could they never stick to the point? 'Who was too soft?'

'Run along now,' Nora said suddenly. She shrugged herself free of Margaret's arm and walked away down the narrow street.

'You're a loony,' Margaret shouted after her, but she didn't look back.

Chapter III

Nora's return, in time for Sunday tea, was a double disappointment to Miss Shard. Taking her own Sunday walk she had seen Nora leaving the Promenade with one of the Mount girls and felt that the police or at least the school should be telephoned at once. 'Better safe than sorry,' was all she would say. She had also been looking forward to eating Nora's fairy cake. It was one with white lemon icing and an orange diamond of tough sugary jelly which she particularly liked. Mrs Fransey had just offered it to her when Nora came into the room, still wearing her hat and coat.

'Good girl,' Mrs Fransey said. 'Take your hat and coat off and I'll give you a nice cup of tea. Go on.' She turned again to Miss Shard. 'She never eats it.'

'I'm not bothered,' Miss Shard said. 'Leave it. She'll want it for sure if anyone else has it.'

She waited until Mrs Fransey had left the room with Nora's hat and coat. Then she turned in her chair and spoke loudly over her shoulder to Nora. 'I didn't know you still had family down here.'

The ladies were silent, waiting to see if Nora would answer; only the television chattered quietly on.

'Miss Gitting. I said, I didn't know you still had family down here.'

'She's got a hearing aid, hasn't she?' Mrs Annerley asked.

'None so deaf as those who don't want to hear.' Miss Shard

grasped both arms of her chair and levered herself into a nearly upright position; then she took up her stick and set out across the room to Nora.

'She was really worried, you know. That other time.' Miss Kess leant towards Mrs Annerley and whispered an advance apology for any badgering of Nora that Miss Shard might be about to do.

'Did she have family down here then?' Mrs Annerley asked her.

'Oh I believe so. Lived here all her life. On her own for a good many years though. I think that's why she's gone a bit funny. Mind you. If my girls could see me! They thought I was bit funny then. Of course, I was always on my own'

Mrs Annerley felt obliged to contradict something. 'Ah but you had your girls,' she said. As if that could ever be the same.

'That's not the same, is it?' Miss Kess smiled. 'Still. Mustn't grumble, must I?'

I don't know why not, Mrs Annerley thought. Without Jim, without Guy, what would have been the point of it all? She had hoped that Miss Kess didn't know she'd been cheated.

Miss Shard walked around Nora's chair and stood over her, demanding attention. 'I didn't realise you still had family down here Miss Gitting,' she said, and waited for an answer. Sitting there in Irene Crose's chair all day. Or wandering about worrying everyone stiff. If there was something going on Mrs Fransey ought to know about it.

'No more run a sweetshop than a pair of babies,' Nora said. 'That useless girl, and him wingeing on.'

'Who was the little girl from the Mount, dear?' Miss Shard said loudly. 'Family, was she?'

'I don't think she's got any family.' Miss Kess lowered her voice and glanced towards the door. 'I think they've passed on,' she said. 'Or so I understood from Mrs Fransey.'

'Perhaps you'd better ask Mrs Fransey about the girl then,' Miss Shard said. 'You seem to know all about it.'

'No, no, no,' Miss Kess protested. 'Oh, no, I never had more than two words with Mrs Fransey about it. I expect I'm mistaken anyway. It's easy enough, isn't it?' Forgive us our trespasses she seemed to pray, especially those on the very private property of Miss Shard's status.

Miss Shard sighed, feeling the comfortable weight of her responsibilities. None of them could equal her experience; not even the married ones. "You see it all in a surgery," she told them. Ellen Kess wouldn't understand in a thousand years what someone like that woman could get up to. She began the return journey to her chair. 'I'll just mention it to Mrs Fransey later on.' This was a reference to her unique position at Bideawhile. She took her evening cup of tea with Mr and Mrs Fransey on Sundays, representing the ladies, passing on their grievances without naming names. 'Better safe than sorry,' she said again. The mumble of agreement consoled her. No one could get any sense out of that woman, she thought. I've done my best.

There had been other ladies at Bideawhile whose behaviour, for one reason or another, had been quite as eccentric as Nora Gitting's. Mrs Shreeve's deafness sentenced her to a state of chronic misunderstanding. Miss Arnold used to collect empty milk bottles in which to trap the poisonous rays in the atmosphere. But Nora had taken Irene Crose's place. Taken her room, her chair, her pigeon-hole for letters. She had arrived on the evening of the funeral, noisy and confused, before anyone'd had a chance to move a picture. Poor Mrs Fransey had had to clear the room out on to the landing while Dr Walsh sat in the office with her. "It's not decent," Miss Shard had said. She had never forgiven Nora. Or Dr Walsh. Nora was the doctor's spiteful reprisal for her intervention in the matter of Irene's thyroid deficiency. Miss Shard overdid it regularly, half hoping to deny Dr Walsh the satisfaction of neglecting her through a lingering illness in the geriatric ward of the local hospital by going off suddenly like Irene Crose.

The other ladies had no special reason to dislike Nora. She was not so very different from most of them. But they respected Miss Shard's feelings in the matter and left her to herself. It's kinder, really, they said to each other. She doesn't understand. Talking only worries her.

Mrs Annerley couldn't see it. 'Shouldn't we encourage her?' she asked. 'Try and take her out of herself?' She was beginning to share Mrs Fransey's doubts about the advisability of living within oneself.

'You go ahead dear,' Miss Shard said. She leant back in her chair and closed her eyes. The walk along the Promenade had tired her. 'Done me right in, all that walking,' she said. 'I'm chilled to the bone. There's no heat in the sun. What with the breeze off the sea.....' She settled her purple mohair stole around her shoulders. 'Chilled to the marrow.'

Miss Kess looked anxious. 'Miss Shard's used to that sort of thing,' she told Mrs Annerley quietly. It was always the same with someone new. New young teachers used to arrive, straight from college, full of new ideas, wanting to change everything. They had to learn the ropes. If things were as they were there was usually a very good reason for it. It took a little while but most of them saw it in the end. Of course, Miss Kess had had her failures. 'The awkward squad,' she called them, joking with the older members of her staff. They never lasted long. Mrs Annerley, on the other hand, was here to stay. Miss Kess thought her a very nice woman – very nice – but wished she could avoid upsetting Miss Shard. She had a tiring habit of questioning everything long established and self evident. Miss Shard had dealt with people like Miss Gitting all her life; if anything needed doing she would have done it already. It had been the same with the matter of the handles. Miss Shard would certainly know whether or not brass was obtainable. Mrs Annerley's remark about getting anything if you paid for it was in very poor taste. Miss Kess didn't think her husband could have been a professional man. How pleasant to see her niece, her niece's little girls, the very nice professional man her niece had married. How kind he had been, motoring her all the way home in time for tea, coming in even and having a little joke with Mrs Fransey. Oh no, she thought. Mrs Annerley was a good-hearted woman but you could always tell. Her own mention of the conversation she'd had with Mrs Fransey – about Miss Gitting's family – had been tactless, perhaps, but not in the same class as Mrs Annerley's persistent insensitivity. 'Quite used to that sort of thing,' she said, more firmly than at first.

Poor old soul, Mrs Annerley thought. Miss Kess, having retired twenty-six years ago – or did she say twenty-five? – was, at eighty-six, nearly ten years older than herself. She must be one of the youngest. The conclusion didn't cheer her as much as she had hoped it might. They were a nice friendly crowd. Guy had moved heaven and earth to get her in here. It was one of the best homes in the area. She'd heard it said herself, often. I've got through worse than this, she thought. Ah, but through it. There had never been a problem that didn't offer its hope of resolution; the good times ahead had been unlikely but possible. This was different. There was to be no going through it. Only staying in it.

'You mustn't let it upset you,' Miss Kess said. 'I expect she's quite happy if only we knew.'

'I'm not upset,' Mrs Annerley said. 'but you can't help wondering, can you? I get in a panic and then I start thinking is this it? Is this the end of everything?'

Miss Kess looked shocked. 'Don't you let Mrs Fransey catch you talking like that,' she said. She laughed, but Mrs Annerley could see that she wasn't joking.

'Oh, don't take any notice of me. I've been a bit down this week. I'll be better when that son of mine stops rushing about making money and writes me a postcard.' She revealed the source of her pain casually, to this near-stranger, and then wondered why she had done it. It wasn't like her. Nothing was the same, in here. Had she changed, already? I'm bound to change, she thought. Nothing else can change now. Only me. Through Miss Kess to Miss Gitting, perhaps. If her heart held out. She began to hope that it would not.

Nora sat facing the window, letting her tea grow cold. Behind the curtains, drawn for her Uncle Ned, her parents were quarrelling. What could Pa have done this time? She sat on the hearthrug by the empty summer grate, trying to understand. Ned was drowned. They were all drowned. Where was the money her brother had trusted to him for a decent burial? 'You've drunk it I suppose.' It was the worst quarrel she could remember. Her mother threw the china cat with the crest on its flank, her father looked wild enough to have performed the unnatural feat of which she accused him. They both forgot that Nora was there and said terrible things which undid, piece by piece, the carefully built pattern of her respect for them. It made them ordinary for her. How could they bury a drowned man, lost at sea, she thought. Why had Uncle Ned trusted her father with money? No one else did. Ma ran the boarding house, paid the bills, kept them straight. 'Because he'd no more sense than your father,' her mother told her when, after a day or two, she had judged it safe to ask. Nora thought that if she had had a brother, and he drowned, she would have spoken of him in a different way. They didn't even wear black in case it upset the boarders.

Maureen took her mother's side, in this as in everything. She was only two years older than Nora but they seemed to be the two that mattered. To hear them talking together about turning sheets or a cheaper kind of custard made Nora feel quite alone.

'Don't you care about Uncle Ned?' she asked her sister. They shared the attic room at the back; Maureen had exclusive use of the dressing table under the skylight, Nora propped up her mirror on the painted chest of drawers.

'Of course I care,' Maureen said. She sat at the dressing table, putting her hair up. Maureen was the pretty one.

'We ought to wear black then.'

'Someone's got to be practical.' She secured a wisp and leaned back in her chair for a longer view. 'How do you think the boarders would feel? Real cheerful holiday, that'd be.'

Nora couldn't see that it was ever very cheerful at the Carlton Guest house; she wondered why certain families came back year after year. "Better the devil you know," her father said. Their own unvarying holiday, a week in London with Ma's sister, taken between Christmas and spring cleaning, was evidently another example of the same cautious policy. Nora soon learnt that a change was not as good as a rest. 'Why can't we go somewhere exciting?' she wanted to know.

'Oh, and I suppose you'd like to pay for it?' her mother always said.

They worked so hard for so little and thought her so stupid for wondering why. The heroic smallness of their expectations filled Nora with a certain appalled admiration and the will to be different. At fifteen there wasn't a lot that she could do, but she decided to make a start with the boarders by being nice to them only when she felt like it. This apparently natural course of action contrasted so sharply with her sister's attitude – described by Maureen herself as 'only civil', by Nora as grovelling – that the younger sister was soon labelled stuck-up. The occasions on which she felt inclined to be nice became rather rare.

It was hot in their room under the roof. Nora sat on her bed (Don't. You're creasing the counterpane.) and watched Maureen smile at the mirror. Poor Uncle Ned. He was the only one of them who knew how to have any fun. She was sorry he had drowned, though it was something exciting to think about for a change. Fancy them wearing their ordinary clothes and pretending nothing had happened. Even when something does happen here they pretend it hasn't she thought. Not that he'd've cared. Two tears rolled down, one each side of her nose, for Uncle Ned not having any more fun.

'For goodness sake,' Maureen said. 'We never saw him more than twice a year.'

'He always brought us presents.'

'Well I must say. Your own uncle. And that's all you can think about.'

This volte face, as unfair as it was irrational, got the better of Nora. She rolled over on the white cotton counterpane, buried her face in her pillow and cried without restraint. Maureen raised both eyebrows and went to help her mother with the menus.

'At least he was a proper man. Not like Frank,' Nora shouted after her.

Frank's parents kept the sweetshop behind the Plage. He was their only child, expected to own the shop before long. They were neither of them young. Maureen planned to marry Frank in a year or so and help him run it. An arrangement so suitable, so sensible it was too neat by half for Nora. 'But you've always known Frank,' she objected. 'It won't be like marrying at all.' This was as near as she could get to defining her uneasy feeling that they would sit there in the sweetshop locked in permanent adolescence. 'I'm going to have a proper man,' she said. Maureen cried to her mother and Nora did early teas for a week.

I was right though, she thought. No more run a sweet shop than a pair of babies. She'd helped them out enough times. Especially after the war when Betty came along. Poured money into it every time Maureen cried. And she'd had plenty to pour in those days. Worked the old Carlton – Sunnyside, she called it – into a nice little business. She used to wish her father could have seen it. But Ma wouldn't let go till he died. Then she went. All of a sudden, all to pieces. Must have been fonder of Pa than she made out, Nora thought. She sighed, remembering her mother's reluctant abdication, her rapid decline into a critical, carping dependence.

'Fancy me seeing Betty's child,' she said. Betty's child was forty-two and lived in Loughborough.

'Tell us about Betty,' Mrs Annerley said quickly, wedging her foot in a closing door.

Perhaps because her voice was less familiar than that of Miss Shard, or her motive more gentle, Nora was drawn to respond. 'My sister's girl,' she said. She even turned in her chair a little, though not sufficiently to face Mrs Annerley.

'I didn't know you had any family down here Miss Gitting.' Miss Shard closed the door with a sentence.

'I don't think she's got any family,' Miss Kess whispered, half to herself.

'What's that?' Miss Shard said. She felt, rather than heard, what Miss Kess intended. Miss Kess rearranged the contents of her handbag and moved her post office book from her knitting bag to its front compartment, next to her pension book and the photograph of her niece's little girls. 'There,' she said.

Miss Shard combined a sniff with an upward jerk of her head. She glanced at Mrs Shreeve to see if she had replaced her battery and could be relied upon for support. Mrs Shreeve had closed her eyes and lost control of her lower jaw; she looked drawn and defenceless. Much use she is, Miss Shard thought. The loss of her friend, Irene Crose, swept suddenly through her, taking an unfair advantage, making her throat ache, her eyes sting. 'I know what you're thinking,' she said, looking from side to side. 'Don't bother telling me you're not.' They hated her, the lot of them. She knew all about Miss Arnold and her milk bottles but this was quite different. There had always been this feeling, ever since the first day when Dr Stacey brought her here in his car and insisted on having tea with her in the office. It's envy, she told herself. Pure envy. She had joked with him about it at the time. 'You'll get me into trouble,' she'd said. He had, too. The other ladies had never been quite easy with her. Except Irene, of course. Miss Shard sniffed again. 'That wind's like a knife. Treacherous. Got myself a chill now I shouldn't wonder.'

The ladies accepted this as the nearest thing to an apology for her incomprehensible attack that they were likely to hear and offered, in return, all sorts of advice. A teaspoonful of cider vinegar with honey and hot water was agreed to be one of the finest remedies for a chill. In the early stages only. Once it had taken hold there was nothing to beat hot whisky with lemon. This was no more obtainable than the honey and vinegar, but even the mention of it seemed beneficial. A warmth grew in the room; the ladies who had knocked back a few in their time laughed knowingly and Miss Kess, who hadn't, increased their pleasure in hinting at past excesses by pretending to be shocked.

'Dr Stacey liked his whisky,' Miss Shard said. There could be no harm in mentioning it now she thought. After all, he was only human. She liked a glass herself, on occasion, but even her drinking was more keenly enjoyed by being related to Dr Stacey, experienced at one remove through the agency of Dr Stacey. 'Never while he was on duty, of course. Never.'

The ladies did agree that this was a praiseworthy abstinence and only what you'd expect from Dr Stacey but lost a little of their party spirit.

'Well I don't know,' Miss Kess said, keeping it going. 'I'm not at all sure I oughtn't to report you to Mrs Fransey.'

She liked to play schools for them from time to time – it was one of her favourite jokes. Some of them laughed. Miss Kess could be annoying but she meant well, was the general feeling. Miss Shard herself smiled. 'We'll have to behave ourselves, then,' she said. Stiffly, performing in an unaccustomed mode. This time the laughter swept round the room, missing only Nora. Even Mrs Shreeve laughed. She didn't know why, but she did enjoy a good laugh. Keeps you young, she always said.

For a moment the laughter held them close. They removed their spectacles and dabbed their eyes with scented tissues, joined in a long diminuendo of sniffs and sighs, resting together like a bunch of tired athletes, as though their present contentment had only been achieved by a severe effort of will.

'I don't know.'

'You have to laugh, don't you?'

'You go like this before you go altogether,' Mrs Shreeve said. That set them off again into a quiet coda of snorts and chuckles. She closed her eyes and resumed her private dream, still smiling faintly until her jaw slipped down again in sleep.

'It must be nearly time for Songs and Hymns,' Miss Kess said. 'Shall I turn it up?'

'Would you dear?' Miss Shard asked her.

The ladies put aside their knitting and folded their empty hands, ready to be blessed.

The nice young man confirmed that it was, indeed, nearly

time for Songs and Hymns. It would come, he said, from All Saints, Bidhampton. A camera zoomed in over some sunlit stubble and showed them the very church; then, miraculously, peered in to the darkness through dissolving doors at stained glass, white flowers and brass altar plate, coming to rest on a well-heeled vicar smiling welcome.

Nothing had changed. The ladies were comforted. There it was, the church of their childhood, before it all happened. Before Dr Stacey, before Jim, before Guy, before the teacher training college. Before Arthur who went and got himself killed for that matter, though Nora, still staring at the drawn curtains, needed no reminding. She wouldn't have done it if it hadn't been for Maureen. Everybody thought Maureen such a blooming marvel. Even Arthur. All he could talk about was Maureen. Coming there with his bunches of flowers, hanging around being smarmy to Ma, and all for Maureen. Maureen had got Frank. What did she want with Arthur? Not much to choose between them, Nora thought. At least Arthur had a bit of gumption. He took her to the pier, didn't he? Him and his precious pen.

The camera had zoomed back to the stubble again and the ladies were being asked to consider the point that though they ploughed the fields and scattered the good seed on the land this was not, of itself, enough. They were thanking the Lord most cheerfully for all the good gifts around them when Nora began to shake.

'Quick dear. Mrs Shreeve. Ring for Mrs Fransey. She's having a fit,' Miss Shard said. Mrs Shreeve looked about her sleepily but made no move towards the bell. Miss Shard reached for her stick.

'Are you sure?' Mrs Annerley said. How offensive, Miss Kess thought. Of course she's sure. 'Let me just see.' But before she could ease herself out of her chair they became aware of a wheezing choking sound which spoiled the hymn for them and made their thanks ridiculous. For no reason at all as far as they could see, Nora was laughing.

Chapter IV

The period between junior supper and junior bedtime was the dangerous bit. Margaret had noticed. Breakfast, lessons, lunch, games, tea, with hardly an unsupervised moment between them – a whole day might be passed in reasonable safety. And after tea there was an hour and twenty minutes of preparation, ruling margins in new books, filling little squares with sums, all in a supervised silence made even more pleasant for Margaret by the sighs of her enemies struggling with work she found easy. No one spoke, neither the children nor the teacher who sat with them; it was quite the nicest part of the day, Margaret thought. She dreaded the bell and always put her books away slowly in order to join the supper line at the last possible moment. But after supper. That was when it got dangerous. That was when you needed all your skill and cunning to survive.

The Mount comprised both old and new buildings. The old was not very old. Not as old as the style to which its architect referred. But the grey stone had weathered very pleasantly and the occasional happy touch – linenfold panelling in the library, heavy oak shutters folded away at each side of the windows in the larger rooms – had impressed parents. The new was new only for Miss Byfield. To her the new gymnasium with its stage and its chapel, the new dining hall with sleeping accommodation above, were a permanent source of pleasure. She had laid out her father's money well, bullying the architect she employed to make the necessary alterations into using every available inch on the ground plan; he had retaliated with the panelling, an extravagance she fought at the time and now cherished. Attacks on it were simply not worth the known penalty of five hundred lines; it remained nearly unblemished.

The junior reading room was part of the old building. Intended, perhaps, as a billiard room, it was large enough to accommodate two billiard sized tables, a dozen wheelback chairs, a window seat, and several sofas too heavy to push or tip. A radio, tuned to the Home Service, was screwed to the elaborate cornice and switched on or off by means of a dangling cord, the kind more usual in bathrooms. In winter a log fire burned behind a fixed metal guard in the fireplace. Most of the juniors could have stood beneath its huge stone arch – especially in the middle, where its double curve rose to a gothic point.

The period between junior supper and junior bedtime, the dangerous bit, was to be spent in this reading room. From seven till eight thirty the juniors laughed, quarrelled, played 'off ground' over the heavy mahogany furniture, and it was possible to do almost anything except read.

The danger, as Margaret saw it, lay in the absence of any adult. The teacher on duty stayed in the library correcting books and only emerged if the noise became excessive. Some of the new girls were left alone; Margaret was not one of them. Everything she did seemed to arouse curiosity, spiteful or friendly. She just didn't have the knack of being ignored.

Her decision to be separate had been made in a moment, on that first evening at the Mount, and never since questioned. She had simply gathered together all her energies and dedicated them to finding ways of being separate in safety. The first problem to be overcome was that of escaping from the reading room. Margaret decided that if she waited as near to the door as she could without making her intention obvious until Julie O'Connor made a joke, when everybody would laugh, even the new girls crying in the corners, it would be possible to get away unnoticed. If she was spotted creeping past the open door of the library she planned to say 'I've left my book in my desk, Miss,' but she managed it beautifully. Out of the reading room, past the library door, along the low corridor with windows on one side and lacrosse sticks pressed into rusting clips on the other, to her classroom in the new building. There she met Harris.

'I've left my book in my desk.'

'You better get back with the others.'

'They didn't say I had to.'

'They didn't say you had to come in here and get under my feet neither.' He had pushed all the desks together in one corner and was sloping arms with a wide broom.

'You can sweep the floor with me here just as well.' She was not being difficult; merely asking his permission to stay.

'Cheek,' he said, and smiled. Margaret climbed over the desks till she reached her own and slid into the seat.

The desks had been one of Miss Byfield's most worthwhile economies. They were the old sort, older even than the original building. Both desks and seats had been cut from slabs of solid wood and bolted into cast iron frames. They were dark with age, worn to a brown landscape of ridges and valleys which swerved from time to time to avoid a glassy knot and made writing impossible unless you leaned on an atlas. It was easy enough to run your pencil along the soft valleys and make shining lead grey rivers; the ridges were tough. Even with a penknife it took ages to do one letter. But the desks did bring a touch of tradition to the raw plaster and metal of the new building, Miss Byfield thought. Something earnest, rugged, and not quite comfortable. Life, as she was fond of saying in assembly, was not a bed of roses.

Harris was short and muscular, with thick brown hair and a lumpy pink birthmark which nearly covered the left side of his face. He picked up a bucket and scattered a strong-smelling pinkish sawdust over the wood-block floor. It was exactly the colour of the birthmark. How could the birthmark and the sawdust be unrelated? Margaret didn't hold the idea up and examine it, but gave it a sideways glance, half fear and half delight. The sawdust could have caused the birthmark. Having to know would spoil the fun. It was less than belief, but a lot more than mere invention. She determined to walk with the utmost care when she left the room, in case any remaining crumb of the vicious stuff should eat through her shoes and make horrible marks on her feet.

She sat in silence, watching Harris sweep the classroom floor, wishing he would talk to her, wondering again if Gran would be there on Sunday. She didn't talk much either. But she probably thought a lot. About Betty's child and things like that.

'I wonder if your Granny will be in the shelter today,' Miss Fernihough said to her as they set out for the Sunday walk. She sounded bright but desperate. The walk along the Promenade was an unshakeable routine. More of a tradition, really, Miss Fernihough thought. She valued tradition as much as Miss Byfield but just now she longed to suggest some variation. An expedition to the foot of the Downs, perhaps. A visit to the museum?

'Yes Miss,' Margaret said. Miss Fernihough was holding her hand again. She summoned up the shelter and willed the old woman to be sitting in it. 'Can I take her home?'

'May I take her home,' Miss Fernihough said.

'Yes. Can I?'

Miss Fernihough wished that she had mentioned Margaret's grandmother to Miss Byfield. Straight after last week's walk. It was getting more difficult by the minute. If she said anything now and Miss Byfield got in touch with the parents she was bound to hear about last Sunday. There had been no harm done in letting Margaret walk her home, but that was not how it would look. Not now. Miss Fernihough tried a few openers. Oh. By the way. Did I tell you? I met Margaret Maildon's grandmother on the Promenade last Sunday. A tiny bit unkempt, actually. More or less senile. So I let Margaret leave the promenade and escort her to her home, which, for all I know, might be a pile of newspapers under the railway arch.

'Can I Miss Fernihough?'

Miss Fernihough drew breath, held it for a moment and exhaled noisily, as though lack of oxygen had forced the decision out of her. 'All right,' she said. 'All right. But I think it's time you realised. This school isn't being run for your benefit.'

Margaret felt the truth of this. 'No of course not, Miss Fernihough. If she's there, I mean.' She saw that Miss Fernihough had gone all red – even redder than usual. 'She probably won't be,' she said. This seemed to be what Miss Fernihough wanted to hear.

She was, though. Sitting there exactly as Margaret had willed her to be. She pulled her hand free and ran to sit beside Nora. One of the first rules for survival that Margaret had learned since she had been at the Mount was not thinking about home. So she had thought instead about Nora. Or someone very like Nora. By a persistent process of forgetting the bits she didn't like and substituting all kinds of other qualities, between one Sunday and the next she had thought Nora into just the Gran she needed. 'Hello Gran,' she said, superimposing this gentler image without any trouble at all.

Nora's smile was vague but kind. She appeared to have forgotten that Margaret had called her a loony. Miss Fernihough stood by, not quite making up her mind to say anything, wondering if even now she could withdraw her permission. Think up some reason or other, put a stop to all this worrying nonsense.

'I won't go far.' Margaret read her correctly. 'Just to Granny's house and back.'

Miss Fernihough hesitated.

'It's only the same as the others,' Margaret said.

'Ah, but they're not leaving the Promenade.'

Aren't grown-ups stupid,' Margaret thought. More than half the second years would be in the Marine Arcade at this very moment, buying sweets, playing the machines.

'Of course not, Miss Fernihough. But this is different.' Margaret linked arms with Nora, defending a sacred bond. 'She's family.'

Miss Fernihough gave up. 'You'll see she gets back on time, won't you Mrs er.....only I am responsible.....in loco parentis and so on.....Right.' She adjusted the strap of her should bag and walked quickly away towards the bandstand.

'Gran,' Margaret said.

Nora stared at the sea.

'Gran. Who couldn't run a sweetshop?'

A ripple of irritation disturbed Nora's stillness; she shook off the question with no more thought than a horse twitching away a pestering fly.

'Tell us, Gran. Go on. Who couldn't?'

Nora turned her head and looked at Margaret, not intending any answer, merely to identify the source of the question.

'Was it Betty? It was, wasn't it? Was it Betty who couldn't run a sweetshop? Mum, I mean.' As she was Betty's child. Out of the corner of her mind Margaret could see this mother. Helpless in the shop, needing her, letting her eat the sweets.

44

'Run off after that Pole of hers. I'd've told her. But not Maureen. Too soft. Or too proud. One or the other.'

Margaret became anxious for her sweetshop mother. 'What about my Dad though?'

Nora stared at the sea till Margaret began to think that the answer might appear over the horizon at any moment and stared with her. 'Was he a sailor?' she asked, when no boat came. She had lost this father before she had properly found him. Why did they do it? Stop the minute anything got interesting. And anyway, what had it got to do with this Maureen person. She looked at Nora's left hand and noted, for the first time and with a shock of disappointment, that she wore no wedding ring. She had some important questions to ask, stuff they all knew at school and wouldn't tell her. She jumped to her feet and stood in front of Nora, fists clenched by her sides, feet apart. 'Why do you keep pretending? I know you can hear me. Tell me about Betty and the sweetshop.'

Nora set about tidying the little room behind the shop while Maureen sat and cried. 'Go and wash your face, Maureen. And do your hair. I don't know what you're worrying about. They'll never take him with those glasses.' Trust Frank, she thought. He's only doing it to frighten her. Although... she considered the empty shop, dustily unappetising, the spikeful of unpayable bills... anything might seem preferable.

'He's all I've got,' Maureen sobbed. 'I might never see him again.'

'On the other hand you might,' Nora said briskly. 'Back from the wars, round about teatime, still moaning about the state of this place, still looking like Crippen on a bad day.'

'How can you, how can you?' Maureen abandoned herself to grief. 'When I think what I may have driven him to. You of all people should understand.' This spiteful reference to the Arthur who had gone and got himself killed was no more founded in feeling than the pretence of guilt which preceded it.

'For goodness sake, Maureen. Get up out of that chair and see to the shop. I don't mind helping but I'm not doing the lot.'

They had taken him though. Not for France. Taken him for a clerk, somewhere in the midlands. And even then he moaned, Nora remembered. Letter after letter about how his boots hurt. Poor Maureen. Nora sniffed. Children, both of them. Like children. 'No more run a ...' she began.

'Oh Gran.' Margaret jumped up and down in exasperation. 'Show me the sweetshop. You promised.' They hated being caught breaking promises. Sometimes they got very angry and went on about how that was before you did something or other and wriggled out of it; sometimes they pretended to forget; sometimes they just lied. But they always got angry. She waited to see if Nora would get angry. Of course, she hadn't really promised. But all that beginning to tell and then stopping was as good as. Or very nearly.

Nora didn't look like an adult under pressure. The mention of a promise seemed not to concern her. 'Like your mother,' she said. 'Always wanting it now.' She leaned forward, trying her weight, estimating the effort required to stand up in an unhurried manner while Margaret hopped about in irritation. When she was on her feet at last she turned to Margaret. 'Well. What are you waiting for?'

Margaret took her hand and went with her along the Promenade to the steps, across the parade, and up the little street beside the Plage Hotel. She was glad that they were going the same way as before in case Miss Fernihough could see them.

They turned left almost at once and stopped in front of the empty shop.

'Come on, Gran.' Margaret pulled at her.

'They'll be round the back,' Nora said. She pushed aside the lidless dustbin which stood in the narrow passage between the shop and the tiling company.

'Who will?' Margaret wanted to know, but Nora was ahead of her, lifting the rusted latch on the side gate as if she had every right to do so, standing in the yard behind the shop, rattling at the locked back door.

Margaret stood beside her and looked into the empty room, not knowing whether to feel relieved or disappointed. There wasn't a real sweet-shop. Or a Betty. Suddenly she was no longer Betty's child but Margaret, dangerously near to remembering her own mother. 'Come away Gran. I don't think we're supposed to.' She ran across the weedgrown concrete to the back gate and looked out into the passage. No one seemed to mind. Perhaps she lived there. Upstairs where you couldn't see. 'Is this where you live?'

'Never thought they'd've taken him with those glasses,' Nora said. She bent down and started to move a little pile of bricks and stones, apparently searching for something but not finding it.

'Have you forgotten your key?' Margaret guessed. She was becoming tired of all these uncertainties; in the absence of any solid information from Nora of the kind usually imparted by grownups it seemed safer to invent her own. Using her limited experience of the known world she concluded that Nora forgot things because she was old, lived here because she was trying to get in, and couldn't get in because she'd forgotten the key. 'Shall I see if I can get through the window? I bet I can.'

She climbed onto the windowsill and slid her small fingers beneath the transom; it swung towards her, dangling on one hinge.

'That Frank,' Nora said, shaking her head.

The remaining hinge pulled away from the rotten wood and the little window slid past Margaret, powdering the sleeve of her raincoat with dusty spiders' web, shattering on the concrete below. She looked at Nora to see if it mattered.

'Sit there and look at it till it fell to pieces, he would,' Nora said. She had known how it would be from the start. As a husband, in the shop, in the army. Useless.

'Who would?' Margaret said. She climbed down from the windowsill and brushed the dust from her new raincoat. 'Is it who lives here?'

Nora looked at Margaret as though she were trying to remember where they had met and why. 'No one lives here. Not now,' she said. What was the child thinking about? 'You better be getting back to that school of yours.'

Margaret fidgeted. If she was going to get sensible how to explain about not being Betty's child. 'My Mum is called Betty,' she said. 'But it might not be the same one. And I only called you Gran because you're old. I didn't really think you lived here,' she added, making a thorough job of it. 'It was a joke.'

The muscles of Nora's face, stiff with lack of use, pulled it into a smile. 'That's all right then,' she said.

Margaret began to feel quite hopeful. She took Nora's hand. 'Why don't we walk to where you really live?' she suggested.

This piece of innocent cunning, transparent, persuasive, touched some nerve. 'You're one for getting your own way, aren't you?' Nora said. Appreciatively, not at all displeased.

'Come on then.'

For the second time that afternoon Margaret allowed Nora to lead, to be in charge, to be a proper grown-up. The old woman in the shelter on the prom was nearly forgotten. She waited while Nora replaced the rusted latch and then took her hand again. They walked together in a companionable silence, out of the alley and along the little side street behind the Plage Hotel, turning left into the wide flat road which led directly away from the sea.

'Is it far?' Margaret asked. She didn't think it could be. Partly because old ladies didn't walk very far, but partly because she had already given up to Nora the responsibility for her safe return at the proper time.

'Not for your young legs it isn't,' Nora said, very reasonably.

They walked to the next side street and paused at the kerb, Nora restraining Margaret with automatic care. At the gate of the house on the opposite corner Nora stopped. 'You run along now.' She rested her free hand on the latch.

Margaret looked from Nora to the gate. 'Is this it?' she asked. 'Your house?' She frowned, unconvinced, at the large red house made of dark red bricks, with blind windows, net curtained every one. It was too ordinary for Nora. And much too clean. 'It's very big,' she said. 'Do you like it that big?' Another thing that made them angry was being caught lying.

'Like it?' Nora said. Her little laugh was the sad kind that, in Margaret's experience, usually accompanied irritating remarks about knowing soon enough. 'Didn't get asked, did I?'

'Nor did I,' Margaret said. 'Were you just sent?' It worried her to think that it happened to them too. Having your own way, however bad for children, was obviously O.K. for grownups. They had it all the time. Or so she had thought. 'How could they do that?'

The window to the right of the front door was different from the rest. Big and modern looking, one great piece of glass, more like a shop. It made Margaret think of the altar behind the fishmonger's. 'What happens in there?' she asked. And then, answering her own question because Nora took so long, 'There's a telly on, isn't there?' She peered through the folds of white net at a muted flicker of pink and blue and green. 'You've left the telly on.' Her attention wandered away from the window to a painted board which swung on two short chains above the porch. 'Bideawhile,' she read. 'Bideawhile. What does it mean?'

A corner of curtain was twitched aside and immediately replaced.

Er-bide with me, Margaret remembered. 'Why only awhile?' she persisted. An unhappy feeling was growing in her, near her stomach. She had found out enough for one afternoon; this was one question too many. 'Anyway it doesn't matter,' she said suddenly. 'I've got to go now or Miss Fernihough'll be furious.' She snatched her hand away and ran from the answer.

Chapter V

Twenty years ago, when the new buildings were new and Helen Fernihough was making her mark as the first, and the best, head-girl that The Mount was to have, she had christened the new junior dormitory 'the horse-boxes'. Miss Byfield, who came to hear of it and liked to think that she could take a joke with the best of them, had found this immensely funny; she referred to it in morning assembly and the name, shortened almost at once to 'the boxes', stuck. It was a fair description. The area above the new dining hall had been divided into wooden boxes with seven foot walls of varnished yellow tongue and groove. They lined the huge room on three sides, or stood back to back in the central space, and a narrow corridor ran between them, a U shaped strip of waxy brown lino. With the exception of the single boxes at the lower corners of the U which were reserved for prefects they each contained two beds. A flowery curtain hung at the entrance to each box, and even prefects were supposed to knock on the yellow wood before twitching it aside because Miss Byfield thought privacy so important.

The pleasure Helen derived from the public approval of her joke was nearly unmanageable. She blushed, she frowned, she stared down into her lap; her hands were still shaking when she stood up in front of everyone to read the lesson. It was not until the afternoon game of lacrosse a game chose by Miss Byfield because the nearby convent school played hockey – that she was able to discharge it in an ecstasy of physical effort which left the defence red faced and breathless and the goal-keeper in tears. 'Well played!' her side shouted. The air was clear and cold, the ground still hard with frost. She stood there listening to them all, sniffing, wiping the sweat from her forehead with the back of her hand. Oh that she might live at The Mount with Miss Byfield for ever.

Miss Byfield thought that this would be a good idea too. Helen Fernihough was no academic, though persistent hard work kept her from falling below the middle of the class. But she had other, rarer qualities. Such a kind, sensible, loyal girl. The juniors adored her. Not quite leader material; not, at least, in any larger world. But here, at The Mount. A natural second-in-command. At the end of the summer term she made her offer. Would Helen care to stay, to work with the juniors as a student teacher for her board and a small amount of pay? She could take her time over the A levels which would qualify her for entrance to a university, or perhaps a teacher training college. Find out if she really had a vocation for the teaching life before committing herself to one course or another. It all sounded so reasonable. Helen presented the golden opportunity to her parents, confident that their delight would match her own.

She loved her parents and was well used to doing as she was told. The Mount had seen to that. By September she was working, and moderately happy, a groom at the local stables. She had accepted their inexplicable resistance to Miss Byfield's offer; it didn't do to harbour grudges and she simply adored the horses. It was not until November the eleventh that she understood. Her mother had gone to church and her father, who had been too young for active service in the first world war and too old for the second, was drinking whisky.

'We got you out of that all right, didn't we Nelly?' he said.

Helen had avoided the dining-room since breakfast because it was where he always sat drinking whisky on November the eleventh, but she needed the carving knife. 'What do you mean?' she asked him.

In a sentence or two he brought about the very thing he had tried so hard to avoid. He said things about Miss Byfield, things which she could not and would not examine, things which made it impossible for her to live at home, ever again. Then, when he saw what he had done and would have given his pension to undo the maroons were fired. For two minutes they stood and faced each other in silence while the time for conciliation ran out. Helen's anger cooled to a small hard crystal, knowing only how to reproduce itself. On the following morning she packed her clothes, took her savings from the post office and went back to The Mount. To show him, with her life, that he was wrong.

Twenty years on, the moment was closer than yesterday, celebrated – and misunderstood – in chapel on each Armistice Sunday; even his death had not released her from it. She didn't feel middle-aged. She didn't know where the years had gone. Her sense of fun and fair play were untouched; generations of juniors had found them increasingly grotesque but she stuck to her guns and accepted their laughter as though it were meant kindly. This couldn't be it. Her life. Here at The Mount. Surely this was only the beginning, she thought. She could no longer afford to think it in words. The idea fought its way to the surface from time to time in restless bouts of planning which worried Miss Byfield less as the terms went by. 'You'll never leave The Mount,' she told her second-in-command, mistaking inertia for loyalty.

Margaret was one of the twentieth generation of new girls to be told, by Miss Fernihough, that she was to sleep in a box. Like most of them before her, she laughed. You had to. Whether from pity or politeness or plain self-preservation she didn't stop to consider. You laughed. And there had not been a lot to laugh about on that first, awful, evening. When Miss Fernihough had said it she had just made up her mind that she would probably never laugh again. But of course, this was different. Like they said about games in the prospectus. Compulsory.

She shared her box with a girl called Sheila Makepeace whose name followed hers on the register. Margaret had assumed that the sharing would lead at once to their being chums and having larks in the dorm, but in this, as in so many of the ideas about boarding school derived from her mother's old Annuals, she was mistaken. Sheila existed at a level of homesickness well below speech. Even before lights-out she hid under the bedclothes and only moved to turn her pillow when it became too wet. Margaret thought this behaviour both boring and mean. She needed someone – anyone – to fill the silence.

'Is it clean socks?'

Sheila remembered the well ordered sock drawer in her bedroom at home and moaned.

'I'll take yours if you like.' Margaret hunted about among Sheila's clothes for her dirty socks.

'Leave my things along,' Sheila snapped at her.

'I was only...' she began, but Sheila was back under the bedclothes, sobbing.

Margaret lay on her bed and stared up into the girdered roof void. The boxes had no lids. Rotten cow, she thought. She had hated it at Fairmead Juniors. Marlene Brandon had been almost as bad as Julie O'Connor. Nicking her dinner-money and then making her pretend she'd dropped it on the way to school. They never believed her, either. It was part of the reason she was here, at The Mount.

'She's a very unusual girl, Mrs Maildon' the headmaster had told her Mum. 'A very bright girl. One of our high fliers. When she wants to be. Eh, Margaret?' He had smiled at her until she simply had to smile back and then they believed her less than ever. It was all very well for him. Smiling and smiling. Marlene

Brandon wasn't in the same maths group as she was. Or French. That meant two lots of maths homework and two lots of French, for a start. Even if she let her copy the history and showed her how to change it a bit and looked up everything in the library for her English project.

'She gets very easily tired,' her mother had said. 'I really wonder about next year. Do you think she'll be able to cope with that huge school? I mean just sheer weight of numbers…'

That's when they'd thought up The Mount. The unusual school for the unusual girl. I must be really unusual, Margaret thought. I'm even unusual here.

The curtain was drawn aside and a scuffling giggling bunch of girls, driven by Julie O'Connor, crowded into the box.

Sheila got out of bed, took her towel and hurried away, not looking at Margaret. They let her go.

'Here,' Margaret objected.

They sat on Sheila's bed, shoving at each other to move up, make room. They were clean and hot and smelt of talc; they looked at each other but not at her. Only Julie remained standing. She drew the curtain again and held it close.

'We've come to see you,' she said. 'Aren't you glad?'

The girls on the bed snorted at each other.

'Shut up,' Julie said. 'Well?'

Margaret was not deceived. Big fat stupid idiot, she thought. Bet nobody ever called her unusual. On the other hand. Julie O'Connor did Chinese burns to people. 'Very glad,' she said. 'Have some chocolate.'

They ate all the chocolate she would get until next Saturday.

'Thanks,' Julie said. She was a well brought-up child. 'What we want to know is, who's that old woman you keep going off with? On the walk. Miss Fernihough says it's your Gran.' Clearly she was offering the benefit of the doubt.

For a moment Margaret considered accepting it. It would be good telling them how she'd fooled Miss Fernihough. Should she join them? Suck up to Julie O'Connor? Follow her around like the others, laugh at her jokes? There would be no going back once she had told them. No secret. 'Of course it's my Gran,' Margaret said. They probably wouldn't have let her join them anyway.

The news was received in silence. Margaret had handed them a weapon against herself so powerful and so delicate that even Julie O'Connor hesitated to use it. 'She's a bit ….. peculiar, isn't she?' she said, after a longish pause and under pressure from the obligation to entertain.

Margaret took over. 'She's terribly peculiar,' she said. She felt shaky and excited. They were all looking at her. 'That's why I have to take her home. She can't do it without me.' They were all listening to her, Julie O'Connor was a fat fool, she was better than the lot of them. 'She's absolutely rich only she wears those clothes so nobody'll know,' she said rapidly. 'And she lives in this big house with colour television. I'm going there to tea on Sunday.' She said this because she could see they weren't that impressed by the colour television.

'Liar,' Julie said. But she had lost her balance. 'Come on you lot.'

They followed her out into the corridor although Margaret thought that one or two of them would have liked to stay and hear more. When they were gone she bounced about on her bed for a while, feeling brave and cunning. Lions had come right into her tent and she had cleverly talked them out of eating her. The bit about going to tea on Sunday was awkward. But it was ages till Sunday. Anyway I might, Margaret thought. It really seemed to her as though she might.

Later, lying awake after lights-out, she began to feel afraid.

What would they do to her for not being one of them? She was better than they were. Except in their stupid way. Their way made everyone better than her. Even stupid boring Sheila Makepeace was better than her, the way they saw it. 'I don't care,' Margaret said. She rolled over and whispered it into her pillow. 'They're all bloody fools.' She lay on her back again and gazed at the pattern of girders thrown against the sloping roof by the prefect's bedside lamp. The prefect was reading. You could hear when she turned the page. Margaret's throat felt dry. I wish I could have some cocoa, she thought. Hot, sweet cocoa. And fingers of soft white bread with cold butter spread so thick that you could dip them into the mug without losing them. How was it possible to want something this much without getting it? There had to be a way. She could hear the prefect, walking slowly down the narrow corridor between the boxes. Her torch moved this way and that, sending the shadows swinging. Wouldn't it be lovely if she was bringing it, Margaret thought. She raised herself up on one elbow, almost hoping, and a shaft of torch light got her right in the eyes.

'Go to sleep,' the prefect said. She let the curtain fall and went on down the corridor.

Nobody likes me here, Margaret thought calmly. The conclusion was an interesting and surprising fact but it didn't seem to have any feelings to go with it. Not one single person, she tried again. They were standing at their front doors, leaning out of windows, waiting for her. Some of them had hung out flags. A banner, right across the road, strung between lamp posts, read 'Welcome Home Margaret'. Here she comes, someone shouted, and they began to cheer. She leaned from the taxi, school scarf flying, waving her lacrosse stick. She's back, she's back, they all said. She's come home. The milkman – the nice one with long hair – smiled. Her parents held out their arms to her, too proud to speak.....

The prefect, without her torch, came softly out of the darkness, fell on top of Margaret, and took her by the throat.

'Kiss me,' she whispered. Her body was a suffocating ten stone, her face in close-up like orange peel, and she didn't seem to be joking.

Margaret giggled in terror.

'Shut up or I'll kill you,' the girl hissed. She let go of Margaret's throat and rolled off the bed. She appeared to have sobered up. 'You better not tell anybody, right?' It was hard to know if she was threatening or pleading. She looked at Margaret with hatred and left.

The boxes had seemed to Margaret a kind of refuge. However strongly her heart thumped out the contrary message there wasn't really anything in the darkness that could harm her. Now she knew better. Not even the darkness was the same here. The small night sounds were no longer human and friendly. The barely audible creeping feet, hot on the cold lino, were creeping in her direction, the little explosions of laughter, stifled by pillows were all about plans for her destruction.

There was only one thing to do, Margaret thought, staring at the curtained entrance to her box; she would have to stay awake all night. The decision was almost immediately effective. The very thought of it made her eyes heavy. She maintained a muscle-aching tension for a good twenty seconds before the weight of it dragged her under.

Miss Fernihough found the dark evenings rather difficult. The summer was such a busy time for her. Tennis coaching for the sixth form, gardening – she did the flowers for the hall and Miss Byfield's study – walks along the chalky paths at the foot of the

Downs, the occasional picnic with a thermos of tea and a library book – nothing you could do in the dark. From time to time she had started societies; drama, music, debating, mah-jong. They were not well attended. 'Such an upheaval, the Autumn term,' she explained to herself and to Miss Byfield. 'New friends, new classrooms. Before you know where you are it's Christmas.'

She had never felt really at ease with Miss Byfield. Her father had seen to that, she thought. She thought this every time she considered the relationship between herself and Miss Byfield, as though she might lose the right to her anger against him if it were not regularly exercised. She had never even managed to call the headmistress Clarrie, except to her face. Privately it was always Miss Byfield.

I've got to make some definite plan this year, she told herself, and meant it as she meant it every year. Only there was always something. This term it was Margaret. That poor child, she thought. A hopeless misfit. I don't know what Miss Byfield was thinking of. It never does. Never. What little confidence Miss Fernihough had relied on such judgements. The unsuitableness of Margaret for The Mount made her feel cosily correct. A round peg in a round hole if ever there was one.

She had come to her room after supper for yet another early night. It made it easier for the younger members of staff. She was, of course, entitled to sit in the common room, but she always felt that her position as senior mistress – vice-principal really in everything but name – inhibited them. Not that an early night was any hardship. Miss Fernihough loved her room. Three years ago, when the stable had been converted into a bootroom, an improvement made possible by the death of Miss Byfield's mother and the consequent small legacy, Miss Byfield had advertised for an odd job man to occupy the old groom's quarters above it. Harris, the only applicant, refused to give up his own place. It stood to reason, he said. Miss Byfield thought it over. Harris had everything. References, a quiet manner, an unattractive scar. Well, she thought. It's sad, of course, but you can't be too careful. She offered the job to Harris and ` the room above it to Fern.

"My flat," Miss Fernihough called it. A slight reduction in her salary had paid for the plumbing. She didn't always enjoy turning out on a wet evening to cross the stable yard but the pleasure of climbing her own wooden stairs, lighting the gas fire, switching on the electric kettle, locking her own front door against the world and sleeping beneath her own sloping roof was compensation enough for any inconvenience.

Just now she was sitting in front of the fire, thinking about Margaret Maildon's grandmother. She had pulled her skirt up over her knees and the dry heat was mottling her shins in red and purple. Ought she to have told Miss Byfield? Ought she, even now, to tell Miss Byfield? One thing she had quite decided. There was to be no more leaving the prom. She yawned, looking about her for some reason to stay awake, avoiding the pile of uncorrected books and the Spanish cassette. It was always the same on lacrosse days. She had hardly been able to keep her eyes open during prep. Very pleasant, really. A smooth round peg in a smooth round hole.

She sipped her tea and reached for another biscuit. The feeling of well-being drained slowly away. Hole was right. What on earth was she doing here? This was it, her life, her only one. The argument was familiar and circular. Mind you, I haven't done too badly, it began. Considering I'm not qualified. Of course. I should have sat for those A levels. Right away, at the proper age. It would look ridiculous now. Imagine if the children were to find out. Especially if I failed. I wouldn't have a scrap of authority left. Anyway it's too late for that sort of thing. I simply haven't got the time. I suppose I could study during the holidays but my God, surely I'm allowed some time to myself? All very well for Miss Byfield to keep on about it. When does she think I'm going to do it? If she'd really wanted me to get on she'd've given me the time to do it. Instead of filling my timetable from morning to night with extra this and extra that until I'm too exhausted to do anything but fall into bed. I can't leave, the argument continued. I can't teach anywhere else without qualifications. What am I supposed to do? Work in some shop? Throw away twenty years' experience?

'She'd love that,' Miss Fernihough said. She ate another biscuit and imagined Miss Byfield confronting her across a counter. Her shock, her embarrassment. The mood of vengeful exultation only lasted a moment; working in a shop was a high price to pay for the pleasure of embarrassing Miss Byfield. A sense of fair play led naturally to the true target. 'It's not her fault. It's his.' He had ruined the chance of a lifetime. That she had taken, in spite of her father, the chance of a lifetime and so far failed to make much use of it was neither here nor there. You could hardly expect anything to be the same after that. Refreshed by this little spurt of anger she returned to the argument.

There's absolutely no reason why I couldn't do a degree. There are plenty of mature students. I might even get a grant. Take the A levels in the summer and apply for a grant.

She dug her heels into the hearthrug and pushed her chair a little farther from the heat. Tiring, lacrosse days. Very pleasant, but tiring.

Of course, I should have taken those A levels. Right away. Ridiculous now.

She sighed, not sadly. There was even some relief. It's too late, she told herself. You have to be realistic. Anyway. It could be worse. She looked again at the attic room, its red and white checked curtains, its varnished horse brasses glowing in the gas light. I'm lucky to have this flat, she thought. And the job, if it comes to that. She had ventured to the outer limits of her territory, inspected her defences; now it was good to be home.

Chapter VI

In the morning Margaret thought about Sunday, and tea with Gran. Perhaps they would watch the colour telly together. Put the crumpets and the teapot in the grate to keep hot and balance the plates on their knees.

The prefect who had visited her box was in charge of the junior breakfast line. Several times she looked in Margaret's direction, fearing to meet her eye, defying her to tell. She need not have worried. The events of the previous night were only part of a larger nightmare. One summer Margaret had removed the stone wedged in front of the garden roller and stood by, helpless, while it squeaked off down the slope and smashed into the fence. The mount reproduced in her just such a feeling of detachment; she was the powerless spectator of someone else's disaster.

No, the real stuff, the picture that filled her head all day and landed her in trouble for inattention, was tea with Gran. And Julie O'Connor standing outside in the cold, looking through the big window, seeing her having it.

Sunday came, and still she believed. Even when she caught sight of Julie O'Connor and Fiona, giggling behind her at a cautious distance as she went with Nora along the flat red pavement towards Bideawhile, the vision of crumpets persisted. 'Just this once more then,' Miss Fernihough had said. Well. She could hardly disappoint the poor woman if Margaret had definitely promised. But this would be the last time. It was all Margaret needed. Just this once more, to show them. 'Nearly there,' she said. They'd see.

She opened the front gate for Nora. 'Come on Gran. I can't stay long. Where's your key?'

Nora followed her up the path and rang the bell. Jack Fransey opened the door to them, wearing his white jacket. 'She's out,' he said. 'She didn't say nothing about visitors.'

Margaret could hear Julie O'Connor and Fiona, still giggling; they were right outside the house now, hidden by the hedge. 'It's all arranged,' she said. Nora offered no explanation. Margaret couldn't be sure that she had heard. 'Isn't it Gran?' she said loudly. He wasn't going to let her in. She tugged at Nora's hand. 'Tell him, Gran,' she whispered, urgently. She had to go in. They were actually laughing. 'Is he your butler?'

Now he was laughing, as though she had said something really stupid. Everyone was laughing at her. She sniffed noisily and` wished she could die, right there, in front of them. Then they'd be sorry.

'Butler!' Jack Fransey kept on saying. 'That's a good one. Her bloody butler!' He went laughing back to his Sunday film, leaving them standing at the open door.

Miss Shard came slowly into the hall, leaning on her stick. Just because Mrs Fransey had gone to her sister's for half an hour. It was always the same. Take advantage soon as look at you. And that poor man as much use as a wet rag. She didn't know how they'd manage when she was gone. 'Goodness Heavens, shut the door at least,' she said. 'It's perishing in here…' She stopped to stare at Margaret. 'Well,' she said. 'We've got a little visitor, have we?' She gave Margaret the neutral smile she had always used for new patients. How did she know they weren't registered with some other practice and just trying it on? The smile reserved her the right to advance or retreat. 'Aren't you one of the Mount Girls?'

Margaret thought about Julie O'Connor and Fiona, laughing out there on the pavement, and stood her ground. 'That's right,' she said. 'I've come with Gran.' The old woman was taking her coat off. She seemed to belong here. But who were all these people? Through the open door of the lunge she could see lots of them, sitting there, looking at her. She should have said, Margaret thought. She should have told me. A terrible thought occurred to her; her real Gran was in a Home. 'It's no good her moaning. We can't cope with her any longer. She'll have to go in a home.' She was sent, just like the old woman was sent. This must be it. The Home. Margaret tried to squint at the ladies in the lounge without turning her head. It gave her flushed miserable face a shifty look.

Miss Shard was encouraged to resume the attack. 'I didn't know Miss Gitting had a little great-niece at The Mount,' she said. She drew the line, for the moment, at debiting the unmarried Nora with a grand-daughter.

'I know,' Mrs Annerley called out. She was pleased with herself for remembering. 'You're Betty's child. Her sister's child. Grandchild, more like it. Now aren't I right?' She eased herself out of her chair and came to join them in the hall. 'You mustn't mind us,' she said. 'We're not used to young people here.' She held out her hand to Margaret. 'Come on lovey. Come and get warm. Just for a minute. We won't bite. She took Margaret's hand and made a present of her to the lounge. 'Look what I've got here,' she said.

A fat leather cushion, patterned with camels and pyramids, was agreed to be just the thing. Mrs Annerley dragged it, panting a little, into the centre of the room. 'There you are,' she said. 'You sit there. Then we can all see you.' She silenced the television and returned to her chair.

The cheek of the woman, Miss Shard thought. She was too

angry to speak. You'd think she owned the place.

Margaret sat on the pouffe and faced the ladies. Miss Kess found some barley sugar in her knitting bag. Mrs Annerley gave her a lavender-scented tissue because the cold made your nose run, didn't it? Only some rather unpleasant illustrations she had once seen in a book about Hansel and Gretel stood between her and the wholehearted enjoyment of being fussed over. She blew her nose, ate the barley sugar and kept her eye on them.

Nora took no part in the fuss. She came wandering into the room as though she'd forgotten every word about her great-niece. It made it easier, Margaret thought, but she worried that they'd think it peculiar. 'Gran's very tired,' she said. And then, quickly, before they could ask, 'I always call her Gran. She's not my real Gran, but... but... I just call her Gran. It's a sort of joke.' She looked anxiously at the ladies, searching their faces for some sign of belief.

'Of course it is, lovely,' Mrs Annerley said. 'What a pity Mrs Fransey's out. She'd have found something nice for you.'

Miss Kess gave a small, barely audible sniff.

'Barley sugar's very nice,' Margaret said. She knew what it was like to be got at.

Mrs Annerley was genuinely sorry. 'Open me mouth and put me foot in it,' she said. 'That's me all over.' I didn't mean that dear. No, I just thought the little girl could've stayed to tea – what's your name dear?'

'Margaret.'

'Margaret could've stayed to tea, couldn't you?'

'Perhaps next week,' Miss Shard said. She had found her voice at last. 'Then we can arrange it properly.' Instead of this overhasty makeshift, with no one any idea who anyone was and the teacher worried out of her mind for all they knew. Really. Some people had no sense.

'I can't next week,' Margaret said. 'I'm not allowed to. I have to stay on the prom.' She raised both eyebrows and opened her eyes as wide as she could, overacting the part of another Margaret telling the truth. This was, in fact, the truth, but it didn't feel like the truth. Not without the performance.

'Oh. What a shame,' Mrs Annerley said. Margaret dared to look at their faces and` was comforted. Except for the ones that were asleep they looked disappointed. The room was too hot, but she didn't mind. She had something special, something they all wanted and did not have. What it was she couldn't say, but they envied her for having it. It was why they wanted her to come again. She sat on her pouffe and `held court, allowing the ladies to warm themselves at her radiance.

'You'll be too hot in that mackintosh,' Miss Kess said. It was thought that she should take it off in order to feel the benefit when she went outside.

Outside. Margaret, who had drifted into a kind of queenly drowsing, remembered Julie O'Connor. And Fiona. And Miss Fernihough. She stared about her, looking frightened. They might have gone without her. Back to The Mount. And she might not know the way. She would have to stay here. They were going to keep her here. 'I have to go, I have to,' she said. She jumped up and ran to Nora. 'Goodbye Gran.' They smiled, the ladies, but they made no move to prevent her. When she had used both hands to open the heavy front door and run down the path to the pavement, she rather wished they had. They seemed to want things without even trying to get them. 'Stupid old women,' she said aloud to the empty Sunday street, keeping her courage up.

They were waiting for her at the zebra crossing. 'Come along, Margaret,' Miss Fernihough said. She was too relieved to be more than irritable. 'And I hope your grandmother understands. We can't have this sort of thing.'

'Yes Miss Fernihough,' Margaret said. Tea at The Mount with the rest of the juniors seemed almost desirable.

'She can walk with us.' Julie and Fiona took an arm each. 'Can't she, Miss Fernihough?' they dragged her to the tail of the crocodile. 'We'll bring up the rear, Miss Fernihough, shall we?'

Well, Miss Fernihough thought. That is nice. She realised that they found some of her ways a bit old-fashioned. Bring up the rear, indeed. But she didn't mind being teased as long as there was a firm basis of respect, underneath it all. And it was very nice to see Julie O'Connor showing her better side for once. Really putting herself out. Very nice.

'Right,' Julie said. 'What did you have for tea?'

'What do you mean?' Margaret asked her. 'you're hurting my arm.'

'I said what ... did ... you ... have ... for ... tea?'

'Crumpets,' Margaret invented, 'don't.' Julie kept jerking her own arm in a way which seemed designed to dislocate Margaret's shoulder.

'With jam or butter?'

'Both.'

'Pig.'

'No I'm not.'

'What else?'

'Chocolate cake. With icing. And hot scones.'

'And?'

'Sandwiches. Sardine sandwiches with brown bread, and...'

'Just what I thought,' Julie said. 'The Oick's made a pig of herself. You won't want your cake then, will you? Or your jam?'

'Yes I will,' Margaret protested, between jerks.

'You can sit with us today then. We'll help you with your tea, won't we Fiona?' they looked at each other and laughed till they staggered.

I don't care what you say, Miss Fernihough thought. There's nothing like the sound of children's laughter.

The ladies sat in silence and thought about Miss Gitting in the unexpected light of Margaret; only the television, restored to life by Miss Shard and unaware of the marvel, chuntered on. They were so nearly detached from the world outside. Evidence of the smallest connecting thread was of the utmost importance. Indeed, it largely determined their status at Bideawhile. Those ladies now sleeping against the wall, with the exception of Millie, whose daughter came from Scotland once a year, had thrown in their hands. But three of them still played. Miss Shard, Miss Kess and Mrs Shreeve. Mrs Annerley, though she sat in their half-circle, facing the television, had not yet fully understood the rules. These had been arrived at, without discussion, over a period of years. To be remembered, by letter or postcard, was to score. Phone calls hardly counted, on the grounds that they were less trouble for those who made them and considerably more for those called. The phone was in Mrs Fransey's sitting room, the conversation limited by deafness and the need to apologise. They were perfectly well, perfectly happy, and must ring off because they didn't want to keep poor Mrs Fransey waiting about any longer.

The glut of mail at Christmas time tended to devalue the postcards but a letter always scored. Visits were high. An invitation to stay even higher, to stay because you were needed, to baby-sit for instance, a rare bonus. But a child. Not dragged there by a dutiful parent. Alone. Of her own free will, apparently. Could they have been misled about Miss Gitting?

Mrs Annerley was the first to speak. Her attitude to Nora

required no re-arranging. 'What a beautiful little girl,' she said, with honest envy. 'I wish mine'd come and see me like that.'

'Never come back,' Nora said. She was in the little room behind the sweetshop again, trying to console Maureen. Never thought he would, she remembered. Not once he got away. The war did that to a lot of them. He came back on leave from time to time. She used to watch him, counting the hours while Maureen grumbled. 'It's all very well for you,' she used to say, over and over again. It wasn't though. Not all, not any of it, not for either of them. She got the letter just after she found she was expecting.

'He'll think different when he knows,' she sobbed, and wrote to him at once. It was one of the few things Nora had ever seen her do right away, there and then, soon as she thought of it. Not that it made any difference.

'You'll just have to put up with it like everybody else,' she told her sister. 'I know people left with six.' It wasn't very kind, but you had to face it. Frank wasn't much of a loss. A baby without a husband would suit me fine, Nora thought. Especially without a husband like Frank.

'Six,' Maureen cried. The thought of it set her off again, though whether she was crying for the five she wouldn't have or the one she would was hard to tell.

'I'll help,' Nora said. And she had. Night after night, while Mrs Piercey held the fort at Sunnyside, she was round there straightening out the books, ordering stock, washing nappies. Sunnyside and Maureen between them had eaten her up. Even now she couldn't be sure why she'd let it happen.

'I said what a beautiful little girl your great-niece is, Miss Gitting.' It was difficult to shout kindly but Mrs Annerley did her best. 'Beautiful. And such nice manners. You don't always find that nowadays.'

'Eh?' Nora turned her head, very slowly.

'Lovely little girl,' Mrs Annerley repeated, encouraging her. 'I'm sure she'll come back. She seems so fond of you.'

They waited for some response, but none came.

'It's nice when they've got time for you, isn't it?' Mrs Shreeve said, after a moment or two. She had put in a new battery and was feeling like a chat. 'It's all promises to start with.' She laughed, without much bitterness. It didn't seem reasonable to expect more from her daughter than she'd done for her own mother. And then they tired you out, children. A little went a long way. Still. A letter'd be nice, once in a while.

'Ah,' Miss Kess said. 'I used to ask my pupils. At the end of the Christmas term.'

They waited, patiently, After all, she had been a headmistress.

'What's the one present we all find it hard to give?' Miss Kess looked from face to face, confident that no one would answer. Mrs Annerley, who had not heard it before, owned herself stumped.

'Time,' Miss Kess said, triumphant, expecting applause.

'What's that, dear?' Mrs Shreeve adjusted her hearing aid until it whistled.

'Time. She said time.' Miss Shard was anxious to return to the subject of Miss Gitting's putative great-niece.

'Now that's very true,' Mrs Annerley said. That really was very true. Miss Kess glowed. 'Did you make it up?'

'Well,...' Miss Kess glanced at Miss Shard, aware of her irritation. 'It's the one thing we've all got the same amount of, isn't it? I've often thought that's why we're not very generous with it.'

Again, Mrs Annerley was impressed. 'No millionaires where time's concerned, eh?' she said. 'Three score years and ten all round. Barring accidents, of course,' she added.

'We must be richer than most then,' Miss Shard said. 'I've had more than my share already.'

'Ah but that's anti-biotics.' Mrs Annerley didn't mean to imply some dangerous meddling with the natural order of things; she was concerned to defend the old testament. 'They didn't have them then.'

'Well.' Miss Shard smiled disparagingly. 'I don't know where that gets us.' She turned to Nora, determined not to let the matter drop. 'Why don't you come and sit over here...' by the fire, she had been going to say, forgetting the television, '...away from the window?' 'There's a shocking draught,' she told the inner circle, as though her invitation required some defence.

Miss Kess forgot all about Mrs Annerley and looked at Miss Shard in admiration. That was what she called a truly Christian act. Considering everything.

Mrs Annerley supported Miss Shard's suggestion as though it had been the most natural thing in the world. 'Yes, why don't you dear?' she said. 'I'll help with the chair.' Good Heavens, she'd been lugging the hoover up and down stairs a month ago. She could see how some of them went. It was all too easy.

It took several minutes to arrange. Mrs Annerley had first to persuade Nora out of her chair. Miss Shard had made her contribution and was not asked to move. Instead Mrs Annerley pushed her own chair a little closer to that of Miss Kess, and Nora's was dragged, with some difficulty, to its new position. Miss Shard's approval was not sought in words. She would have repudiated the slightest suggestion that it was any of her business.

'Come along dear.' Mrs Annerley took Nora by the arm. 'You come and sit with us.'

Miss Shard thought about Irene Crose. 'I don't know how she'll get the trolley past these chairs,' was all she said.

Miss Kess opened her handbag and transferred her post office book to her knitting bag. The action was more nervous than deliberate. Had they done the right thing? Miss Shard had merely suggested...she did wish Mrs Annerley wouldn't... well, never mind, she supposed it was too late now, but...

Mrs Shreeve had not heard the invitation because Miss Shard had turned towards Nora as she made it; her hearing aid worked very much better when she could lip-read. What could they be thinking of? She smoothed the tartan rug over her knees and waited for trouble. She wasn't worried. Let them worry. Anyway, she thought. I can always switch off.

Even Mrs Annerley was flustered. She tried to laugh at herself. What a performance about moving a chair. They ought to have seen her when she got into one of her changing-it-all-round moods. Jim used to pretend he thought he'd gone next door by mistake. One chair, she thought. That wretched woman had only asked Miss Gitting to join them because she knew the poor soul'd do no such thing. If I'd just sat there like the rest of them she'd still be staring at the curtains, she thought. Of course, there were five of them sitting together now. It wouldn't be the same. She could see that. Put me foot in it again, she recognised. Second time this afternoon. 'Isn't it Songs and Hymns soon?' she said. Cheerfully, into the silence.

'You are getting ahead of yourself,' Miss Shard said. 'We haven't had tea yet.'

Mrs Fransey came back from her sister's and wheeled in the tea. 'Goodness,' she said, 'you've been moving the furniture.' She looked to Miss Shard for an explanation, but Miss Shard's patient sigh disclaimed responsibility.

'We thought Miss Gitting'd be better sitting with us,' Mrs

Annerley said. It was quite ridiculous; she felt as though she were owning up in order to prevent the others from being kept in after school. 'There's a bit of a draught by that window.' She regretted it at once. That wasn't why she'd thought Miss Gitting would be better sitting with them. It sounded exactly like the excuse it was.

Mrs Fransey was affronted. 'I don't think you'll find there's any draught from that window,' she said. She left the trolley standing in the middle of the room, took hold of the heavy velvet curtains and shut out the last of the day. 'I don't think you'll find there's any draught.' She returned to the trolley and began to pour out the tea. 'I'll asked Mr Fransey to have a look at it in in the morning.' She hoped that Mrs Annerley wasn't going to start complaining. It only took one. That sort of thing spread like wild-fire. She hoped that Mrs Annerley hadn't been a mistake. No wonder that son of hers was desperate. Mrs Fransey had seen marriages founder and sink on smaller rocks than Mrs Annerley. 'And what's this I hear about visitors?' she asked them. 'Case of "While the cat's away", eh?' She laughed, indulgently, not quite concealing her annoyance.

Again Mrs Annerley felt obliged to explain. 'Miss Gitting's great-niece came back with her. She didn't stay five minutes. Lovely little girl,' she added.

Mrs Fransey looked from Nora to Mrs Annerley. 'Is that what she told you?' she said. 'Great-niece?'

Miss Shard's patience gave out. 'She didn't say anything of the sort. It's one of the Mount girls. Doing a kindness, I shouldn't wonder. Helping her across the Parade. I've seen them together before. Talking to the teacher. One Sunday, on the promenade. Last Sunday it was. Or the Sunday before.'

'Well…as long as the teacher knows I suppose it's all right. But don't go inventing nieces, Mrs Annerley. She's confused enough as it is.'

"I beg your pardon,' Mrs Annerley said. You should beg mine, she meant. 'Are you suggesting…?'

'Now don't go getting upset,' Mrs Fransey said. Her manner was offensively soothing.

Mrs Annerley hit the roof. 'There's nothing wrong with that poor woman that a bit of ordinary human behaviour wouldn't cure,' she shouted. The tears pouring down her face. What's happening to me, what's happening? she thought.

Mrs Fransey took a brown glass bottle from the pocket of her overall and shook one small yellow tablet onto the palm of her hand. 'You take this with your tea dear. I'll get Dr Stacey to have a word with you in the morning. As for ordinary human behaviour, …' she turned to the ladies. If they considered her behaviour inhuman let them say so.

Mrs Annerley's courage seeped away into the silence. She blew her nose and accepted the tablet. 'I didn't mean…' she began. What was the use? It was hard enough without fighting anyone else's battles. The doctors must know. If there was something they could do they'd have done it already. 'I just meant talk to her a bit,' she said.

'Yes dear. You do. I'm sure that'd be very nice,' Mrs Fransey said, humouring her.

Miss Shard smiled; Mrs Shreeve, who had switched off when Mrs Annerley began to shout, drank her tea in tranquil neutrality; Miss Kess searched for her post office book among her knitting patterns. A young boy in cassock and surplice maintained with dazzling purity that if he had wings he would build him a nest in the wilderness. 'Far away, far away,' he sang. The very accuracy of his intonation pierced the layers of angry muddle and arrived at the heart of Mrs Annerley's grief. Guy had sent her away. Not his wife, who was a good girl in spite of everything. Not their children, her grandchildren, who in the midst of choosing wall-paper for their new rooms had had the grace to cry. Not death or sickness or any other disaster beyond their control. Guy. Her baby, her boy, the son who had promised her grapes and a Rolls-Royce. I must be going simple, she thought. Any fool could've seen it coming.

She looked up and caught a sideways glance from Miss Kess. 'Don't take any notice of me,' she said. 'I'm still a bit unsettled.'

'Now that's where I was lucky, really,' Miss Kess said. 'I'd nobody to leave.'

'That's one way of looked at it.' Mrs Annerley soldiered on, jauntily philosophical; the yellow tablet was winning. 'Don't you have any family, then?'

'My mother would be a hundred and twenty if she were still alive,' Miss Kess said. 'She had me rather late. A bit of an afterthought.' She laughed, to conceal the hurt. 'A bit of a mistake, I daresay, if the truth were told.'

'She must have been very proud of you, doing so well,' Mrs Annerley said kindly. The exercise of patronage pulled the edges of her own wound together like a skilfully applied plaster.

'Funnily enough,' Miss Kess said, 'she never…'

'I think we'd all like to hear the sermon,' Miss Shard interrupted her. 'Unless you'd rather talk?' She leaned forward in her chair, demonstrably willing to turn off the television.

'I'm so sorry,' Miss Kess whispered. She lay back in her chair, eyes front, hands folded, in an attitude of passive receptivity.

Mrs Annerley said nothing. The effort of resenting Miss Shard was hardly worth making. After all, what did it matter? The vicar was all for effort, and fighting the good fight. I've fought mine, she thought, surveying the facts from a nearly painless distance. Much good it did me. Out of the corner of her eye she observed Nora. She seemed to be watching the telly. But then she had seemed to be watching the curtains. I bet she talks to that little girl. You wouldn't find a child putting up with it. All that staring into space, bits of this and that, starting and never finishing. And not even her real gran.

She summoned up her own grand-children; the picture was clear enough, the feeling muted. I don't know what they put in those pills, she thought. She glanced again at Nora. I did that, though. I got her over here. She could've stared at those curtains till the cows come home. That she still had the power to make things happen gave Mrs Annerley intense satisfaction; she smiled at herself for an old fool, but nothing could spoil her pleasure in the achievement.

'All right dear?' she asked the unresponsive Nora. Then she turned to face the television and closed her eyes.

Chapter VII

On the following Sunday the shelter was full of strangers. Only Miss Fernihough's presence prevented Margaret from crying out. She stood quite still and stared at the bench where Nora should have been sitting as though the strength of her need could force the old woman to materialize.

'Your Granny's not here today, then,' Miss Fernihough said. 'It's a bit cold I expect.' The late September sun was brilliant.

The two statements, one unnecessary and the other inaccurate, restored Margaret's confidence. 'She told me she'd be a bit late today,' she said. 'She asked me to wait.'

It was very tempting. A deck-chair behind the bandstand with Monday's Spanish and the evening free for an early night with the telly. Margaret, wide-eyed and unsmiling, willed her to believe. 'I supposed you'd better sit here and wait then. But don't forget, Margaret. There's to be no leaving the Promenade.' 'No Miss. I mean Miss Fernihough. Thank you Miss.' Margaret found a place on the bench and sat knees together, hands clasped in her lap. Then she leaned forward and peered around the side of the shelter, indicating the direction from which Nora might be expected to come. Any minute now. Out of the corner of her eye she could see Julie O'Connor and Fiona, down by the breakwater, waiting. They talked and laughed together, seeming unaware of her, but every now and then they glanced at the shelter, turned quickly away and laughed more loudly.

Bitches, she thought. Bloody fat bitches. Gran must come. She had to come. Curiosity, strong as hunger, had been growing in Margaret all week. Why was there no one in the sweet-shop? Who would look at a window till it fell to pieces? And when did she talk? She had never met a grownup who didn't talk. Boring stuff, mostly, but they talked. All the time. Gran was just the opposite. She hardly said anything, and when she did she never finished it.

It's just about the worst thing in the world, Margaret thought. Stories without endings. Books with the last page missing. There were several of those in the library at The Mount. She always made sure of the last page now, half-closing her eyes to blur the print. The other worst thing in the world was people who cheated and read the end. Or told it to you before you'd got there.

'No pleasing some people,' Nora said loudly.

Margaret jumped. 'Hello Gran. I didn't see you coming.' The family of strangers gave each other speaking looks and said they supposed they'd better be getting a move on; they huddled together at the end of the bench, packed their thermos flasks and left.

'Dream yourself into trouble one of these days.' Nora sat down beside Margaret. 'Like your mother. All dream and no sense.'

Margaret had never heard her say so much or sound so ordinary. It seemed a shame to waste the moment in quibbling over the facts. 'You said you were going to tell me about Betty this time,' she invented. Nora looked at her, not speaking. Was she frowning or smiling? 'Please,' she said, like someone trying the last key of the bunch. It didn't fit. 'Oh Gran,' she whined. 'You're doing it again.' She took hold of the old woman's arm and hugged it to her. 'Come on Gran. Tell me.'

'Well now,' Nora said. 'What is it this time?' She supposed it would be money. It usually was. 'The coalman or the milkman?'

Margaret giggled. 'Honestly, Gran.'

'What is it, lovely?' Fancy sending the child to ask.

This was more like it, Margaret thought. She wriggled closer to Nora, still holding on to her arm. 'Tell me about when you were a girl,' she said. 'With Betty and all that lot.' She could see Julie O'Connor and Fiona skimming stones at the bright water. Their laughter came from a long way off, clear, but not quite real. Like looking down the wrong end of a telescope, Margaret thought. It was hard to believe that she had ever cared about them. 'Go on, Gran. Tell me about where you used to live. About your house.'

'My house,' Nora said, as though that would indeed be telling.

'I mean where was it?'

'Where was it?' Nora said. Margaret sighed. Did she have to say everything twice? 'You could see the sea from the back attic,' she told Margaret, remembering. How they'd fought in that attic. Poor Maureen. 'I never moved out. Not even when I could've had the pick. No point in wasting a good let. And I was always full. Always,' she said. 'Never short of boarders.'

'Oh I see,' Margaret said intelligently.

Nora appeared to believe her, which was a pity. She stared at the horizon and offered no further explanation. Margaret swung her legs to and fro, scuffing her lace-ups, trying to kick a can ring as far as the stones. Sunday lunch and the warmth of the afternoon sun were making her sleepy. 'You haven't got any sweets, have you?' she asked, without much hope. 'Only I'll have to go soon.' She stopped kicking. 'We've got to be at the bandstand by half past three.'

She thought about Gran's boarders and wished that she could have been one of them. She bet Gran's school wasn't anything like the Mount. She could have explained to Gran about Julie

O'Connor. She wondered if Miss Byfield could possibly get to be as quiet as Gran if she lived to be a hundred. She'd still be going on on about her little bird and what it kept telling her, Margaret thought. She leaned against Nora, temporarily abandoning the search for facts, allowed her to expel Julie O'Connor for torture – she herself had saved the lives of several small first-years – and smoking in the toilets.

Nora was thinking about Andrew. About the summer with Andrew McManus. It was the summer when everything changed. Nothing went right after that, she remembered. It was one of her regular couples who had recommended Sunnyside. Andrew's mother had died just before Christmas and they felt sorry for the boy. Not that he wasn't perfectly capable of looking after himself. Too capable, they told Nora. He could sit there in that empty house and get old before he noticed it. He needed a bit of fun. A nice change. It seemed to them that Nora and Sunnyside were just the ticket.

She gave him the table in the window. Kept the glucose on which his well-being seemed to depend with the sauce bottles. 'Shall I keep it down here for you?' she said. 'Save you bothering?' He wore a dark green paisley pattered scarf in the open neck of his white sports shirt on that first morning. Why that should have seemed moving and pathetic she couldn't say. Everything about him moved her. His thin boyish awkwardness, his freckled skin, red after only a day, his well pressed flannels, his wiry ginger hair, his wiry ginger moustache dusted lightly with glucose. To see him sprinkle that glucose on his porridge she could have died for him. You're an old fool, she told herself. You're ten years older than he is if you're a day. Eleven, as it turned out. It made no difference. He's another Arthur, she thought. She had worked herself into the ground forgetting Arthur. Not because he'd ever meant anything to her. Rather because he hadn't. But for me he might still be here, the argument ran. It was what his family thought; they made that very clear. Nora accepted their view of the affair and resisted a series of urgent invitations to make the happiest man in the world out of four or five of her unattached boarders. She would keep remembering Arthur, and the terrible consequence of settling for second best.

'He's not good enough for you, I suppose,' Maureen said, after she had turned down the third applicant. No, he's not, Nora thought. Why should I pretend?

Flick was different. He played on the bandstand during the season. "Flick Flyssen and the Debonnaires.' He never stayed at Sunnyside after the first time; he took a room at the Plage. 'Your lot put me off me breakfast,' he used to say. 'The Plage don't care. Long as you pay.'

Nora thought about those afternoons between concerts and the Plage with Flick. She always worried about leaving Sunnyside for too long, even with Mrs Piercey keeping an eye. 'Stop thinking about that blessed place for five minutes,' Flick would say. But on the whole the arrangement suited him as well as it did her.

'You're lucky I've got it to think about,' she told him. 'I might start thinking about wedding bells and orange blossom.' That shut him up.

Three summers they had. He never came again after Andrew. He played on the bandstand for another couple of years. Well. You could hardly expect him to turn down a good booking. But he wasn't liked, locally. Not after the business with Andrew. Then one year he didn't come. Got a better offer, she supposed, but he didn't come again. She had known it would happen, sooner or later. Flick didn't count as settling for second best. Or any other kind of settling, for that matter.

He arrived at the beginning of each summer with his charm and his nerve, paint-fresh from some regenerating hibernation, sure of himself and of her. She never asked him how he spent the winters, or with whom. It would have been, she felt sure, a mistake. Occasionally a card arrived with a foreign post-mark; once he had written to her on the headed paper of a London hotel. He hadn't actually said that he was playing there but this was clearly the impression he hoped to convey. Again, Nora didn't ask. It wouldn't suit everybody, she thought. But it suited her well enough.

'I don't know how you can,' Maureen used to say. Her husband's desertion had left her views on the sanctity of marriage untouched. 'I mean. At least I've got my Betty.' Not to mention me, Nora thought. Her money, advice and help had proved to be a more than adequate substitute for the gentle Frank. In every way, as far as Maureen was concerned. Remarks about Nora's 'goings on' were moderated by a sensible degree of self-interest. 'We can't all be the same, can we?' she said often, to Betty.

'She knew which side her bread was buttered,' Nora said suddenly. Margaret thought she sounded fierce, but recognised the cheerful smile that grownups smiled when they said a bad thing would happen and it did. The mention of bread and butter reminded her of tea. What kind of jam would it be and would they let her have any? There was cake as well for Sunday tea, but she tried not to speculate on the variety and whether it would be iced. Julie and Fiona were bound to eat her cake. Whatever happened, she wasn't going to walk with them. She decided to be first at the bandstand and say to Miss Fernihough 'Please can I walk with you?' as though it would be special treat. Which, compared to getting jerked all the way to the Mount by Julie O'Connor, it would be.

'I'll have to go now Gran,' she said. 'But I'll see you next Sunday, won't I? You come here every Sunday. Don't you?' She looked Nora straight in the eye. If she had possessed a gold watch on a chain she would have swung it gently in front of the old woman's face. She had seen it done on the telly and it always worked. 'Every Sunday,' she repeated. It was pretty clever, really. They couldn't get you while you were with a grown up.

She looked this way and that, up and down the Promenade. Then, catching sight of Miss Fernihough walking slowly round from the side of the bandstand, slid from the seat and ran to join her. She left Nora sitting in the shelter and began at once to recall the weekday Gran of her imagination, the one with the cut glass jam dish and the lace tablecloth. She had learned to hop from one to the other, using either Gran with equal facility.

For Nora the choice was less simple. Not between real and imaginary; between now and then. The habit of living now, weakened in the long descent from Sunnyside to Bideawhile, had been broken finally by the actual removal from one to the other.

'We can't leave her like that,' Dr Walsh told the department. Nora's life had crazed and cracked into so many fragments, so delicately balanced in mutual dependence, that any attempt to save it was bound to damage it further. 'We'll have to get her in somewhere,' Dr Walsh insisted.

Nora experienced her rescue as a rather troublesome distraction, a helpless dream-like interlude after which real life would recommence. Meanwhile it was up to her to hold on. To Maureen and Frank and Arthur and Andrew and Flick – poor Flick, he hadn't meant any real harm. He hadn't met anyone like Andrew. People like Andrew didn't belong in his world. Nor in her own, it seemed. A fortnight, they'd had. And that much upset the boarders,, specially one or two of the regulars. She had favoured him shamelessly; breakfast at all hours, with extra this and extra that. No sandy towels hanging from his window. She washed them herself every time he went for a swim and dried them on the airer above the kitchen boiler. The leave taking of several couples was cool and pointedly final. Well. You couldn't bring children into this sort of thing. No, they were sorry, but you couldn't.

Discreet afternoons at the Plage were one thing. "What the eye don't see…" was the generally held view. This was different.

It was different, all right, Nora thought. Lord, what a fool. But he talked so beautifully. And he read to her, up there in the little back attic. Stuff he'd written himself. It made her remember her own plans, her own determination to be different. Of course, she had changed the old Carlton. Sunnyside, with its bright cream paint and its orange curtains and its long list of regulars was different. But that wasn't it. That wasn't what she had meant, even then. Andrew talked about another world altogether. He was going to be a poet, he said. He was only working at the bank to save enough. Then he was going to start.

'Enough for what?' Nora asked him.

'Poets eat too, you know,' he said. Quite as though he would have preferred to manage without.

It didn't take Flick long to catch on, she remembered. He wasn't used to playing second fiddle. Or first. Running the whole show was more his mark. She might have known not to trust him. Even Arthur had his doubts.

'But they won't want to hear my kind of thing,' he said, when Flick told him about the talent contest.

'They will if it's any good,' Flick said.

Baited with this romantic challenge the hook was irresistible. 'I could keep it short,' Andrew said. 'One of the love sonnets, perhaps. One or two.'

'Fine,' Flick said. 'It'll make a nice change.' He sat by the fire in the back attic, looking as though butter wouldn't melt in his mouth. I could have seen it coming a mile off, Nora thought. Would have done, if I hadn't been knocked all of a heap by that poor boy.

They should never have met, Flick and Andrew. She hadn't meant them to, but Flick came round, following his nose, after the Sunday concert. And took to the boy. Asked him all about his poetry, appeared genuinely impressed; no "What's he doing in your room?" or anything of that sort.

The bastard. She could see him sitting there with a red carnation in his navy blue chalk-striped suit. Poor Flick. He did love that suit. Always wore it, with a carnation, for the Sunday concert.

'I know it's not the money that counts,' he told Andrew. But there's the prizes. Five pounds for the first. I mean, even we artists have to eat.'

'That's just what I've been telling N... Miss Gitting,' Andrew said. The coincidence seemed to please him enormously.

'Bastard,' Nora said loudly. A mother wheeling a pram along the promenade put out a protective arm and hurried the child at her side past the shelter.

The talent contest was no new idea. Flick always ran one on a Saturday. 'They'd rather watch each other than me any day,' he said. 'And it gives the boys a break.' Except for the pianist, of course. He had the worst of it. They'd all troupe up, ready to sing, no idea of the key; he'd be lucky if they knew half the chorus. Often it would be little kids, all starch and ringlets, kept up past their bed-time and pushed on half crying. Or a pub tenor, red with beer and winkles, clinging to the mike-stand as though it, and not he, were in danger of falling over.

Sometimes a thin brown child in a bathing costume and

plimsolls would stand on her head and do back-bends; or a father might fancy himself as a comic, and Flick would alert percussion to fill in any awkward silences with drums and cymbal. He saw his amateurs as obstinate children who would insist on attempting difficult and dangerous feats well beyond their strength; he smiled paternally through each act and lead the sympathetic applause for total disasters. The holiday crowd loved him for it. When they had voted by a show of hands and the prizes had been awarded, they loved the way he picked up his baton and led the band into something fast and flashy, winking over his shoulder at them. Here's how it's really done, he smiled. Just between you and me, aren't you glad I'm back?

It was immensely reassuring. They settled back into their deck-chairs. Those who had remembered to bring rugs and thermos flasks began to be glad. The man changed the numbered card in the stand at the side of the platform, near the ferns, and they consulted their numbered programmes. Ten down and ten to go. It usually got rather chilly by the end, but they'd paid for twenty and it seemed a shame to miss any.

Nora watched Andrew sitting at the back, behind the band. He kept fidgeting with the clasp on the locked diary, bound in red leather, which contained his manuscript poems. His skin was too burned to look pale. The other competitors whispered and giggled together but he sat at the end of the line of gilt chairs, staring ahead, hardly aware of them. Flick was putting him on last. It's the best place, he had assured them.

She gazed at her beautiful poet, half smiling, no more than pleasurably apprehensive. It was not until Flick began his introduction of Andrew that she understood.

'And now,' Flick was saying. He glanced only briefly at the band but Nora saw at once they were all in on it. 'Now we've got something for you that's a bit different.' He paused, and the audience, trusting him absolutely, waited for the difference to be explained. 'So quiet you lads at the back there, and give the ladies a chance.' The blond young trumpeter tipped back his chair, gave one shout of laughter and was suppressed by his colleagues with frowns and hisses and grotesquely disapproving looks even more disruptive.

'No, now, be fair,' Flick pleaded. Fair, Nora thought. Her eyes filled with tears of pure rage. 'A hearing, please, for Mr Andrew McManus, our very own…poet.'

The audience hovered uncertainly on the edge of nervous laughter. A poet? Did he mean a real poet? Or was it a joke? They looked to Flick for guidance, caught him struggling to be kind, and fell. The laughter started, as he had intended it should, with the boys at the back. He had treated them earlier at the local. Filled them with beer and told them all about the poet. How sensitive the poor young man was. What he wouldn't do to them if they laughed.

Andrew attempted to leave the centre of the stage, but Flick seemed determined to secure him a hearing. 'Now, ladies and gentleman. And that doesn't include you lot at the back.' That set them off again. 'Come along now. Fair's fair.' He held up a hand for silence and smiled encouragingly at Andrew.

Andrew opened the diary and began, fatally, the first love sonnet. 'Could I but lay my head upon thy breast,' he was heard to say, in a voice sharp with misery.

'That did it' Even Flick laughed. He staggered, leant against the wooden upright of the bandstand, covering his eyes with one hand, fairly shaking with laughter. He had done his best. Some things were more than flesh and bloody could stand.

Poor Andrew, Nora tried to think. Poor boy. How can they be so cruel? But even while she said these things to herself an awful clarity began to grow in her. Oh why can I never believe in anything for more than five minutes, she cried in despair. I don't know who's the bigger fool. Him or me. 'Could I but lay my head,' she persevered, searching for any remaining crumb of magic; then losing heart, she gave up the attempt and laughed with the rest.

Afterwards she wondered why she had laughed; it wasn't that funny. She never saw him again. Not even to explain. He walked from the platform, his face rigid with hurt, and threw his poems over the railings, round behind the bandstand. She supposed he's meant to throw them into the sea, but the tide was out. She went after him as he left the platform, excusing her way past knees and shopping bags and trailing rugs, but they always packed them in on Flick's amateur nights. The deckchairs were too close, it took too long and she missed him. She spotted the diary though. Ran down onto the beach, hobbling over the stones in her pretty shoes, and rescued it from the wet sand below the bandstand. But by the time she got home with it he had left. Bundled his things into the great Gladstone bag he brought with him, paid Mrs Piercey with more than a pound to spare, and left. She sent it on to him with a letter, but the parcel was returned, unopened.

Poor old Flick, Nora thought. It wasn't so much what he'd done to Andrew. All's fair, as they say. But she couldn't forgive him for making her laugh. First Arthur, then Andrew. Before the war, it was, she remembered. Not Arthur's war. The other one.

She watched the whirlpool of dusty sand on the concrete floor, felt the cold of another night to come and took automatic care to survive it. She wasn't sure of much, but she knew where the warmth was. Past Maureen's road, past her old road, along the new red brick pavement to Bideawhile. When Miss Fernihough marched her girls from the bandstand the shelter was empty.

Chapter VIII

Mrs Fransey was a nurse who had married her patient. Out of greed, or pity, her friends said. They couldn't decide which was worse. The case prepared on his behalf had been settled out of court for a substantial sum – his firm had admitted negligence in the matter of safety precautions and were glad enough to pay up. And of course the poor man was never going to recover. What a terrible mistake, they told each other. She doesn't know what she's letting herself in for.

She knew very well, being an intelligent young woman; and she could see that that was what they were bound to think. You couldn't ignore money. She'd be the first to admit it. You couldn't help feeling sorry. Anybody would who knew anything about it. But that wasn't the half of it. Not one of them understood how she hated nursing. It had taken her seven years to admit it, even to herself; then she had not been able to explain how she hated it. And now here was this handsome boy. A bit slow. A bit irritable. Needing her like no one else would need her, making demands she could meet without fear. An honourable retreat from all that dying.

She married him, bought Bideawhile, and surrounded herself with ladies so unthinkably old that even now, at thirty-eight, she seemed to them and to herself not much more than a girl. 'You're a good girl,' they said to her often, appreciating some small kindness.

She did her best. Kept their hair nice for next to nothing, encouraged them to buy new outfits from her catalogue – she liked them to look smart for visits – 'They're my children,' she used to say to families. The only thing she couldn't put up with was illness. 'I'm not geared to it,' she would explain. 'It wouldn't be fair. To me or to them. Besides, they need proper nursing,' she told the doctor at the very first hint of a symptom. 'I can't give them that here.' Only those ladies who were too quick for her died at Bideawhile; most of them made it to the hospital. In return, she had had to oblige the doctor once or twice. Nora Gitting, for instance. She had been one of Dr Walsh's emergencies. Not her usual sort of lady at all.

'There've been some changes in ten years,' she said to her sister. 'Well, of course – we're none of us getting any younger, are we?' She preferred to avoid the more natural converse of this proposition.

Her sister agreed that they weren't. 'Will you need me for putting them down tonight?' she asked. Her question supported the fiction that the ladies were suffering from some temporary incapacity.

'If you would dear. Unless Ray minds?'

'Not him. He's glad of the extra. Be round about six then. No point keeping them up half the night, is there?'

Ten years ago her ladies had managed for themselves; now there were only five of them who could get through the tiring and confusing business of dressing and undressing without help. Mrs Fransey's sister had been coming round morning and evening for the last three years. At first she had watched and chatted. 'Keeping an eye,' she called it. Now it was quite a job, even with the two of them.

'You want to go for the younger ones,' she advised. 'Like Mrs Annerley, for instance. More that sort.'

'No thank you very much,' Mrs Fransey said. 'One trouble maker's enough.'

Mrs Annerley would not have recognised herself in this description. 'There's trouble enough without making any extra,' she always used to say to Jim. 'I'd rather make a bit of peace and quiet.' At Bideawhile this was proving to be less simple that she had at first supposed. Who would have thought they'd go on like that about Miss Gitting's chair? Miss Shard, sighing every time she had to walk round it as though it made her hard life that little bit harder. Miss Kess, leaning forward and raising her voice when she wanted to speak to Miss Shard. She's two foot farther off at the very most, Mrs Annerley thought. She had offered to change chairs with Miss Kess, but oh no, that wasn't good enough. Miss Kess had always sat in that chair. About time you tried something different, she wanted to say, but the yellow tablets made her see that it was not worth the bother.

On Sunday evening, when the wall ladies had been led away to bed and Miss Shard was drinking her tea with Mrs Fransey, Mrs Annerley switched off the television. 'Like hitting yourself on the head with a hammer,' she said cheerfully. 'Lovely when it stops.'

'I don't know that Mrs Fransey would like it.' Miss Kess glanced at the door and began to fidget.

'She doesn't have to,' Mrs Annerley said. 'But I don't mind. Really. I'll put it on again if you were watching something. Were you watching something?'

Miss Kess looked guilty. 'Well. No. Not actually watching,' she said.

Mrs Annerley laughed. 'Neither was I. I haven't the faintest idea what they were on about. Couldn't tell you a word of it. Not for love nor money. What about you, Miss Gitting?' She turned to Nora, refusing to exclude the possibility of some response.

Nora continued to stare at the empty screen. 'I know what I meant to ask you. Did you see that little friend of yours this afternoon?'

'All dream and no sense,' Nora said.

'She's one of the dreamy sort, is she?' Mrs Annerley held on. 'My grand-daugther's like that. It's a lovely age, isn't it?'

Something in her manner, gentle but insistent, made Nora frown. 'Why they couldn't leave me alone,' she said.

'I know, love,' Mrs Annerley comforted her. 'I know.'

'Perhaps we should switch it on again,' Miss Kess said. 'Only I wouldn't like Mrs Fransey to think…'

'Goodness, don't upset yourself dear.' Mrs Annerley leaned forward in her high chair and stood up, breathless with the effort. 'It's not worth upsetting yourself. There.' She switched on the Sunday film, a ghostly black-and-white affair which had outlived most of its actors. 'I just thought we could talk,' she said. They were a funny lot and no mistake.

The film was the kind Miss Fernihough most enjoyed. They suffered all right, those well-spoken young people. But they did it so beautifully. As though a reasonable providence, seeing their preoccupation with higher things, had thought it only fair to relieve them of more usual problems. Loneliness, stupidity, putting on weight, owing money. They did sometimes arrive at loneliness, but only by way of tragic loss: Miss Fernihough had no one to lose. They were articulate, greyhound slim and possessed of a private income; Miss Fernihough was not. And yet she wept for their unhappiness and avoided, whenever possible, the appearance of an occasional survivor, sadly changed, on a late-night chat show.

These were her myths, pre-natal evidences of the life, if not hereafter, at least here-to-fore; the clouds of glory trailed by Miss Fernihough were back-lit by Warner Bros.

This evening's film was a particular favourite. She made herself a thermos of tea and got into bed. It's a bit early, she thought, but who's to know? The rain beat down on the stable roof. She turned up the sound. Good news, if it had required her to move, would not have been welcome; the sound of footsteps in the bootroom below, terrifying at another time, filled her with a rage of exasperation that overcame fear. Couldn't she even have her Sundays to herself? They didn't know the meaning of privacy. She got out of bed, putting her dressing gown around here. Unlike her day clothes, a collection of pastel skirts and blouses relentless frilly, the dressing-gown was navy blue no-nonsense towelling. She had bought it at the local menswear shop, thinking how useful it would be when she took junior swimming. Worn for this purpose with her old patrol leader's whistle on a lanyard it gave off no special magic. With striped pyjamas it was a knockout.

'Who's there? Who is it?' she shouted down the stairs.

Harris looked up from the bootroom. 'Sorry Miss. It's only me. Left me fags.'

'Well good heavens, you surely haven't come all this way just for that.' Harris lived some distance inland, at the foot of the Downs and cycled to work each day. 'Couldn't you have got some from an off-licence or somewhere?'

'I could if I had any money,' Harris said. 'Sorry to bother you. Hope I didn't give you a fright. I'm just waiting for the rain. Can't keep going much longer, can it?' He smiled in such a very friendly way.

Miss Fernihough had this much in common with Sleeping Beauty; her parents' fears for her had rendered her nearly defenceless. 'Well you can't wait down there,' she said. 'You'll freeze. You'd better come up.' Well he couldn't, she thought. How awkward. She didn't suppose he would stay long. Just her luck, right in the middle of the film. The sheer inconvenience of it obliged her to make the offer. She had been trained to put herself out.

From where Dave Harris was standing, in the bootroom, it looked rather different. It looked, as he explained to his mate on the following evening up at the allotments, like the old come-on.

'What a turn-up,' the mate said, politely. It didn't sound like one of Dave's best efforts.

He only stayed for ten minutes. She made him cocoa and sat by the fire with him while he drank it. The rain persisted, but he said he had to go anyway.

She watched his rear light wobbling away down the drive, got back into bed and switched on the television. What a thoroughly nice man. Very sad, that birthmark. Must have been difficult. At school, for instance. Children could be so cruel, she always thought. Funny. She must have walked past him hundreds of times on the way to her flat. When he wasn't seeing to the boilers or stacking chairs in the gym he was nearly always in the bootroom. Scraping mud from the children's wellingtons, soling and heeling the leather shoes, polishing lace-ups for the Sunday walk. Hundreds of times. 'Good evening Harris.' 'Good evening Miss.' Never thought of him like that. Like what? Miss Fernihough attacked her pillows and tried to concentrate on the film.

After a while she noticed that she was making a detailed comparison of Gervase from the riding school and Harris. Her father used to tease her about Gervase. 'How's love's young groom today?' He hadn't thought much of Gervase, and Gervase was public school; she couldn't imagine what he would have thought of Harris. She planned a scene in which Harris asked her to marry him, she accepted, and then went to tell her father. 'Pity you ruined everything, isn't it? I might have stayed at the riding school and married Gervase. You'd've liked that, wouldn't you? Very Court Circular.' Harris, marked, too young, a member of hoi polloi, was a natural in the part. An inspired piece of casting.

The climax of the film went unnoticed. The well spoken young people loved, lost each other, found each other. A list of the dead rolled past against a black and white sunset. Miss Fernihough crawled to the foot of the bed, switched off the set and continued to dream. It would jolly well serve him right, she thought.

Mrs Annerley was really quite enjoying the film. It was really quite good, once you got into it. She liked the black and white. More than some of the coloured pictures. 'Doesn't it make you think?' she said. 'I had a hat like that. Exactly the same. And a veil with spots. Little velvety spots.'

Miss Kess smiled. 'Fancy,' she said, embarrassed by the admission.

'Ah, and look at those milk bottles.' Mrs Annerley remembered the wide-mouthed milk bottles with cardboard tops and Guy, sitting at the kitchen table, telling her about school. 'It's as well we can't see into the future,' she said.

Miss Kess smiled again. She was a good soul, Mrs Annerley. Inclined to ramble, but well-meaning. 'I think I'll go up dear,' she said. She removed her glasses and searched her handbag for the empty case. The first case she found, a red one, contained her reading glasses. She zipped it back into an inner compartment and snapped the bag shut. Then she tried her knitting bag. When this contained no case at all she began to display signs of anxiety, looking about her in a vague but desperate manner, covering her open mouth with one hand as though to stifle a cry.

'What is it dear?' Mrs Annerley said. The hat had prejudiced her in favour of a girl who was clearly no better than she ought to be. She had made every allowance and was reluctantly transferring her allegiance to the blonde one with the jabot.

'Only it's the one I keep my batteries in, Miss Kess said. 'The blue one.'

'It's in your bag. I saw you put it there.'

Even the relief of finding the case, empty except for the card of tiny batteries for her hearing aid, did not prevent her from recognising the irritation in Mrs Annerley's voice. Or resenting the idea of being overlooked in this way. What else had she seen? She opened her bag again, pulled out her post office book and mimed pleased surprise at finding it quite free of any forged withdrawal.

Mrs Annerley drew breath to tell Miss Kess what she could do with her post office book and sighed instead. What was the good? She'd probably be like it herself if she lasted that long. 'I'll say goodnight then,' she said, and returned her attention to the film.

Mrs Fransey enjoyed Sunday evenings. Miss Shard wasn't a bad old thing, whatever Dr Stacey had said. Besides, Jack couldn't get awkward with her sitting there. Well, he could, but he didn't. He cared what they thought, the ladies. Pity I'm not one of them, she pretended, laughing at the idea.

There was no getting away from it, Jack could be awkward. But it was only what you'd expect. Vera Fransey, having failed so painfully to distance herself from her patients had managed better with husband. She counted what she gave him, calculated that enough was enough, and stopped. Well. You had to draw the line somewhere. She didn't mind a chat of an evening, but drew the line at switching off the telly; she didn't mind sex, but drew the line at children. 'He's all the children I need,' she joked to her sister. Her sister thought she was marvellous and didn't know how she put up with it.

On Sunday evenings she didn't have to. Miss Shard sat between them on the sofa, a neutral observer of their private struggle. Patronage was in the air. Both she and Mrs Fransey felt that they gave more than they received. It made them kind to each other and to Jack. Miss Shard carried on a dignified flirtation with him, allowed him to tease her about the old films they watched together. 'Here comes your sweetheart, Miss Shard. Don't you wish you'd said yes? Poor man. Now he's all unhappy.' 'What nonsense you do talk, Mr Fransey.'

It was warm in the little room. There was hardly room for the three of them.

'Jack dear, what about a cup of tea?' Mrs Fransey said. 'While the commercials are on. I don't know about you Miss Shard, but my tongue's hanging out.'

'Well… if you're having one, I wouldn't say no.' Miss Shard had said no to a good many things in her time, but never to a cup of tea.

'Some biscuits'd be nice,' Mrs Fransey called after him. She leant forward and cleared a space for the tray on the low table in front of them. She had left everything ready. The kettle was filled, the tray laid, the biscuits arranged on the glass plate with the plastic doiley. If everything was ready he could manage. She'd forgotten the milk once and he'd brought in the whole bottle, straight out of the fridge. She'd laughed, and he had got angry. It didn't do to laugh. She remembered the scene, with

Jack banging about in the kitchen and her trying to pretend nothing had happened. Had Miss Shard noticed anything? She could never be quite sure. Of course, she was pretty deaf but… As if it mattered, she told herself, and was not convinced.

He carried the tray into the sitting room and laid it carefully on the table. It was perfect. He'd even got the tea-cosy to fit. 'Thank you dear. That is nice,' she said, as though it were his treat.

'Can't have her tongue hanging out, can we Miss Shard?' he said, with unexpected venom.

The tears rose to Mrs Fransey's eyes. That was all the thanks she got. And after last night, too. You wait till next Saturday, my lad, she thought. Saturday nights were, to Vera Fransey, a kind of currency. Payment for the week past, a bargain struck for the week ahead. She had done her part. He could be a bit of a trial, could Jack. And then to say that. Right out, in front of Mrs Shard. She stared at the beautiful young people. They were standing on the balcony now. Oh he's got his white tie and tails, she thought. Heaven knows who paid for them. I haven't heard work mentioned. And I should think that dress would be a bit out of range for a florist's assistant.

She watched them kiss and hated them for lying to her. As though that was all there was to it. Then she helped herself to a custard cream and began to pour out the tea. They must be older than I am now, she thought, more cheerfully. Or dead. And Sunday was as far from Saturday as you could get.

Chapter IX

The ladies of Bideawhile were all agreed; you'd hardly know it was autumn. More like summer, really.

'You'd think it was from the crowds,' Miss Shard said, and everyone laughed.

It was quite the thing to despise the crowds. One or two of them had depended on these same crowds for a living; they laughed with the rest. The summer crowds were small enough, and dwindling by the year. Family parties mostly, wanting somewhere quiet and not too expensive. But they filled the tea shops, giggled arm-in-arm along the parade, roller-skated up and down the Promenade. So, to the ladies, they were trippers, vandals or little nuisances, and their departure a powerful satisfaction. The first ice-cream kiosk to padlock its shutters, the first sighting of the deck-chair lorry, were signs of the season's end, welcome in their turn as the first cuckoo. Mr Fransey put up the heavy winter curtains and the ladies shook the moth-balls out of their fur pieces. They had survived invasion, united against a common enemy and were all the closer for it. Very cosy, it was. And then, (behind the closeness), and there again, they thought; it was something to have outlived another green summer.

This year the summer hung on for dear life. The fine September days persuaded Londoners that sea air was the very thing they needed. Couples on bikes, families in cars, walkers zipped up in puffy nylon jackets.

'The new shelters were crowded out,' Miss Shard said. 'I'm surprised the Residents' Association doesn't do something about it.'

Even in October it had been warm enough for most of the ladies to take their Sunday stroll. Now, early in November, it began to rain. Margaret watched the sky and worried. Would it rain on Sunday? If it rained they didn't go for a walk. She had asked. If it rained they stayed in the reading room or the classroom. All day. The prospect of a whole unbroken day spent hiding from Julie O'Connor made her wonder if her pocket money, what was left of it, would be enough for a ticket to London. She could phone home from London. She could hear her mother's voice, high pitched and panicky. 'Stay in the phone box darling. Don't you talk to anyone. Stay right where you are. Daddy's coming.' That part would be all right. It was afterwards that wouldn't. 'But we thought you loved it there.' 'Shall we go and have a little talk with Miss Byfield?' or, worse, the unanswerable 'You're not going to tell us we've spent all that money for nothing?'

The way Margaret saw it, they had spent it for considerably less than nothing. She had adapted naturally and at once to being disliked. Another child might have cried and waited. Not Margaret. She wasn't the kind to demand a recount; they had voted against her, they had failed to see that she was beautiful and clever, they belonged with the enemy. For the moment there was nothing she wanted from them, nothing they could give her. She excluded them from her plans for getting through the day, ignored them in her dreams and simply asked that they leave her alone.

Of course, she had been disliked before, but only between nine and three thirty. Here she lived with the enemy. So in the gym on Armistice Sunday she knelt on her hairy blue hassock and prayed, against reason, for fine weather. 'Rain before seven, fine before eleven,' she reminded God, over and over again in a passionate mutter. Mr Bury smiled. He didn't usually approve of early confirmation, but some children came to it sooner than others.

In the classroom before chapel they were all talking about Miss Fernihough. Julie O'Connor had come in from IIB and was telling the first years what to look out for.

'You can turn round when it gets to Oh Valiant Hearts. She shuts her eyes. But you can tell she's crying. She goes all red in the face.'

'She doesn't,' they said.

'She does.' The verb was delivered in two swooping syllables, doubly convincing.

'But why?' they wanted to know.

Julie, who had seen the phenomenon once, in her own first year, looked about her for some fresh inspiration. Margaret was sitting at her desk, pretending to read Black Beauty. 'You better ask her,' she said. 'She knows everything.'

'I don't know anything about it.' Margaret wished at once that she had kept quiet.

'Thought you were supposed to be reading.' Julie waited for her laugh. 'Come on then. Tell them.'

She ought to have laughed with the others. She knew it, but she couldn't. Stupid fat pig. 'Tell them yourself,' she said; her voice squeaked with fear and resentment. To Julie it was irresistible. She sighed in mock humility. 'We can't all hold hands and be teacher's little darling, can we?' she asked them.

'Who'd want to?' somebody daring called out, and everyone except Margaret shouted with laughter.

A prefect looked in. 'Keep quiet in here. Have you all got chapel-money?' She offered a plastic bag full of ten p pieces.

These were handed round on Sunday mornings and collected again during the offertory. As there was no possibility of spending them in the interval and there was hell to pay if the number collected failed to equal the number distributed the coins were quite devalued as currency. Their surrender stood in for giving, a charitable rehearsal entered later on each child's bill.

Margaret kept very quiet. It showed God was on her side sometimes. She hoped he would realise that she needed the fine weather as well. He didn't usually answer two prayers running. In fact, it occurred to her, if he didn't answer all of them you couldn't really tell if he'd answered any.

'You better get back to your own classroom Julie. Mr Bury's in the vestry.'

'I'm giving a message. For Miss Fernihough,' Julie said. Several first-years snorted.

The prefect was not going to argue with Julie O'Connor. 'Well hurry up then,' she said, severely, and left.

Julie slid down from the desk on which she had been sitting and faced the class. 'Now. Where was I?' she asked them. 'Ah yes. Margaret Maildon. With dates please. What was the name of Miss Fernihough's lover and which war did he die in?'

The juxtaposition of sex and death was too much for the first years; they lay back in their desk and giggled with shock. Miss Fernihough! The Fern! As if she could ever have done That! With an actual soldier!

Julie, high on success, shouted for silence. 'You can come up here and tell the class,' she said.

Margaret was dragged from her desk and delivered to Julie. She took it all back about believing in God. 'You stupid fat bitches,' she mumbled, wanting them to hear, afraid of what would happen if they did.

'Louder,' Julie said. She grabbed at Margaret's hand, pushed

up the sleeve of her Sunday jumper to the elbow and took hold
of her forearm as though it were a sheet she intended to wring.
'Go on then.'

'But I don't know anything,' Margaret shouted, exasperated
out of her caution. Pain burned round her arm in a thin red line,
a bell rang, and the children scrambled to be first in to chapel.

'You better find out then,' Julie said, losing interest. First in
got the window seat. She pushed Margaret from her and ran to
her own classroom.

Half way though the sermon the sun began to shine. 'That's
it, God,' she prayed. 'Keep it up.' And by the time the juniors
were assembled in the reading room after lunch the full extent
of his mercy became apparent; the trees were sparkling, the
pavements steaming, and Miss Fernihough had decided that the
juniors should risk it in wellingtons.

Margaret walked along beside her in a mood of high
optimism. The walk had happened. Anything could happen –
and probably would. She held Miss Fernihough's hand quite
willingly and found it easy to forget that the walk must end.
Today Gran would tell her about the sweetshop. She was in the
shelter now, waiting to tell her. About Betty and the sweetshop
and her school.

'I don't expect your Granny will be feeling like a walk today,'
Miss Fernihough said. She wondered if Harris ever cycled down
to the front on a Sunday afternoon.

'Oh yes. She comes every Sunday.' Margaret sounded as
though she thought Miss Fernihough's not knowing this rather
stupid. 'They have to. So they can clean their rooms.' It wasn't
true on the way up but it became true as she said it.

'Goodness.' He might fish from behind the bandstand, Miss
Fernihough thought. At high tide. They fished in all kinds of
weather behind the bandstand. Though she supposed she would

have seen him before now if he fished. 'It's a bit cold for sitting still dear. I think you'd better come with me today. We'll walk to East Point and back. Get some colour in those cheeks.' They fished from East Point too, she remembered.

'But my Granny'll be there,' Margaret explained.

It was not immediately possible to see into the old shelter. A little crowd of the puffy nylon jackets, blue and orange, was gathered round it, arguing in high angry voices.

'Come along, for goodness sake. What's the point? Will you come along? Well you can stay. I'm going.' A mother dragged two children behind her and a father followed them, pausing once to turn and threaten some action or other.

They left Nora sitting alone, her eyes closed. It was difficult to believe that she had taken any part in the discussion.

'What did she mean, Mum, what was she saying?' the children wanted to know, but their mother wouldn't tell them. Later when they fell asleep on the journey home, she laughed about it. 'Wicked old woman,' she said. 'They're the worst, the old ones.'

Margaret was only glad that they had gone. 'Hello Gran,' she said. What a cheek. Those people probably didn't know and she'd had to explain it to them. It was obvious to Margaret. However full the other shelters got no one ever seemed to sit with Gran; if the shelter hadn't belonged to her they would have done. So the shelter belonged to her. 'I'd better stay with my Gran,' she told Miss Fernihough. 'In case they come back while she's asleep.'

'There's only the paddling pool at the west end, Miss Fernihough thought. 'If you're sure she won't be any trouble,' she said, automatically respecting Nora's seniority. Nora, with her eyes shut, looked quite untroubled; it was Margaret who had offered protection. 'You'll look out for us at the bandstand won't you dear?' She hurried away towards the eastern end of the

Promenade, not thinking about Monday's Spanish.

Margaret leaned against Nora and watched her go. Funny, the way she walked. So fast and leaning forward like that, sticking her bum out. You'd think she'd fall over if she stopped. She waited until Miss Fernihough was right past the bandstand and then began. 'Gran.' Two syllables, each with a rising inflection. Pay attention, they said plainly. I'm going to ask you a question and I shall go on asking it until I get an answer. It was the economical use of the language familiar to children. 'She do-oes,' Julie had said, silencing the doubting first-years. 'Are you calling me a liar?' would have been the long way round.

Nora twitched. Now what did the child want?

'Gra-an.' There was a loving persistence in the single word with its two urging syllables that was hard to ignore.

She opened her eyes and turned to look at Margaret, leaning away, frowning, trying to focus. 'Pestering me like that,' she said. 'I ought to call a policeman.'

Margaret's face, hot and miserable beneath her pudding basin Sunday felt with the tight elastic, began to quiver out of control. 'I didn't mean… I mean… I only meant…' she mumbled at her knees. This unexpected attack let loose the flood she had spent all term damming and diverting. 'They're rotten horrible pigs,' she sobbed suddenly, and buried her face in Nora's coat sleeve.

'Shush, shush,' Nora said. Always the same. Maureen, Betty, Betty's child. Whether they wanted something or didn't want something they always came crying to her. She had done her crying alone.

'They don't like me, nobody likes me.' Margaret continued to sob. 'I'm not like them.'

The present held for Nora the half-remembered confusion of distant childhood, which, in its dependence at least, it closely resembled. There were, of course, differences. No prizes now for understanding more clearly; only sadness and a little fear. With eighty seven years from which to choose Nora seldom chose the present. Margaret's demand for comfort offered a rare luxury. But between them there were doors to be opened, connections to be made. Some of the paths were overgrown and nearly impenetrable, others lost altogether. Well lost, it seemed to Nora. Let them all get on with it. She had done her share. She turned away again and stared towards the horizon.

Margaret's crying hiccupped to a standstill. Out of the corner of one red eye she could see Julie and Fiona emerging from beneath the bandstand. She leaned against the old woman, drawing what comfort she could from their closeness, and thought about Sunday lunch. Roast pork with apple sauce and double pudding with custard. You could always have double of dead dog. Nobody liked it much. Margaret liked almost anything, especially with custard. She wished she could have it all over again for supper. As much as she wanted, double of everything. Wave after wave dragged at the stones, each time a little closer to the shelter. Margaret chose a chalky white one and defied the water to reach it. One wave failed – then another. Julie and Fiona were the sea, she was the stone. Safe, unreachable. Before the incoming tide could prove her wrong the red eyes flickered once and closed.

Nora felt the weight and warmth of the child at her side and smiled unmaternally. They all did it, she thought. It was a child's trump card, that look. She could see Betty, worn out after some selfish tantrum, sleeping like an angel on the ottoman in the room behind the shop. She could even see herself, using the look and getting what she wanted. Whoever invented original sin knew what he was talking about. It was all there, right from the start. Just hadn't wormed its way to the surface. Children. Nothing but trouble.

It was an old argument, no more convincing now than it had ever been. I should have had it, she thought. For one whole week she had held to the idea of having Flick's baby. It would have meant giving up everything. Sunnyside, being the strong one, Nora who was good at everything. I might've been good at that, she thought. But Flick's child. Poor Flick. What a father to land a child with. Should've been Andrew's, by rights. She'd've had it and the hell with the lot of them if it had been Andrew's. Ah, but how could she have managed? As it was she'd had to spend the money she'd saved for repainting the outside. It showed, too. Down-at-heel, the place had looked, the whole season. That was when the business started to drop off. She lost the last of her regulars. Had to take anyone, casuals, all the wrong sort.

And then no one had told her how she would feel. Why hadn't they told her? They must have known. She'd only to look at a pregnant woman to come over queer. It was the same with prams. She'd sat next to a pregnant woman on the bus once. Had to get off before her stop and walk right up from East Point. To hear that doctor talk you'd think he was the council come to collect the rubbish. He did a good job though, I give him that, she remembered. So he ought, he charged enough. No one knew. Not even Maureen. She had thought about telling Maureen but what was the good? She'd never've heard the last of it. Didn't tell Flick neither. The Great Lover. Wouldn't even see him after that business with Andrew. He'd tried all right but she wasn't having any. No, she'd arranged it herself and paid for it herself. And gone on paying for it, she thought. By the time she cared enough to try it was too late. There wasn't any Sunnyside worth saving. 'I don't know what's come over you,' Maureen kept saying and it was true, she didn't.

'You're a fool to think about it,' Nora said fiercely.

Margaret sat up, startled and cross. The pattern of Nora's

sleeve was imprinted on one hot cheek. 'No I'm not,' she said, and looked for the chalk white stone. It had gone with the rest. 'Think about what?' It was all no good. There wasn't any sweet shop. It was all lies and she didn't care if she never sat in the shelter again. 'I probably won't be able to come next week,' she said. Then you'll be sorry, Nora was to understand. She wriggled from the bench and stamped off without looking back.

Over by the bandstand the juniors were beginning to assemble. Unusually, there was no sign of Miss Fernihough.

'Perhaps she's fallen off the pier and drowned,' Julie was suggesting as Margaret joined them.

Margaret was unable to resist knowing better. 'No she hasn't she's gone to East Point,' she said, and was immediately sorry.

'You better go and get her then, hadn't you?' Julie said. 'Before we're all soaked.' There was some sense in what she said. The sun had gone in and you could see the rain already, coming at them across the water. The sky looked top-heavy, with ragged grey bits hanging out underneath. 'You can ask her about her lover on the way back.'

A shout of laughter went up. Several girls were obliged to hold on to each other in order to remain standing. Margaret decided that when she was forty she would buy a gun and hunt down Julie O'Connor to the ends of the earth and completely kill her. Meanwhile, she supposed that she had better go and look for Miss Fernihough.

Away from the crowd she began to feel important. How God must love her in her new uniform. How that stupid old woman would miss her. Next week, when she walked straight past, talking with her friends, not even looking. Margaret, the darling of the dorm. The faster she thought, the faster she walked; her cheeks burned with the effort. This was more like it. The captain of the first eleven, protecting the weak, punishing the bullies.

It took some believing, but she could do it. Alone, she could do anything. It was better than the real stuff any day.

She stared, unseeing, at the real Miss Fernihough for several seconds without recognising her. A couple leaned together against the dark green railings. The man had a fishing rod but he wasn't fishing; he seemed to be waiting for the woman to speak. As he turned towards her, half smiling, Margaret saw the birthmark. Harris! How could Harris be here? Harris belonged to the bootroom. Then the woman laughed, a high pitched, awkward sound. Miss Fernihough and Harris. Harris and Miss Fernihough. Margaret was hardly able to believe her good fortune. She had found the lover.

'Er…please Miss,' she said, with offensive delicacy.

Miss Fernihough looked as though she had been caught picking the lock of her own front door. Her face was pink with frustration. How could she clear herself of any impropriety if no one was going to accuse her of it?

'Really Margaret,' she hissed.

'The others said I had to,' Margaret explained. She knew they were rotten to people who told tales, but they were rotten to her anyway.

'It's always 'the others', isn't it, Margaret?' Miss Fernihough, cornered, resorted to a self-righteous blustering. 'Very well then. I'm sorry.' She turned to Dave Harris, all tight lips and raised eyebrows. 'We'll just have to discuss this later.' Some deep matter beyond the understanding of a child concerning the arrangement of boots in the bootroom, she hoped to convey.

Dave smiled. That much embarrassment was definitely promising. 'Right you are then Miss Fernihough,' he said. His manner, formal and business-like, acknowledged the necessity for some kind of performance.

Miss Fernihough felt the risk. She had accepted a gift from

a stranger. Where might this reckless behaviour not lead? It made her anxious in a way which was unfamiliar but not unpleasant. 'Come along then, Margaret,' she said, matching his performance with her own. She took Margaret by the hand and dragged her away towards the bandstand at a breathless pace.

Margaret hopped and skipped along beside Miss Fernihough, re-running the only sex education programme she had ever seen on her internal video. You were supposed to be young. And beautiful. She didn't know ugly old people could do it. I mean. You had to take all your clothes off. Margaret looked quickly up at Miss Fernihough; then she stretched her powerful imagination to its limit and undressed Harris.

'Am I going too fast for you, dear?' Miss Fernihough said. The child looked quite done in. No stamina at all.

'No Miss. It's all right. Really,' Margaret said. Just wait till they ask me next time, she thought. Just wait. And it wouldn't be any good Julie O'Connor pretending she knew already. Because she didn't. She'd tell everyone straight out if she knew. Stupid fat pig. She wasn't going to tell them. Not yet, anyway.

There was no doubt in Margaret's mind about the accuracy of her deduction; only the pure joy of knowing Miss Fernihough's secret and the joy, less pure, of knowing how she would use it. Just wait, she exulted. Delightful sensations of power made her smile more cheerfully than she had smiled since arriving at The Mount.

'That's right dear. That's what I like to see. A nice cheerful face. I knew it wouldn't take long. Once you join in the fun and start making friends. Next thing I know you'll be crying because it's time to go home!'

Margaret perceived that this was a joke and gave a token laugh. Joining in someone else's fun was boring. She preferred her own. And as for making friends. The process seemed both dull and dangerous. If you didn't pretend you liked what they liked they suddenly hated you, and what was worse, they made everyone else hate you. The idea that she might, even for a moment, endure the painful vacuum and wait for the world to rush in had not occurred to her. She worked at her dream as though her life depended upon it, and after a while it did.

The reference to home she did her best to ignore. Talking about it, just like that, was exactly the kind of thing you had to expect from grownups. They didn't seem to have any sense. Still. She didn't think Miss Fernihough meant to. It was probably being in love and thinking about her lover. Margaret made allowances and began at once on the reinstatement of Nora as her weekday Gran; Harris and Miss Fernihough she was saving up for later.

Dave Harris packed up his fishing tackle. I'll call it a day, he thought. Might as well get back before this lot comes down. He wheeled his bike from the Promenade, head bent against the first heavy drops of rain and made for home.

Chapter X

Mrs Annerley was expecting a visit. Guy had phoned Mrs Fransey to say that he was on the way back from somewhere, on his way to somewhere else, and would be able to fit in an hour on Sunday evening; Would this be convenient? It all sounded amazingly convenient. Mrs Annerley had to admit it. She wished it could have been slightly less so. She wished that he had phoned to say that he had cancelled vital meetings, postponed the discussion of some lucrative deal, had dropped everything and was coming because he wanted to. To Mrs Fransey she said only that it would be nice. 'That's nice,' she said, and tried to look as cheerfully appreciative as Mrs Fransey evidently thought she should.

Since receiving his message on Saturday evening she had not been settled in her mind. Even the yellow pills seemed less effective than usual. Would he come alone, or would he bring Sally and the children? It wasn't so very far – but then perhaps it would be late. After supper. And what with school in the morning...no, she didn't think he would bring the children. Would he bring Sally? She's a thoroughly nice girl, underneath it all, Mrs Annerley told herself; it was less an expression of affection than a declaration of policy. She had decided from the start that she wasn't going to be one of those mother-in-laws. Whoever Guy married. It had been a good thing, as it turned out, having it ready planned, or she might have said what she thought. Been caught on the hop and ruined everything. Privately she thought Sally a self-centred snob, a whining horse-faced kind of girl who never stopped talking about her family. My son's your family now, she wanted to say. And my grandchildren. She didn't, of course. It made it easier for Guy. I was always making it easier for Guy, she thought, staring at the ceiling of her bedroom on Saturday night, unable to sleep. Well, it was easy enough to see the mistakes now. She dozed off at last, only to wake a short while later in a state of heart-thumping anxiety. She couldn't remember his face. Guy. There he was in his newest suit – the grey with the pinstripe – overweight and worrying about it, tall but not as tall as he would be if only he'd stand properly. He's almost as bald as Jim already, she thought, trying to trick herself into seeing the face. Their wedding photograph was on the dressing table, next to hers. She reached out for her bedside lamp, almost crying. You soppy 'aporth, she thought. Going on like a wet week. She put on her glasses to look at the photographs. Of course I know what he looks like, she maintained, reasonably; the image resisted her for a moment longer and then gave in. She closed her eyes quickly, not quite confident of holding on to it, and felt about under her pillow for her glasses case. What she wouldn't give for a cup of tea. Even at home they didn't like her wandering, as they called it. 'Sally's only afraid you might fall,' Guy used to say. 'She has got a point.' She'd got a point all right and that wasn't it, Mrs Annerley thought. Didn't want me bumping into her precious guests. 'We've got guests tonight, Granny dear…'

Mrs Fransey walked in without knocking.

'Goodness, you made me jump.' Can't call your soul your own here, she hoped the woman would understand.

'You won't leave the light on dear, will you? Shall I turn it out for you? Save you bothering? That's better. Sleep well dear. You've got that great son of yours coming tomorrow. Mustn't miss your beauty sleep.'

'I'm quite capable...'

'Lovely dear.' Mrs Fransey smiled away into the lighted corridor, closing the door with a warning degree of firmness.

Mrs Annerley huffed herself into a sitting position and switched on the lamp again. 'Well,' she said aloud. 'Well!' She sat there shivering for a minute or two and then supposed that, after all, there wasn't much point in it. I'm only bringing myself down to their level, she thought. She switched off the light. Just childish, that's all. Far better ignore it. Aware of having the edge on Mrs Fransey she lay back against her several pillows and drifted into sleep.

Now she was sitting in the lounge, wearing her best dress – the coffee coloured crepe with the jacket – and her uncomfortable shoes. She usually wore slippers indoors because of her feet, but she knew Sally hated slippers and he might bring Sally. She hoped he wouldn't, but he might.

How she had got through the morning she would never know. She had tried at first to conceal her excitement, feeling it to be undignified, but everyone seemed to expect it of her and by lunchtime she had given up the attempt. She usually took a short walk after lunch on Sundays, but it was understood that this would be far too risky. He might come early. She might miss him. So she returned to the lounge after lunch and waited for him there all afternoon, a tactic which lengthened it remarkably.

When at last Mr Fransey drew the heavy winter curtains, after tea, she pretended to watch television with the rest but her head ached with listening for the doorbell.

'I expect your son'll be here soon,' Mrs Fransey said, as though it might well have slipped her mind.

In the end he came late, and alone. She had gone upstairs to make sure that her hair was all right and had to be fetched by Mrs Fransey. 'I've put him in the dining room dear,' she said.

115

Mrs Annerley appeared doubtful. 'If you're sure it won't be any trouble...' She had been looking forward to showing him off to Miss Kess and Miss Shard and Mrs Shreeve.

Guy stood up as she came to meet him. He was large and clumsy. His coat dragged at the table cloth, disarranging the breakfast cutlery and knocking over the salt. 'Hello Mother,' he said. The greeting was diminished by an excess of warmth; he spoke as though he were determined to compress a month's affection into the hour.

'Hello Son.' This was not the man she had been remembering. She'd got his face all wrong.

'I'll leave you two to have a nice chat,' Mrs Fransey said.

Guy smiled his thanks and something more. What did they know, those two, what had they said, what plans had they made for her further isolation?

'You better not stay too long. They don't like us using the dining room. Not out of meal-times.'

'What's up darling?' He seemed not to know. Tell me everything's lovely, she thought. Then I won't have to worry. 'Oh it's nothing. They've very good. Don't worry about me.'

'Really Mother. Tell me the truth. Because if it's not...'

What will you do? If it's not, she wanted to ask him. 'How's Sally?' she asked instead. 'I thought you might have brought her.'

'Sally?' He frowned, finding this an odd suggestion. 'How could I bring Sally? Didn't Mrs Fransey tell you? I'm going straight to the airport from here.'

'Are you love? Where are you going?'

'Oh, it's only a business trip. The usual. Mother, I haven't got long. Let's have a proper talk, one of our good ones.' He took her hand and trapped it on the table between the sugar and the marmalade. 'Remember how we used to? In the kitchen?'

It was her own kitchen that Mrs Annerley remembered. Not

that stripped pine marvel with the silly German name they all went in for nowadays, Sally's kitchen, ovens stuck up on the walls and a hob like glass that was nothing but a danger to a child. She thought of her own kitchen, cold slate, enamel, black iron, flames you could see, a whole shelf full of marmalade with hand-written labels, not like this rubbish... the back-breaking sweet-smelling scraped scrubbed quiet of it. Talking in there, at the end of the day, was like talking in church. How could they talk here?

But still she needed to comfort him. 'It's all right love. They're very good. I suppose I just never thought it would happen to me.' She smiled, apologising for such a foolish lack of foresight.

Guy spent a large part of each day thinking that it would happen to him; larger than he cared to admit, even to Sally. Especially to Sally. 'Well, we all have to face it, don't we?' he said, doing his damnedest to look like a man who accepted the unacceptable.

'That's right love.' She felt so tired. Almost too tired to talk. And what had they said? Nothing. Really, she wished he would go. 'How are the children?' she asked him. 'They're growing up so fast. I expect I shall hardly recognise them soon.'

'I know, I know,' he said. 'When I think of myself at their age. They hardly seem to have any proper childhood, do they?' They are not babies, they needed your room, he wanted her to understand. I mean the boy's nearly seven. Besides. Better to have her comfortably settled in somewhere before they moved. 'That reminds me.' He searched in his coat pocket with his free hand. 'They send their love and I have to give you these.' He found the two letters for her and waited to be thanked.

'I'll read them when you've gone,' she said. 'Is Sally quite well?'

'Honestly darling.' He tried to tease a smile from her. 'Anyone'd think we were strangers. It's only a month. We'll all be coming to see you soon. I'd've brought them all this evening if I hadn't got to go straight on to Gatwick.' He glanced involuntarily at his watch and then, in case she had caught him at it, stood up and took off his overcoat. 'Now,' he said, as though they had all the time in the world. 'What have you been doing with yourself?'

It didn't seem a good moment to mention the move. And it probably wouldn't happen for another six months, anyway. He folded the coat, inside out, and placed it carefully over the back of a bentwood chair. Her hand still lay upturned on the table where he had left it; he sat down again and covered it with his own. 'Come on then. Out with it. What have you been up to?'

'Oh, I'm a lady of leisure nowadays,' Mrs Annerley said. She had meant to meet his mood but the words sounded bitter.

'Quite right too!' he simulated indignation that this desirable state of affairs should have been so long delayed. 'It's about time you took things easy. Put your feet up, let someone else wait on you for a change.'

She smiled at him a little vaguely, understanding his need to believe what he was saying but hardly able to manage it for herself.

'I could do with a bit of it,' he maintained, defiantly. I'm a money-machine, he though. That's all I am to her and the kids. A money-machine. Except that machines didn't get ulcers.

'Have you had anything to eat?' she asked him. All that rushing about. It couldn't be good for him.

'I'll get something on the plane. Don't worry about me. It's my turn to worry about you now. Are they looking after you properly? Is the food all right?' he frowned at her, suddenly and painfully concerned. Could he have found a better place? It had come at such an awkward time. As far as he could see promotion was going to ruin him. They'd be in it up to the neck with this move. For years. And this was what he'd been working for. Not to say crawling for. He began to wonder why. He began to wonder where his loyalties lay, or whether, indeed, he had any.

He had lost his place, once and for all, when they sent him away to school. Sold one side to the other, again and again, and the loss was always his. Ended up feeling uneasy in both camps, a sort of failed double agent. They must have known it would happen. Must have wanted it to happen, or they wouldn't have sent him away.

'You're looking tired love,' she told him, ignoring the question he had asked and then forgotten.

The pleasure of her son's visit began almost as soon as he had left. Mrs Annerley went with him to the front door, in spite of his being sure that she would get cold and its being unnecessary. She watched him walk quickly to the car and waved to him until he turned the first corner. He didn't look back, but then she didn't expect him to. It would have been quite unsafe. Jim always used to say it caused accidents, all that turning round and waving, not concentrating on the job in hand.

Mrs Fransey found her standing in the hall, making small indecisive movements towards the stairs, towards the closed front door, towards the lounge. 'I thought I heard the door,' she said. 'Well. Wasn't that a nice surprise?'

Mrs Annerley looked anxious. She had been expecting Guy for the last twenty-four hours. Was there something else? Something they hadn't told her? She allowed herself to be led, in some confusion, to the waiting ladies.

'There you are dear,' Mrs Fransey said. 'Have a little look at the telly for a bit. Help settle you down.'

Here the pleasure began. It seemed that Guy had come looking for her in the lounge with Mrs Fransey and they had seen him after all.

'What a handsome great man your son is,' Miss Kess said, in honest admiration. 'A professional man, I expect?'

'Well...' Mrs Annerley was not sure she understood Miss Kess. 'He got his B.A. ... but he went into business.'

'Oh, a lot of them do, nowadays,' Miss Kess said, reassuring her. 'Firms expect it, you know.' In educational matters at least she felt herself to be the unchallenged authority. 'You must have some fine-looking grandchildren,' she added, kindly; here too her opinion was of value.

Mrs Annerley had not seen her so animated. She was encouraged to take a photograph from her handbag and offer it for Miss Kess's approval.

'Oh. May I?' Miss Kess said. She began to search for her other glasses.

Mrs Annerley held the familiar picture at arm's length. Guy and the children, in the garden, under the apricot tree. Last summer, it was. Or the summer before. Guy brown and smiling, sitting on the grass under the apricot tree, hugging his knees like a boy, smiling up at her. Not the clumsy man now driving to the airport; her beloved son, in whom she was well pleased.

Miss Kess, who had changed her glasses, looked for permission to examine the photograph. 'Oh yes,' she said, not at all surprised. 'Just what I'd've thought. Beautiful children. Really beautiful. Like him, aren't they? Especially the boy.'

'Now I can't see it,' Mrs Annerley said. No one was like Guy.

'Everyone says it but I can't see it. Funny, isn't it?'

Miss Shard pressed her lips together and exhaled. Slowly and audibly. At once Miss Kess held out the photograph. 'I expect Miss Shard...' she prompted Mrs Annerley, quietly, with just a touch of reproof.

'Oh, I don't expect...' Mrs Annerley took the photograph and offered it uncertainly.

'I should very much like to see it,' Miss Shard said. To doubt it seemed an offence.

Mrs Annerley assessed the distance between herself and Miss Shard and the likelihood of Miss Gitting's passing the photograph. 'Perhaps I'd better...' she said, and eased herself out of her chair, panting slightly.

Miss Shard waited. She appeared majestically pleased at such proof of the inconvenience caused by Nora's new position in their half-circle. Nevertheless, she accepted the photograph and gave it her careful consideration. 'Yes. I thought so at the time. He's not unlike Dr Stacey,' she said at last. 'Very nice.'

Mrs Annerley felt ridiculously pleased. Well, she thought. The Accolade. She smiled at herself, a little less than she might have done a month ago. Perhaps Miss Gitting would like...

Miss Shard intercepted the idea. 'I wouldn't,' she said. 'She's very easily confused.'

Mrs Annerley supposed that this was so. You can't be forever fighting other people's battles, she excused herself. Fancy them all meeting Guy, though. She tried to remember the man in the dining room, the man getting into his car, driving to the airport, and could only see him where, in fact, she had not seen him; standing at the door of the lounge with Mrs Fransey, winning their admiration with his brown and smiling summer face. Was it last year, the photograph? Or a little while back?

She returned to her chair, replaced the photograph in her handbag and found the letters. 'I'll be forgetting my own name next,' she said, to anyone who cared to listen. 'They've sent me letters, the children. I expect their mother sat over them, but it's nice anyway, isn't it?' Ashamed to be the centre of so much loving attention, she set about undervaluing it to the ladies. Laughing to herself in a knowing way about the selfishness of children, especially her grand-children, appearing to discount the possibility that the letters might have been a spontaneous expression of their affection. Privately she knew their worth, rejoiced in it, felt it to be enhanced by the harmless charade.

'What are their names?' Miss Kess asked.

'Jim – James, they call him – and Clara,' Mrs Annerley said. 'Guy's my son, of course. But James and Clara, the children.'

'Beautiful names. Beautiful, aren't they?' Miss Kess leaned forward a little to include Miss Shard in the discussion She wasn't going to make the same mistake twice.

Mrs Annerley settled down to enjoy her letters At once the ladies withdrew their attention. Miss Shard looked at her watch and wondered what had happened to Mrs Fransey; Miss Kess got out her knitting. Between them they cordoned off the space around Mrs Annerley, made an area of privacy in the room.

Mrs Shreeve woke up. 'I used to do a lot of knitting. Before my hands got bad. Couldn't hold a needle now,' she said, displaying her arthritic knuckles with pride. She glanced at Mrs Annerley, hoping to engage her interest in the knuckles, saw the letters and looked quickly away again. 'They're so short, these evenings now, aren't they? I don't know.' As a further contribution to the isolation of Mrs Annerley she removed her hearing aid and began to fiddle with it. 'Damn things,' she grumbled. 'Never work.' This complaint was correctly transferred by Miss Shard and Miss Kess from the device to the need for it.

'It's a terrible thing, deafness, isn't it?' Miss Kess said. 'I've always thought. I'd rather be blind than deaf.'

Miss Shard looked critical. She was sure she'd rather be neither. Not that she was likely to get any choice in the matter. 'I don't know about that,' was all she said.

The hearing aid responded to being shaken with a piercing whistle. 'You've got it on, dear,' she shouted.

'Can't get a sound out of it. That's a new battery.' Mrs Shreeve put it to her ear and jumped. 'Damn things,' she said, confirmed in her original view.

Nora, too, had seen Guy, she knew the sort all right. They came to Sunnyside. Little boys, she called them. Tired and resentful, playing God and every kind of tyrant to their families. After fifty weeks in the year of maternal regency they seemed obliged by the public strangeness of their situation to take command. Unused to the job, they were inclined to be shaky in their judgement where the children were concerned, winning popularity by overruling vetoes already accepted and then coming out strong against some simple privilege. For the sake, apparently, of 'taking a stand somewhere'. 'You have to take a stand somewhere,' they told her, canvassing for support. 'But Dad,' the children would whine. 'Mum said we could.' She had known whole holidays ruined for less.

She felt uneasy because he had left with nothing settled. She should have got it fixed up then and there. He was a cut above her regulars but he liked what he saw. She could tell. 'I should have got it settled,' she said, suddenly distressed.

'What's that dear?' Mrs Annerley folded the letters from Jim and Clara, placed them carefully in their separate envelopes and returned them to her handbag. 'Did you forget something?'

It was too late now. He wouldn't come back. Nora sighed heavily. Margaret's outburst in the shelter had disturbed her. She remembered a child, crying, and couldn't remember whose child. Not mine, was it? she thought, with a triumphant blaming bitterness. Not having the child had been the failure she hated most. Nora who was going to be different, Nora who didn't live her life caring about what people would say, what people would think. When it came to it, she had cared. She had cared as much as it was possible to care – cared away her chance of a child, cared the poor thing to death. 'You're a fool to think about it,' she said angrily, for the second time that day.

'Think about what dear? What do you mean?' Mrs Annerley asked her.

'She doesn't mean anything,' Miss Shard said sharply, losing patience. 'You'll only wear yourself out worrying if you keep thinking she means anything.'

Could this be right? Mrs Annerley sighed. Such a tiring day. She decided not to wear the shoes again, for Sally or anyone else. Perhaps it was stupid to think that she could help. Miss Shard had worked for years with this kind of thing. Perhaps the poor soul really didn't mean anything and asking for explanations was only drawing attention to it. By 'it' she meant Miss Gitting's problem. The dull cloud which separated her from the other ladies. Seen in the light of Miss Shard's experience the cloud began to assume a hopeless unchangeable aspect, beyond understanding. It's very sad, but what can I do? she asked herself, fighting off the fear behind her relief. Better not get too involved, she thought, as though Miss Gitting's problem might be contagious.

Mrs Fransey and her sister arrived to escort the wall ladies to bed. Mrs Shreeve gripped the wooden arms of her chair, whitening the arthritic knuckles, in a token resistance. No one had so far suggested that she would prefer an early night, but you had to fight for yourself in this world, she always said. She might be deaf but she wasn't stupid.

Miss Kess continued to knit for her nieces's little girls. What a pity Mrs Annerley couldn't see eye to eye with Miss Shard. They had been such a harmonious little group. She didn't wish to be on bad terms with anyone, but… would she be able to count both ladies as her friends? It seemed not.

Miss Shard's anticipation of her Sunday tête-à-tête with Mr and Mrs Fransey was, for once, quite spoiled. What would that woman get up to as soon as her back was turned? Not that Milly Kess was any kind of substitute for Irene. But she'd lost one friend; she didn't mean to lose another. 'I expect you'll be going up soon?' she said to Miss Kess. 'I know I shan't be long.' She looked towards the door from which Mrs Fransey would summon her and sighed; the Sunday ritual of tea and television was a tiresome duty undertaken for the good of others.

'Oh, I was hoping you were going to keep me company for a bit.' Mrs Annerley mimed comic dismay and then smiled at Miss Kess in her most friendly manner.

There you are. I knew it, Miss Shard thought. 'What about your friend Miss Gitting,' she found herself saying. 'You could always have a nice chat with her.' She regretted it before she reached the end of the sentence but didn't know how to stop.

The attack took Mrs Annerley by surprise. "I didn't know whether to laugh or cry," she would have explained it to Jim. That was the trouble with this place. There was plenty going on. Sad, funny, worrying things. And no one to tell it to. She almost smiled, imagining what Guy would make of it. "There's this woman, thinks she's the cat's whiskers, bosses us all around." It sounded more like a play-ground quarrel, the kind of thing that Jimmy and Clara cried over. Second childhood they called it, and she wasn't ready for hers yet. 'What's that dear?' she asked Miss Shard, mildly. None so deaf as those who don't want to hear, she thought, and was rather pleased with herself.

Miss Kess, like Mrs Annerley, had heard Miss Shard quite clearly. She stabbed the ball of pink wool with her knitting needles and began to roll the left front of a cardigan around them. 'I am rather tired,' she said. 'If you'll excuse me...'

Miss Shard was called by Mrs Fransey. Miss Kess went up for an early night. As she was rather tired and if everyone would excuse her.

'Well,' Mrs Annerley remarked comfortably to Nora. 'Here we are then.' She took the photograph from her handbag and held it at arm's length. The television chuntered quietly on. The budgie, wakeful beneath a royal blue velvet cloth, nudged its bell and twittered in minute alarm. The image in her mind of the visitor in the dining room began to fade, to be replaced by something easier; again she saw him as the ladies had seen him, standing at the door of the lounge, a man without flaw. Their unknowing view of him had realised in her a powerful source of comfort. She looked again at the photograph. Was it last year when they made the jam? Baskets and bowls and saucepans full of apricots, more than they knew what to do with. Or was it the year before? Sally and the children helping, even Guy helping, fifty four pounds they made, apricots rotting faster than they could eat them and wasps everywhere. Jim getting stung, Guy remembering she used vinegar (Only for wasps. Bicarb for bees, she reminded him), Jim having Turkish delight in her room to take the pain away. Or was it Guy? He was only a little chap. It would have been a year or two ago, she supposed. The pictures came to her with the most delightful clarity. She was drawn into their bright circle, lived and relived them, willingly surrendering her life-long habit of fixing a date, checking a sequence. (It was on the Wednesday. No. The Thursday.) Whole years, whole decades slipped away. Often she might have passed and repassed Nora; for minutes at a time they inhabited the same world and never knew it.

'Ah dear,' she sighed, luxuriously sad. 'Funny old days, weren't they?' Reluctant to exchange them for the present she thought that perhaps she wouldn't go to bed just yet.

Chapter XI

Margaret had made good use of her amazing discovery. None of the juniors knew the name of Miss Fernihough's lover; all of them knew that Margaret did. A counter-claim by Julie O'Connor that she had known for ages and wasn't going to tell them because she couldn't be bothered was not well received. Julie, used to winning, became angry. She tried pretending not to care but the performance cut no ice. And it didn't help that Fiona had let Margaret use her real leather writing case with the special place for stamps. A lesser leader might have recognised defeat and made for the bunker. Julie felt the ground opening beneath her and did worse than usual in maths.

She found it hard to understand what had changed. At what precise moment it came to her that her word to the juniors was no longer law. When she made jokes they still laughed. Or most of them did, anyway. She still behaved outrageously in class, pushing each teacher to a nicely calculated limit before retreating, wide-eyed, from the very edge of mutiny, and they went off into absolute snorts of suppressed laughter.

But it was all different. She knew it and they knew it. Some of them even talked to Margaret in the reading room, knowing that Margaret had been chosen by her at the beginning of term as their victim, knowing that she could see them talking to Margaret, not caring. Given that something had changed, how had it changed so quickly?

She began to hate Margaret, seeing her now not as the simple sacrifice, necessary and innocent, but as an unexpectedly powerful enemy. Sly, deceitful, full of traps and tricks. Like treading on an ants' nest, she thought, remembering the actual picnic at which she had experienced this piece of treachery. Bloody fools. She felt the tears tightening her throat and slammed in to the attack. 'Bet you didn't even ask her.'

Margaret was sitting at one of the long tables in the reading room. There were other children at the same table. They weren't exactly with her, but neither had they left the customary gap or two or three empty chairs on either side of her as though she were a bad smell to be avoided. 'Didn't have to,' she said, annoyingly unafraid.

'Who is it then?' Julie challenged her. Not because I don't know but because I don't believe you do, she hoped the others would understand. She knew. Of course she knew.

'She made me promise not to say.'

The picture of intimacy and mutual confidence conjured up this downright lie – it was a lie, Julie was sure of it – provoked her to a sudden fury. 'Liar,' she shouted, and began to sob. It wasn't fair, she hated everybody, she wished they would all die and she would be the only one left to rule over the whole world and she could wear stuff like Wonder Woman and everybody had to bow down to her.

There was a moment of shocked silence. No one looked at Julie. The children playing 'off-ground' paused, panting, and then chased off round the easy run of window-seat which preceded the piano jump. Their wilder energy and their more hectic laughter were to conceal her disgrace. The Ludo players rattled their dice more furiously, the two on the sofa who had nearly settled their argument began it again more loudly. Fiona dropped out of the 'off-ground' course and flopped down beside Julie.

'They're stupid,' she offered. The offer was rejected with a sniff. Fiona had treated with the enemy, had made a separate peace and sealed it with the real leather writing case. Julie felt herself to be utterly alone. Her power had lain in her unthinking use of it; now she stopped to consider, and was lost.

On the Saturday following Margaret's last meeting with Nora, the occasion of the amazing discovery, Miss Byfield announced that this afternoon, after lunch, they would play the Game.

She was a lonely woman, Miss Byfield, made unreasonable by lack of opposition. Her father's declared hope for her – that she would marry and make some other man miserable – had not been fulfilled. She had chosen, instead, to manoeuvre herself into a position in which she was likely to become even more lonely and even less reasonable. 'If I tell you to jump out of the window you jump out of the window,' Margaret had heard her shout at a prefect who failed to carry out her instructions. She demanded unquestioning obedience and then valued only those children who refused to give it. The story was that she had once thrown a book at the head-girl and the head-girl had thrown it back. Not very long ago, either. Just before she was elected head-girl, in fact.

Miss Byfield had invented the Game. She maintained that she had played something similar as a girl, with her several brothers, and it had never done her any harm. But the Game, as known to the girls of the Mount, she had invented, along with the tradition that it was always played, once, in the September term. Everyone had to take part, from the head-girl to the newest new-girl. 'You can't learn everything in a classroom,' she explained to the younger members of staff. And the way in which it enabled the stronger to terrorise the weaker was, without doubt, an education.

The Game went like this. Everyone dressed for lacrosse and assembled in the junior playground. The juniors were at once unsettled. To see those great girls, bursting out of their tee shirts, herded into junior territory as though they were no more than children. What further humiliation might Miss Byfield not command? First years who failed to control their nerves and giggled were done for; second years knew better.

When the roll had been called Miss Fernihough went to fetch Miss Byfield and her staff. The head-girl and the vice head-girl stood at opposite corners of the playground, the rest drew back to give them room, and the choosing began.

The Prefect was one of the first to be chosen. There were six prefects, but to Margaret the large girl with the orange-peel skin who had spoiled the comfortable darkness of the boxes for her was always the Prefect. She watched the head-girl smile and hand her the distinguishing band of red braid. These bands made neat diagonals across the chests of thin girls; the Prefect's band rested horizontally, as on a shelf. Julie O'Connor had told them about the Game but she hadn't believed her. Now she believed her. Absolutely. She kept very quiet and made some calculations. There were one hundred and seventy four girls at the Mount. Forgetting that some girl unknown to her might be sick or gone to the dentist or having a music exam she worked it out that she could be last or next-to-last to be chosen. It seemed likely that she would fight it out with Charlene Parsons who was small for her age, wore glasses, and was already crying. In this she was quite wrong. Once the prefects had all been claimed the head-girl and her vice worked their way through all the undersized juniors. Margaret herself was one of the first. She nearly got to be a Red Band, but the Prefect whispered something, laughing, to the head-girl, who then pretended to have meant Charlene, after all. This left Margaret standing in no-man's-land, mistakenly relieved; further consideration might have shown her that her best hope of safety lay in being on the same side as the Prefect, but she was called to be a Green Band and was glad of it.

When the choosing was done the first years were pushed to the front of the two groups. Miss Byfield took up a position from which she could address them both, and explained the rules. There didn't seem to be very many of them, as far as Margaret could see. Julie's account had been an accurate one. The Reds were to go about catching Greens and the Greens were to have five minutes start and any wounded were to go straight to Matron in Dispensary.

The new English teacher (an active member of CND) decided to leave. She had been wondering but now she was certain. A term's notice was going to be a bit tricky. She would have had to hand it in on her first day. She had in fact been tempted to do this and was presently cursing herself for an indecisive fool. If she left at Christmas and the woman complained she could offer to tell the agency about the Game. Would they, too, see it as educational?

'Setting them on to each other, it's like cock-fighting,' she hissed at her neighbour (music and cookery – "Just till we get our replacement dear.").

'Only not so fair,' the neighbour murmured. She had seen it last year.

The grounds of The Mount were ideally suited to the Game. The formal terrace and the playing fields on its south side would have provided little cover and were anyway out of bounds; the neglected shrubbery on the north side, crossed and re-crossed by little moss-grown paths, dank green snails'-trails of pebbles trodden smooth, winding about in the airless undergrowth –

that was a different matter. Rules didn't count for much in the shrubbery. The south side was for speech days and sports days, for public encounters between teachers and parents in which each surrendered to the other and the children swaggered about unchecked in the resulting truce; the really awful things that happened at The Mount happened in the shrubbery. People had accidents there. People threw themselves out of trees or into nettle-beds there. Charlene Parsons had got into trouble for taking her clothes off first in order to make a proper job of it and had been quite unable to explain why. Julie O'Connor was said to have rescued her. Even Charlene said it. Her mother came from Birmingham to visit Charlene in hospital and brought Julie a present. Margaret had learned to avoid the shrubbery.

Miss Byfield looked at her watch. 'Ready Greens?' she shouted. 'Good hunting.' She nodded to Miss Fernihough who stood beside here, sucking on her whistle like an aging baby. 'Come on Fern. What are you waiting for?'

Miss Fernihough blew and the Greens stampeded along the wide cinder track which led to the shrubbery. Margaret ran after them. She had the impression that they had received instructions and were running to order. When could these have been given, she wondered, beginning to fall behind. Not that it mattered. The fearful excitement of the pack quite failed to penetrate her dream. It had simply not occurred to her that she might join and be led, that this might be easier, and a lot safer. She had plans of her own.

For a while they worked well. She slowed to a limping trot, waited until the penultimate straggler had disappeared into the rhododendrons, took off her green band and crept back towards the playground, keeping close to the high privet hedge which lined the cinder track. When she had gone as near as she dared Miss Fernihough blew a second time. Margaret, inspired by fear, dived for the bottom of the hedge and fought her way through it to the shallow ditch beyond. It was a bit wet, and full of leaves. She burrowed into them and watched the feet of the Reds pound past, sending the cinders flying. Then, sustained by the joy of being one against the rest and winning, she crawled out of her ditch and made for the ha-ha.

This circled the terrace, separating it from the playing fields and extending, on the east side of the school, to the wall of the stable yard. If she were to creep along the very bottom of the ha-ha, close to the retaining wall of the terrace, she couldn't be seen from the school. And if she could climb into the stable yard she could hide in the bootroom. She didn't think Harris would give her away. Harris was nice. She dreamed for a moment about not giving Harris away even when tortured by Julie O'Connor and Harris thanking her. Finding that this took the edge off it somewhat she played it a third time without either Miss Fernihough or Harris's birthmark. This was the best of the lot, and made her careless. She decided to see if Harris was sweeping leaves from the tennis courts. On her way to the ha-ha. There was no reason at all to suppose that Harris, unblemished and waiting to thank her, would be in the tennis courts, but Margaret felt suddenly sure that he would be. She was really surprised to see Charlene standing alone by the net.

'What on earth are you doing here?' she said.

Charlene was still crying. 'They said I had to.'

'But why...' Margaret began. Plimsolls skidded on the hardcourt, a hot fat hand covered her face, other hands grabbed at her.

'Red or Green? She's a Green. Where's your band? She's a spy. She's Green, she's Green...'

The voice of the Prefect cut through their squabbling. 'Shut up and bring her here.'

Margaret was pushed through the weak place in the high wire netting which surrounded the tennis courts. The dusty hollow behind it, impregnable from the shrubbery side, made a perfect prison. Several first years were already huddled there; good-hearted ones mostly, lured to the tennis courts by the wailing of the Green's reluctant decoy.

'Right.' The Prefect was holding cricket stump and looking over-excited. 'Where's your green band?'

'It's in the hedge next to that path that goes to the other end of the shrubbery,' Margaret said. 'About half way along. Rolled up. Under some leaves. Shall I go and get it for you?' There was a desperate helpfulness about her which even made some of the prisoners laugh.

'Oh very funny.' The Prefect paced about in the confined space, perfecting her grip on the crickets stump with a jerky little movement, throwing and grabbing; every now and then she took a trial swipe at some trailing creeper which dared to hang in her path and the prisoners ducked. 'You can give me something else then.'

'What else?' Margaret asked. Before she could regret it the Prefect was standing over her, sweating and heavy, using the stump to push her back against a really prickly bush. 'I was only…' she protested. The stump began to imprint a painful red bar on her chest and the branches scratched at her bare arms and legs. 'I don't know what you mean,' she squeaked, outraged but not surprised by the unfairness of it all. 'You can have anything.' What, after all, had she got?

The Prefect released her pressure on the stump. 'Anything?' she said.

'Yes. Anything,' Margaret assured her.

'All right. Give me your knickers.'

The prisoners rolled about in the dust, shaken by spasms of

nervous giggling. Margaret removed her knickers. She dragged them over her plimsolls, caught one heel in the elastic, staggered and fell. Her fellow prisoners, shocked into a momentary silence by this last enormity, collapsed again.

The Prefect hooked the discarded knickers onto the end of her cricket stump and drove its point into the ground. 'Now shut up or I'll have everybody's,' she said. 'We don't like spies here, do we?'

Her prisoners murmured agreement.

They're supposed to be on my side, Margaret thought. Bloody pigs.

The Prefect continued her pacing, radiant and breathless. She'd never been in charge of a prison before. Last year she got captured. She snapped off a dead branch to replace the cricket-stump and dreamed of punishments which even she recognised as beyond her power to inflict.

The prisoners huddled together. Most of them were bored and miserable. Some displayed a fearful tendency to crawl; a few had hung around, longing only to be caught, and now dared retribution in excited whispers. To all of them the outside sounds – of chasing, screaming, fighting, laughing – were enviable but remote. They had forgotten what it was like out there. The Green prison was all their world; they only half believed in any other.

Margaret crouched with the rest in the dark and dusty hollow. She hugged her knees, covering herself as well as she could with her games skirt, glad for the first time that it was so much longer than anyone else's, and hated the Prefect. She hated her completely, with passion. She prayed that God would strike her down. When he didn't she saw that not even God was on her side. Her hatred grew and spread. Now it included all the girls and all the teachers, now it reached out beyond The Mount and accused her parents who had sent her away to live with strangers. It rose in a great flood and left her one small foothold on the very top of the highest mountain till it seemed that she would soon be drowned in her anger and it would all be their fault.

This was the thought that she had tried so hard not to think. This was the worst thing in the world. With the strength of extreme fear she dragged it to her, covered it up and hid it at the back of her mind. Who wants to be like them lot anyway? She asked herself, too proud even to use their language. Toffee-nosed.....bitches! Bitches was about as far as you could go and made her feel better. If Matron asked her about the knickers she would tell exactly what happened. Cheered by the prospect of revenge she looked up, caught the Prefect's eye and stared her out.

'Here.' The older girl woke from her dream. She uprooted the cricket stump and held it out to Margaret. 'You just put those on again. And watch it.' She sounded menacing but Margaret understood that she had lost her nerve.

'Oh Miss. Thank you Miss,' she said, odiously respectful.

The Prefect turned away, pretending not to hear. Little snorts of laughter, sweet as applause, showed that the prisoners understood it too. Margaret was triumphant. She scrambled to her feet, lurched about with the knickers half on and half off, pretending to be drunk, showing off abominably. She was clever and beautiful. They were stupid and ugly. Her audience tired of the performance long before she did. She squandered their small amount of goodwill as though she imagined a limitless supply of it to be at her disposal.

'Shut up and sit down,' the Prefect said at last.

'Yes. Shut up you,' the prisoners agreed.

The tennis-court catchers crawled out of hiding and reported to the Prefect. No one had come for ages and Charlene had stopped crying. Should they take her to the bike shed and try there? If the Reds hadn't got it. A spy was despatched to find out. 'It won't work if she isn't crying,' someone pointed out. The look which passed between the Prefect and the largest catcher made it plain that this was the least of their problems.

'Do you want a go?' the catcher asked, fairly. They ought to take turns with the best bits.

'No thanks,' the Prefect said. 'I'll guard this lot. I don't mind. Honestly.'

Margaret sat down again and curled herself into the smallest possible space. She had had enough of them anyway. They never played anything really interesting. She had much better ideas than they did. She turned her back on them and thought about Harris and Miss Fernihough. What if Miss Fernihough had a baby? If she was secretly married to Harris. She'd have to be married. She didn't know exactly what you did but she knew you had to be married. She wouldn't be able to keep it in the bootroom though. Margaret had this feeling, almost like knowing, that Harris and Miss Fernihough lived in the bootroom. Gran probably looks after the baby for them, she thought. In that big house.

The good witches gathered around the cradle in the front room of Bideawhile, presenting their Christening gifts of barley sugar and' lavender-scented tissues. That's why she takes us to the Prom on Sundays. To find out about the baby. That's why... Margaret rocked with pleasure. Ideas faster than you could think them, doors opening, light flooding in, carrying you away, miles away from all them lot and their stupid games. That's why Miss Fernihough was so annoyed when I wanted to talk to Gran. In case she told. Why the butler wouldn't let me in. Not till they'd hidden the baby. She looked down on her fellow prisoners from a great height. 'I'll tell you about Miss Fernihough's lover if you like,' she whispered over her shoulder, recklessly, to anyone who would listen. 'Tonight. Before lights out. If you come to my box.'

Chapter XII

Nora sat with Mrs Annerley and wondered when the war would end. She ought to be getting back. There was no knowing what those soldiers might get up to. Dutch some of them. And Polish. Well, it wasn't the same as your own, was it? She used to complain at first, to the officer. Made no difference. None at all. Could have saved her breath.

'Dirty devils,' she said, coughing and laughing together.

Mrs Annerley was glad Miss Shard wasn't there. 'Shush love. Don't. Have a little look at the telly. We'll be going up soon.' Nora's war had a lot to answer for. Ruined the end-of-season business, sent her last few boarders scuttling back to their homes, though what for goodness knows. Might just as well have stayed, she thought, from what they said on the wireless. Londoners some of them. She wrote to one or two, later on, when the raids got bad, but they never answered. By the time the soldiers came the place was empty. She walked by when she remembered, keeping an eye, but they'd boarded up the windows. She thought it might be the blackout. You couldn't be too careful, so near the sea. In her room, the attic room – hers and Maureen's that was – she had fixed up a frame for the skylight covered with black twill; four pegs swivelled round on long nails and held it in place. She got the idea from a leaflet. Made the wardens check it for her. 'No one's calling me a spy,' she told them. Spy-mania, some people had. They'd all seen spies. Standing next to them at the food office, pretending they'd lost their ration books. And

their identity cards. What did they think we were, stupid? Mrs
Piercey's sister had seen nuns. Landing on the Downs. Well
not actually landing. But she'd told the police and the Home
Guard sent up a platoon to investigate. They didn't find anything
but then they wouldn't would they? They always buried the
parachutes. It was well known.

The town was buzzing with strangers. Everything changed.
Ordinary things didn't seem to matter anymore. Nora and
Maureen took their aluminium saucepans and threw them onto
the sacrificial heap in front of the town hall; to be transformed, it
was generally understood, into aeroplanes. Betty worked at the
bank and spent every evening at the canteen. Serving char and
wads to the brutal licentious, she said, laughing. Maureen hated
to hear her talk like that. At least she's doing her bit, she said to
Nora. And then some, Nora thought. No good telling Maureen,
though. Betty was as near perfect as you could get. Sometimes
she wondered what Maureen would have talked about if she
hadn't had Betty.

'Her and her Pole,' she said suddenly, making Mrs Annerley
jump.

'What was that dear?' she asked, more from habit than any
hope of an answer.

Nora had been round at the shop the night Betty brought him
home. Lovely looking boy he was in his uniform. Didn't say much.
Just stood there smiling at them, smiling at Betty. She did all the
talking. They were going to be married. As soon as possible. Wasn't
it marvellous? She was so happy. Weren't they pleased? Could they
just see her as Mrs Glagowsky?' 'Pani Glogowsky – my mother-'
the boy said, smiling politely, and they laughed at his mistake.

When it became obvious, even to Maureen, that Betty was
pregnant, they had the kind of row that can only happen once.
Betty was seen to be someone else; not the daughter she had

loved at all. Maureen discarded the dream and redirected her considerable imagination to the cover-up. Betty had in fact married her Pole, only to lose him, tragically, within a week. Shot down over France, she said. It was a terrible time for these young people. Terrible.

'Maureen,' Nora tried to tell her. 'Who d'you think you're kidding' She wouldn't budge though. Nothing would make her. Bought the girl a wedding ring and wore a black arm-band for him when any fool could see it was all rubbish.

'It's the shock, she told Betty. 'What did you have to go and blurt it out like that for?'

'She knew. She must have known,' Betty said. 'Anyway. I'd've told her sooner if she'd listen to anything real for five seconds. Was it Dad leaving or was she always like that?'

'I thought you modern girls knew everything,' Nora said, ignoring the question. 'Facing landing yourself in a mess like that.'

Betty began to cry. 'Don't you start for goodness sake. It's bad enough Mum going on about war-brides all the time. Anyway I'm leaving. I'm not sticking here. I know what they think. Her friends. You can see it all over their faces.'

'Right, aren't they?' Nora said. 'What are you going to do then?' The baby was her desperate concern. They sat together in the shelter between the pier and the bandstand, staring at the sea. Coils of rusted barbed wire hung with seaweed prevented them from approaching it more closely but you could still get into the shelter. 'I've got a bit. Not much. It depends what you're going to do.'

Betty stopped crying and looked at her aunt. 'Are you offering me money to get rid of it?' she asked, shocked and curious in equal measure.

'I'm offering you money to go away and have it. If you've got any sense. Or guts,' she added, accusing herself.

'I got them from you if I have, Betty said. She gave Nora a hug. 'Honestly Auntie. I'll pay you back. If you could help me out this once. Only don't tell Mum. She'll go on for ever about it.'

'What do you mean, help you out?' Nora asked, immediately suspicious. 'If you think I'm helping you to....'

'Listen.' Betty weighed the likelihood of Nora's telling Maureen against the impossibility of getting the money from anyone else. 'I was going anyway. I know where he's been posted to. He didn't want me to know. His friend told me. But it'll be different when I tell him about the baby. I know it will.'

That's what your mother said, Nora remembered. And she was married to the man. Poor kid. She supposed there'd be no stopping her.

In the morning she went to the bank. A cheque wouldn't be any good. The child would need cash. She took it round in the evening with some corned beef she'd got on points and the rest of her meat ration. Hard enough eating for one these days, never mind two. She'd have to take care of herself.

Betty was dressing to go out. She sat by the fire in the back room, stopping a ladder in her nylons with nail-varnish. She looked flushed and excited. Nora gave her the money while Maureen clattered about in the scullery. 'You're never going tonight?' she said, guessing suddenly.

'No point in waiting, is there?'

Nora looked towards the scullery. 'Have you told her?'

Betty applied the varnish to the nails of her left hand. 'Tell her for me. Please,' she said. The words, spoken with a childish urgency, had nothing to do with the careful brushstrokes.

Nora drew breath to protest but Maureen came in, looking so happy because Betty had made a wonderful cake for them – without eggs, from a leaflet, with carrots – that she hadn't the heart. 'You're staying for supper Betty, aren't you?' she said, instead of what she had wanted to say. 'I've brought me corned beef specially.'

They ate around the fire. Betty looking so pretty, Maureen so admiring. 'It's like the old days,' she said. 'The three of us. Round the fire. Pigging it, Mum used to say. Do you remember Nora? How she hated us pigging it!'

They drew her into their make-believe world; she knew they should talk but they seemed so happy. It was not until Betty had left, the dishes had been washed and the crumbs swept from the hearth-rug that she managed to detach herself from the dream.

'What do you mean, gone?' Maureen shrieked at her when at last she found the words to explain. 'But…' she looked wildly about her for some weapon with which to counter this attack. 'She can't have gone. She…' Hanging behind the scullery door, half hidden by mackintoshes and the peg-bag, she spotted Betty's gas-mask She knew it was Betty's. She'd bought her the smart navy cover for the cardboard box, with a shoulder strap and her initial on the popper. 'She hasn't taken her gas-mask.' She stared at Nora for one moment of triumph. Then thought of Betty, bubbling her life away, drowning on dry land, like Frank told her. 'Oh my God,' she screamed. 'Get out of my way.' She snatched at the gas-mask and ran sobbing from the room. Loved a bit of drama, did Maureen, Nora remembered. Even when they told her that Maureen was dead she was unable at first, to control her irritation. Running down the steps like a lunatic, missing a tread in the darkness, falling against the railings. Or where the railings were. That was the trouble, they said. Hit her head on a little sawn off stump of railing. Never came round. Faded away leaving Nora with those awful last words. 'Maureen you're a bloody fool.' Yelled out into the street, in a thoroughly bad temper. While she lay there dying. We'd have made it up, she told herself, reasonably, but what was the use of that?

She couldn't even trace Betty to tell her. The officer had been quite nice about it but she had to see his problem, he said. There were an awful lot of Poles. Without a name there wasn't a lot he could do. He tried some names on her but they all sounded the same. This-offsky and that-offsky. She could ask the police, he said. But then Betty might be calling herself Madame something-or-other by now. With luck she might even be Madame something–or–other, poor girl. Perhaps it was for the best. Nora had not looked forward to telling Betty the manner of her mother's death. You couldn't have stopped her. Maureen all over, that was. Ruins the girl then runs after her shouting please.

Nora sighed deeply and frowned, unseeing, at the television. Years, she'd spent, propping up the pair of them. First one, then both. Maureen had always looked to her for everything and Betty soon caught the habit. You couldn't blame the child for that, she thought. It comforted her to find excuses for Betty.

But that first evening. She had needed some comforting, that first evening. Mrs Piercey had left Sunnyside the year before but she still came round sometimes. She came round that evening, Nora remembered. Very kind. Very kind she'd been. But what was the good of all that now? What was the good of anything? Behind the shock, and the grief, a doubt began to form. While she had pitied Maureen, despised her husband and despaired of her daughter, had they pitied her? For an empty life? No man of her own, not even a Frank. No child, not even a Betty. For all her youthful determination to be different it was Maureen who had taken the risks. 'Ah Flick,' she sobbed, while Mrs Piercey tried first tea and then brandy.

They expected her to be a bit knocked out at first. Mrs Piercey, the officer, even the soldiers. She expected it of herself. They were quieter with her, more distant, as though she inhabited a special planet, designed for mourning, to which, happily, they were strangers. But after a while they forgot, and expected her to forget. This she could not do.

She heard them calling to her and could not answer. A cold weight filled her limbs. Sometimes she forgot how to speak for whole hours at a time. She would sit in her attic room – hers and Maureen's – staring wide-eyed at where the sea would be if only the skylight sloped right down to the floor. They came and asked her things, ordinary things about money or repairs, small but vital things affecting the preservation of Sunnyside against the good time coming. She wanted to answer them but she couldn't withdraw her gaze from some chosen point, a little knot in the skirting, standing proud of the paintwork, or a turned wood pinnacle on the dressing table. She had to stare until her eyes were sore and dry and the questioner crept away, embarrassed.

Decisions were made, she didn't complain, they ceased to consult her. She cooked at night, the little she needed, to avoid them; they seemed to have more right to be there than she did.

Mrs Piercey was moving away, to be with her daughter.

'I know how I'd feel if it had been my sister,' she said, but she didn't. Neither did she consider that this was the proper way to go on. 'I don't like leaving you like this, you know,' she said. 'You've got to make an effort. Snap out of it dear. They'll take advantage. I've seen some.' And she would tell Nora about the latest pieces of wanton damage inflicted on the property of a friend in similar circumstances. 'We don't need Hitler,' she'd say. 'Not while we got this lot.'

Nora felt her leaving. It was the end of the old Sunnyside. She wanted to stretch out her arms to the woman, to hug her and thank her for helping, to laugh with her over their frequent rows, to take her out to the pub and stand her a drink, two drinks, three drinks, to cry about the old days and get hopelessly blotto. But she could not drag her eyes form the smooth worn knob of the left-hand dressing table drawer. So she said nothing and Mrs Piercey went unthanked to her daughter in the country.

She heard them clanking and thumping about downstairs. They had taken up the carpet, thoughtfully, rolled it up and stored it in the attic. All day long she heard them. She supposed they must be doing something useful but she didn't care to discover what it was. She went out to buy her rations, talked to no one, came back and ate them alone. Once, returning form the shops, she had wandered without thinking into the dining room. A huge wooden frame filled the centre of the room, stretched over with coarse dark net; young girls stood on either side, weaving a pattern into it with earth coloured tapes. They were laughing with one of the soldiers, who seemed to be in charge of this curious operation. They stopped when she came into the room and waiting for her to speak.

'Good morning, ma'am,' the soldier said, into the silence. His young neck looked quite raw, she thought. A girl on the far side of the netting glued a cigarette between vermillion lips and started whispering about for a match. Clearly she was holding up the work, whatever it was. The girl was young, and so pretty. Half her bleached blonde hair was folded back from her face in a golden crest as high again as her high forehead. The rest hung straight past her cheekbones into a rolled gold frizz. Like Betty, she thought, and felt, ridiculously, faint. They helped her upstairs, the soldier and another plainer girl. The laughter from the dining room followed her all the way from the attic. She didn't let them in, though. She wanted to say 'Come and have a cup of tea,' but she watched them hover awkwardly on the landing and closed the door, saying nothing. She knew this behaviour to be unfriendly and ridiculous. When they had left she tried to make herself go downstairs and invite the lot of them up to have tea with her. The girls, anyway. She supposed the soldier wouldn't be allowed.

But something fixed and frozen in her mind prevented her. She made the tea in the small pot and took some aspirin. Their noise made her head ache. She took a few more aspirin with the second cup and lay on the bed, crumpling the white counterpane. Then, because it seemed wrong to lie on the counterpane just because Maureen could no longer tell her not to, she got up, folded the thing neatly and placed it on the ottoman at the foot of the bed.

'Nora Gitting, you're a fool,' she said; decisively, as though the counterpane proved it, once and for all.

Mrs Annerley reached out and patted her hand. 'I think you've been dreaming dear,' she said.

The gentle touch confused Nora. Now what did they want? There was always something. Money for this, money for that. She didn't have any money. It was all Betty's money.

She had watched the post, waiting to hear from Betty about the baby. When a whole nine months passed with no word she despaired of the baby and waited only to hear from Betty. Of course it was up to her where she went. You could hardly call her a missing person. She was twenty three now and for all Nora knew a married woman. The police had enough to do. But she worried about the money. Like everything else in her life since Frank let her down Maureen had left it to Nora. Why not her daughter? Nora asked the bank manager to whom Maureen had entrusted her will. Why not Betty? It seemed that Maureen had not trusted Betty any more than she had trusted herself. 'She said she knew you'd see to it. I think she was leaving you Betty as well.' Very likely, Nora thought. Again, the undercurrent of irritation. Trust Maureen to think up a stupid arrangement like that and not even tell her.

The bank manager found her a buyer for the sweetshop. A greengrocer from London, bombed out he said, wanting somewhere quiet. It's quiet all right, Nora thought, but he made a go of it. She used to get her vegetables there. It hurt, but she couldn't keep away.

Not that it was always so quiet, she remembered. They went over night after night on their way to London. The steady drone of their engines and the erratic percussion of the ack-ack kept her awake often enough. But they never seemed to hit any planes and the planes never seemed to drop any bombs. Their town was too small for real war. Occasionally – if they had a few bombs left over, so as not to waste them – they'd chuck 'em out on their way home, just before they got to the Prom. Mrs Piercey's old place got hit like that. She came up from the country, specially to see it. Talked about the Hand of God and tried to persuade Nora to come and stay. She couldn't leave, of course. Betty would be bound to come the minute she left.

She often sat in that shelter. They'd taken the barbed wire away now. She supposed they knew what they were doing. Visitors came in the season. Walked up and down the Promenade, laughing and quarrelling, just as though there'd never been any war. Children shouting in the water. She only hoped they'd found all the mines. Terrible it was at first. Mines floating about in the seaweed like dumplings in a stew. And what else she didn't like to think. Someone had swum into half an airman, the top half, rotting away in a life-jacket. Nora frowned, trying to sort it out. She thought it might be a while ago, all that. She thought that she might soon go back to Sunnyside and knew in her heart that she would never go back to Sunnyside. They were kind, but they would keep her here. They could do it. They could make her stay. Somewhere along the way she had lost the right to protest. Handed it over in exchange for a warm bed and three meals a day.

Fair exchange is no robbery, they used to say, Maureen and her. Poor Maureen. How she loved that girl of hers. Betty in curlers, drinking half-and-half cocoa in the room behind the shop. Sharp as a pin and all self. Proper little madam. But could you get Maureen to see it? Sometimes she wanted Betty to come back just so that she could tell her about Maureen and how she had died as she'd lived – running after the girl. Trust Betty not to be there when she was needed. Getting out from under was her speciality. Even now she didn't come herself. Sent that child. Sitting with her in the shelter, large as life, pestering her for stories. Her and her Pole, Nora thought. I bet he told her a few. She began the wheezing, shaking laugh which so worried the ladies when they heard it first.

'You have to laugh, don't you?' Mrs Annerley said. 'What rubbish they do put on nowadays.' She was not convinced that Nora's laughter was a response to the rubbish but you never knew. Miss Shard was still in Mrs Fransey's room 'Did I show you the photographs of my grandchildren? My son's children?' she asked. She took them from her handbag and offered them to Nora.

After a moment or two she withdrew them, a little awkwardly, and put them back in her handbag. She was glad Miss Shard had not witnessed their rejection. She had a way of looking at the ceiling with her lips pressed together which said I told you so plain as a pikestaff. 'I think I'll go up,' she said to Nora. The film was over, Miss Shard would be back to collect her mohair stole, making some remark about it for certain. Checking up on her, finding out if she'd ignored her advice and shown Nora the photographs.

And then she liked to be in bed when Mrs Fransey brought the pills round. Yellow for day and pink for night. Her dolly-mixtures, she called them. She'd never been one for pills but you had to admit it, they were a blessing. Especially the two pink ones. She slept better now than she'd done since Jim died. Talk about sleep! She had her work cut out to get down in time for breakfast. 'Good night dear,' she said.

Nora sat alone and wondered when the war would end. A pair of bishops, seated in buttoned vinyl chairs, applied their personal brand of middle-eastern mysticism to the solution of yet another problem. Inner-city violence, they were doing tonight. They flickered away at each other in purple and black and white, baring their teeth in appreciation of each telling point, fairly glowing with protein.

A sweet-sour smell of dried urine and talcum-powder lingered in the ladies' lounge.

'Goodness it's stuffy in here,' Mrs Fransey said. 'Come along dear. Time you were in bed.' She helped Nora to her feet. 'That's the way. Ups-a-daisy.'

Miss Shard collected her stole and stood by to turn off the television. 'She could have gone up before this,' she said. 'She's not been watching it. It's a waste of electricity.'

Chapter XIII

The brief and only affair of Helen Fernihough owed its life to her father and Dave Harris's disfiguring birth mark. It was made possible by her desire to hurt the one and compensate for the other. That her father had been beyond hurt for some time made no difference. Neither did the fact that Dave Harris had known how to attract more than adequate compensation, over the years, of just the sort she had in mind. Between anger and pity she found all the justification she needed for this reckless departure from normality.

It came about as Dave had intended it should, right from his very first cup of cocoa. He forgot his cigarettes, again, the Sunday they met on the Prom. It rained, again. Over the second cup of cocoa he laughed at his inability to cook in spite of frequent attempts. Since his wife left him and took the children. Over the third he went on about the extreme cosiness of her little room and his own loveless pad. They watched the first episode of a three part serial together and planned to watch next week's over supper. She bought a slow-cooking electric saucepan, made him Irish stew and was in bed before the gravy had congealed on the plates.

It wasn't so surprising really. Apart from the birthmark, which made her loving an act of Christian charity – or very nearly – there was his accent. She conjured up her father, drinking whisky on Armistice Day, saw him cringe and was glad. What was so special about you? she thought. He's worth ten of you. There was condescension in it, spite, need, flattery and the extreme difficulty of saying no when asked nicely.

Dave, not fully aware of his advantages, was impressed. 'Where have you been all my life?' he asked her. No point in wasting original material.

'Here,' she said, working it out.

Once she had abandoned the difficult notion of love Miss Fernihough took to sex like a duck to water.

'It's easy,' she said, as though he had maintained that it was not.

'What did you think it took? O levels?' he asked her.

'No but, well, I mean, we shouldn't really be…it's wrong isn't it?'

'How'd you make that out?'

'I should have thought the burden of proof…'she began. No, that wasn't it. She began to see where she might have made her mistake. Got off on the wrong foot, so to speak. They had always said it was wrong and she had believed them. Why hadn't she been the one to demand proof?

'Aren't you supposed to love the person?' she tried again. Perhaps none of it was true.

'Thought I just had,' Dave complained.

'That's not love.' Miss Fernihough sounded shocked. Here at least she was on terra firma.

'Course it was,' he said. 'It's only a word, anyway.'

He was pulling away the foundation of her life, brick by brick. 'Well in that case.' She lay down and curled up against him.

The juniors were quick to sense the change in her. She didn't need them any more, she didn't care if they liked her or not. She didn't care about much, that November. She set homework that had to be corrected in class and her Spanish went completely to pieces.

'What's wrong with you, Fern?' Miss Byfield asked her.

Nothing was wrong with her. Her figure, her hair, her stripey pyjames, her cocoa, her loving. Dave enjoyed them all. 'Nothing,' she said. 'I'm fine.'

She would have admitted to being a bit taken aback when she heard that Dave was not yet divorced from the wife who had left him and taken the children. Not that she expected him to marry her for heaven's sake. I mean, good lord, she was years older than he was. Three or four years, anyway. He must be over thirty. And thirty eight wasn't the end of the world. There were lots of very successful marriages where the husband was miles younger than the wife. But that wasn't the point. Surely to goodness two mature adults (she claimed the status with less than perfect confidence) could come to some sensible arrangement.

If Dave couldn't see her sometimes – (She never asked him why. The programmes on it always said to avoid being possessive.) – she watched her films, delighting in the difference; she was no longer standing on the outside with her nose pressed against the window pane. She floated through the days, avoided the bootroom, waited for him every evening and tried not to guess the end of the story.

When it came she knew that it was exactly what she had been expecting. It was then that she found out about love. She had not thought it possible to suffer so acutely. I simply wouldn't have thought it possible, she told herself. That things could change so. And all in a month. She had always imagined love to be a gentle thing. This was more like a disease. She felt ill, feverish, sick; the first time she saw him with the new English teacher she thought she was going to faint. In the bootroom, they were. Right underneath where... actually, she thought she was going to die. The prospect seemed to offer such a blessed relief from pain that she contemplated – not for long, and not without a horrified disgust that she could have given the idea house-room, as her mother used to say – she considered the possibility of accelerating the process with aspirin.

That was only on the first day, the day she found out, but it showed her clearly how low she had sunk. Suicide, indeed. She had always despised people who took this cowards' way out. With no thought for those they left behind. Miss Fernihough took stock of those who would be left behind and failed to find a single grief-stricken mourner. Miss Byfield would be worrying about the scandal. The juniors? She'd be something exciting to fill out their Sunday letters home. She thought Margaret Maildon might be a little sorry. She'd done her best with Margaret and the child did seem to be settling down. Settling down, she sobbed into her pillow. Is that it? I helped a child to settle down. She threw out the pillow because it smelt of his hair and sobbed again into the mattress.

'What's wrong with you, Fern?' Miss Byfield asked her.

'Nothing,' she said. 'I'm fine.'

After a week of avoiding him in order not to know that he didn't mean to explain, of sitting in the staff room every evening pretending to read until his bicycle was no longer padlocked to the stable gatepost, of trying not to overhear the fragments of gossip among the younger members of staff which showed how well aware they were of this latest development and – fresh horror – of wondering if they could possibly have known of her own involvement with Dave Harris, Miss Fernihough became ill.

The teacher who was sent to enquire if she were not coming to assembly reported that Miss Fernihough had flu. She had plenty of aspirin, and lemons for making hot drinks. It would be quite unnecessary to call the doctor; she wished only to be left alone. Miss Byfield visited her after assembly and found poor

Fern looking decidedly rough. 'Always the same with that type,' she said. 'Go down like ninepins. I saw it coming. She hasn't been right since the eleventh. Always upsets her, Remembrance Sunday.'

On the following morning Miss Fernihough, sustained by rage, rose again. No one thought she looked up to it. They felt sure she should go straight back to bed. Even those teachers who had been obliged to take her classes for her gave limited support to this idea. They need not have worried. Miss Fernihough's disease had entered a new stage. White faced, tight lipped, she came among the first years and made them know, as she had been made to know, what suffering felt like.

Tests, she gave them. Hour after hours she tested them, as she had been tested; one by one she uncovered their weaknesses, outstaring the insolent, humiliating the ignorant. Julie O'Connor, who maintained during junior prep that her neighbour had said a word beginning in F and ending in uck, was made to stand in the corner with her face to the wall. In the shocked silence with followed this staggering piece of lèse-majesté Julie was actually heard to sniff. One or two of them turned to Margaret, awaiting her reaction; Margaret bent over her work and pretended not to notice them. Stupid fat pig, she thought joyfully. Serve her right.

When the first years had all been tested beyond their strength, Miss Fernihough began on the notes. Page after page of notes, dictated at speed. Those who failed to keep up had to borrow from the fast writers – Margaret was one of the fastest – and copy them out during detention.

'She's gone bananas,' they assured the second years. 'You should see what she's like in class. Somebody ought to tell Miss Byfield.'

No one did, though. The team spirit, so warmly advocated

by Miss Fernihough herself in happier times, failed to unite the
first years. They quarrelled and joked and complained about it
but they didn't actually do anything about it. They were still
quarrelling about it when Miss Fernihough's disease entered
its third stage; quiet despair. She gave them chapters to read,
stories to write, and sat at her desk staring over their heads.
Silent, unreachable. The class returned to its former state of
comfortable anarchy.

Miss Fernihough was waiting. For what she couldn't say. She
heard the world going on outside; it was all very interesting,
but nothing to do with her. There was something she had
missed, some natural conclusion to the events of the past weeks.
Without it she was powerless to move in any direction. She
could no more regret the past than she could plan the future.
So she sat very still with her mind out of focus while pain and
pleasure receded and the first years got away with murder.

Then, on Thursday evening, during prep, it came to her.
Writing the date on the blackboard. Her period was late.
Two weeks late. She stood so long, still holding the chalk, not
moving, that the juniors began to giggle. 'I have to see Miss
Byfield,' she said loudly, making them jump. 'Get on with your
prep. And no talking. I put you on your honour.' She turned
away from them, blushing helplessly. Who was she to talk about
honour? 'Collect the books, monitors, and leave them on my
desk, if the bell goes,' she said, and ran from the room.

Alone in the corridor, she tried to be sensible. Good heavens,
she had missed before. She missed when her father died. It was
probably the flu. What flu? She reminded herself. Oh God, Oh
God. This was the worst thing. Worse than dirty underwear,
worse than being common. You're ridiculous, she told herself.
You don't even know. You're just guessing. It's probably the
change. I'll go to one of those places, she thought. In London.

Miss Byfield agreed to a morning off.

'I'll need the day,' Miss Fernihough said. 'It's something I've got to go to town for. Family business.'

'I didn't know you had any family business. Or any family, for that matter,' Miss Byfield said. 'Still, you look as though you could do with a break.'

Television, Miss Fernihough's link with the larger world, had given her quite a bit of useful information. You needed to take a urine specimen; it had to be mid-stream, taken first thing in the morning and presented in a labelled bottle. She boiled an empty honey jar for an hour, to be sure, and after a whole evening's agonised consideration wrote MRS FERNIHOUGH on the label.

She didn't possess a ring of any sort but thought that perhaps she would be able to keep her gloves on. The left glove, at least.

It was not until she lay down to sleep that all sense of adventure deserted her. She thought about her mother, about what her mother would have said. Then she got up again and made cocoa. Then tea. Then more cocoa. In the end she only just made it through till dawn – perhaps a night specimen wouldn't do? – overfilled the honey jar and had to write another label.

By the time she reached Victoria Station on the following morning she was exhausted. The girl in the television play had read an advertisement in the underground. On the escalator. Or perhaps the yellow pages? She decided to have a cup of tea and a bun before thinking about those places, and how to find one.

She slid her tray past the sandwiches and chose a Danish pastry. With icing. Well, why not, she thought, her spirits a little lifted by the extravagance. No point in saving. Who have I got to leave it to? Miss Byfield was right. No family business. No family. Her only hope of a family was floating – or not – in a honey jar in her shoulder bag. She opened the bag, re-tested the screw top and re-arranged the plastic bread-bag carefully around it. Of what they would look for and how they would look for it she had absolutely no idea. She thought it might be something to do with microscopes. One drop of her urine, magnified a million times. Would it be clear, empty, barren? Or would it reveal a scatter of minute token embryos, neatly spaced as a Laura Ashley wallpaper, proof positive of the true flower growing within? Though she would certainly not have admitted it, Miss Fernihough was beginning to hope for the wrong answer.

There seemed to be no end of those places in London. She went up and down the escalator twice, once to make sure of an address and once to take down the phone number, just in case. She had been at the bank by nine-thirty that morning and had with her two pounds in ten p pieces and five ten-pound notes. She didn't think it could be more than fifty pounds, for testing. If it was they would surely take a cheque. She didn't like carrying large sums of money about; it was simply putting temptation in people's way, she always said.

It wasn't easy to find the street. She didn't like to ask a policeman in case he guessed and the A to Z she bought at the station book stall had such small print. You need a magnifying glass, she thought, and blushed, remembering the specimen. And the street itself wasn't much to write home about. Miss Fernihough could see that they wouldn't want a great shopfront, all bright lights and plate glass, but she had hoped for something a little more dignified.

She thought about the oak-framed picture on her bedroom wall at home. Pre-Raphaelite, surely. There was Gabriel, more beautiful than any girl, and Mary, crouched in the corner, plain with fear. She wondered why they'd put it there. Was that how her mother had felt? 'One was more than enough for me,' she used to joke. Perhaps she had meant it. Or perhaps the picture had been hung there to remind her that there were other less acceptable ways of becoming pregnant. A sudden longing seized her. She hung on to the chipped white-painted newel post and prayed to be restored, alone, to the safety of her gas fire and horse-brasses. Then she pulled herself together and began the ascent to the fourth floor.

The office itself was reassuring. Fitted carpet, magazines, a plastic flower arrangement, a receptionist radiating boredom. Miss Fernihough fumbled about in her shoulder bag.

'Er…should I…I mean do you want?…or shall I wait until…?'

The receptionist didn't smile. 'Name?'

Miss Fernihough blushed. 'Mrs Fernihough,' she said. She got out the honey jar, still wrapped in its bread-bag, and stood it on the desk. 'I thought…don't you um…?'

'Thank you. Take a seat please.' The receptionist took the jar away, went through the private door behind the desk and returned in a moment, empty-handed. Miss Fernihough was still standing there. 'Take a seat please.'

Miss Fernihough, struggling with the heart-thumping lie, took a seat. How could she have said it? How could she have gone up to that woman and said it? Mrs Fernihough. Why had she assumed this stupid pretence to be necessary?

The parental fortress, so lovingly and fearfully constructed around her, began to crumble. After all, she thought. They got it wrong about sex. Could they have got it wrong about babies? And being common and how things would look and what other people would think? Oh God, she had wasted her anger. They hadn't understood any more than she did; perhaps less. A different and more desperate longing overtook her. To come out into the open, breathe the air, belong in the crowd. She looked around her, seeing for the first time the white-faced young woman with her sulky boy, the thin girl with sunken cheeks and flat straight hair, already nursing a child, the older woman – though not as old as herself – wearing a sheepskin coat, reading her own newspaper, wishing to be seen as separate and unconcerned. Miss Fernihough looked on them with the loving eyes of a convert; they seemed to her unreasonably attractive. Was it too late? Could she still join? A young woman in a white coat brought information. Names were called, money changed hands, envelopes were handed over.

'Mrs Fernihough?'

She jumped to her feet in a moment of senseless panic and remembered that her mother was dead. Now the receptionist smiled. 'Take your time,' she said, kindly. The telephone money rolled about the carpet.

'How stupid of me, I won't be a moment, so sorry...' Miss Fernihough collected up the coins and poured them into her shoulder bag. She found her purse. 'Do I er...oh yes, of course. Right you are.' The woman was telling her something and showing her a piece of paper. 'I see. Yes. Thank you,' she said, seeing nothing.

She was sitting in the station buffet again before she understood the meaning of the word. Positive. The test had proved positive. Proof positive. A surge of joy made it impossible not to smile. She tried to be afraid. To look ahead, to foresee the problems. Late pregnancy. Amniocentesis. Unmarried mothers. Telling Miss Byfield. It was no good. Joy obscured the view. She pushed aside her cup of stewed brown tea and stood up. Milk, she decided. I must drink plenty of milk. Still smiling, she went to join the queue.

Chapter XIV

Christmas could no longer be ignored. The shops had been full of it for weeks, Miss Shard said. It was like everything else nowadays. Just a commercial racket. They started earlier every year. Still. She'd found some very nice cards in the shop near the post-office.

For the ladies it was a time of trial. Where would they spend Christmas? Those without families knew the worst. They would spend it, as they would spend it every year now, at Bideawhile. To those with families such certainty was almost enviable. Miss Kess thought that perhaps this year she really would prefer to stay quietly where she was. Such an upheaval. Travelling over the holiday period was so difficult. The cold. And the roads. By the time the letter of invitation from her niece, her niece's nice professional husband and her niece's little girls arrived she had almost persuaded herself, if no one else, that this really was what she would prefer. 'But I can't disappoint them,' she said, and the ladies agreed that she couldn't.

It had to be faced; Christmas was coming, and you knew where you belonged at Christmas. For the rest of the year you could kid yourself but at Christmas time you knew.

'Well. That's you settled,' Miss Shard said.

Miss Kess tried to replace the letter in its envelope without letting anyone see that her hands were shaking.

Mrs Annerley had never given the matter a second thought. 'I'll be spending it with my son I expect,' she had said, whenever

Christmas was discussed. Any doubt expressed was a modest formality. Goodness, she thought. Where else? But now she wondered. Nothing had been said about Christmas. Nothing arranged. Of course, they'd probably taken it for granted. She hardly liked to write and ask. It seemed so unnecessary. Guy might be hurt. Upset, very likely. Mother, she heard him say. Whatever were you thinking about? No, she couldn't write. Besides. She didn't want to give the girl any ideas. Guy would want her to come, but it didn't always depend on what Guy wanted. Poor Guy, she thought. He hadn't exactly made it easy for himself.

She rearranged the tartan rug over her knees and returned to the justification of Guy. It was a soothing occupation, one to which she was quite accustomed. Plenty of people had felt the rough edge of her tongue before now. 'I speak as I find,' she always said. She prided herself on that. And she was always willing to admit a mistake. 'If I'm wrong I'll be the first to admit it,' she always said, though such revelation were rare enough and usually came too late to be of much use. But with Guy it was different. Guy was the whole product of her life, Guy, round-shouldered slippery ulcerated Guy stood between Mrs Annerley and the dark. He was her woman's work, never done, or likely to be, to her own and anyone else's satisfaction.

'What about you, Mrs Annerley?' Miss Kess asked her 'I expect that handsome son of yours will come and carry you off.' Her imagery came oddly from the junior library.

'I'm not bothered.' Mrs Annerley accepted as her due the suggestion of Guy as a knight in shining armour. 'I'm not going unless they've finished decorating. Always upsets me, the smell of paint. Painters' colic, they used to call it. You don't hear it now, do you? I don't know if it was the lead, but I couldn't be in the same house with it, let alone the same room.'

Miss Kess smiled and nodded and sighed in her warmest manner; she knew a well hedged bet when she saw one. Poor old soul, she thought, a reflection that would have enraged Mrs Annerley, whose energies were now almost wholly devoted to changing not the real world, but her perception of it.

'They're doing up my room. For the children,' she explained. 'Can't stop them growing up, can you?' This Canute-like absurdity was to represent the only alternative to her eviction.

'No indeed,' Miss Kess said. 'No, you wouldn't want to do that.' Tactfully she injected the element of choice. Leaving had been an unselfish and entirely praiseworthy decision; a sacrifice to the wellbeing of the younger generation.

Mrs Annerley felt safe enough to display a little, a very little resentment. 'It's all for the children nowadays, isn't it?' she said. 'Makes you wonder.'

'No wonder about it,' Miss Shard said. She had been seated at the desk to the right of the fireplace since breakfast, doing her Christmas cards. 'It's that wretched man Spock. I'd've had that book banned.'

'What book was that dear?' Mrs Annerley said.

Miss Shard caught a hint of patronage in the 'dear' and changed her line of attack. 'Good thing it's only once a year,' she said. 'The price of stamps.' She squared up a pile of envelopes, each containing one of the very nice cards. These are all my friends, she wished them to understand. Have you as many?

'Gracious. You need a secretary,' Miss Kess said, automatically responding with what seemed kind.

'I didn't think you went in for that sort of thing.' Mrs Annerley spoke in honest surprise and then wished she could have bitten her tongue out. Me and my big mouth, she thought. 'After what you said,' she tried to explain. 'I mean, what a racket it all is nowadays.'

163

'It's more a matter of obligation,' Miss Shard said. Her smiled matched the wintry suburban landscape of red brick and white lace beyond the picture window.

Nora stared at the television screen. Mrs Shreeve snorted quietly in her sleep. I'm sure that's what she said, Mrs Annerley told herself. The budgie hopped about in the sand, fluttered upwards to the swing and pecked at its reflection. Just a commercial racket, she persisted. In spite of Miss Shard's convictions there was room for wonder.

She wondered, again, about Guy. Had they done the right thing? Education was all very well, but had it made him any happier? She unravelled the man, started again with her clever twelve year old and reconstructed him as a greengrocer. Helping Jim in the shop. Learning to drive, doing the deliveries. Taking over. Expanding. A nationwide chain of shops, supermarkets. Offices, meetings flying off on business trips. In no time at all she was back where she had started. He's a good son, she assured herself, preferring to accept the distance between them, however painful, as of her own choosing. You have to make sacrifices if you want them to get on she and Jim used to say. But for what? For that girl? She's never been any good to him, Mrs Annerley thought, suddenly bitter, and longed from Mrs Fransey to bring the morning pills.

'She's late with the pills, isn't she?'

'Miss Gosling's very poorly.' Miss Shard raised an eyebrow and sighed. 'I should think she's got her hands full.'

That's me properly told off then, Mrs Annerely thought. Wait me turn. How I'm supposed to know about Miss Gosling beats me. She was dimly aware of Miss Gosling as one of the wall ladies – shrunken as a stored apple, a funny old thing, wrinkled and yellow. 'What's wrong with her?' she felt bound to ask.

'Same as is wrong with all of us,' Miss Shard said. She bared her unnaturally perfect teeth, facing death with a smile for the pleasure of bringing its imminence to the attention of Mrs Annerley.

Miss Kess looked up from her knitting. 'Now dear,' she said in some agitation. A trolley rattled along the corridor. 'There. I thought she wouldn't be long.' She sank back into her chair, relieved of responsibility. Such a very strong-minded woman, Miss Shard. She'd be missed at Bideawhile. Sadly missed. It did not occur to Miss Kess that at eighty six it was a sadness she might well be spared.

Mrs Fransey eased the trolley over the non-slip rug and wheeled it to the centre of the room.

'Aha,' Miss Shard said, recognising the cardboard boxes on the lower tray.

'Yes,' Mrs Fransey said. There was a determined brightness about her. 'Decoration time. Now. Who's going to help me? We like to put on a good show for Christmas, don't we, Miss Shard?' She directed her brightness at Mrs Annerley. 'What about you dear? Would you like to help with the paper-chains?'

'Paper-chains?' Mrs Annerley smiled. It must be her little joke. 'You're surely not going to bother with paper-chains?'

In the silence a car door slammed and footsteps approached the house. Mr Fransey's voice could be heard in discussion with other male voices, quiet but urgent.

'We certainly are,' Mrs Fransey said, giving the faintest nod to Miss Shard's unspoken question. 'One moment ladies.' She hurried from the room.

'What's going on?' Mrs Annerley asked. 'Goodness, I hope poor Miss Gosling …' After an even deeper silence it came to her that poor Miss Gosling was known, by everyone but herself to be dying if not actually dead, and that her remarks were yet another infringement of the rules. Even Mrs Shreeve seemed to have guessed it, heaven knows how. An unaccountable urge to hit back possessed Mrs Annerley, a rage at her helplessness, a determination to have one more shot.

'You're never making paper-chains,' she said to Miss Shard, in a goading voice, heavy with jocular unbelief.

'I shall do it as I do it every year. For Mrs Fransey,' Miss Shard said.

She's lived for Dr Stacey and now she's going to die for Mrs Fransey. Mrs Annerley sniffed. Pity she never thought of doing anything on her own account. Her anger ranged out of control, looking for targets. Why couldn't the woman give them their pills? If the doctor had said she should have them she ought to have them at the proper time. The tears stood in her eyes. She wasn't going to make paper-chains. Catch her making a fool of herself. Let them get on with it. She thought with longing of the coloured strips, banded together in little bundles, red, purple, orange, green, each with a stamp-sized patch of glue on one end. They used to glue the whole strip, she remembered. Wasteful, really. Perhaps Miss Gitting could manage a paper-chain? With help. 'Perhaps Miss Gitting would like to have a go,' she suggested. 'It can't be good for her, sitting there like that. I don't mind giving her a hand.'

'You'll never get her doing anything useful in a month of Sundays,' Miss Shard said.

A month of Sundays was right, Mrs Annerley thought. Month after month after month of Sundays. All her life she had hated waste and here she was, ready and willing to throw them away. Goodness, she thought. There must be something you could do with them. 'No harm in trying, is there?' she said, holding up, for one brave moment, the weight of her seventy-eight years.

'You do as you like dear. It's a free country.' Miss Shard

returned to her Christmas cards. What some people did with their precious freedom was beyond anything, her smile implied.

Mrs Annerley held one hand with another, as if to restrain them from further useless action, and rested them in her lap. Then she closed her eyes. Doubt after doubt opened up in the darkness. Why had they done it? Because it was good or because it was difficult? It hadn't made any difference. They'd been dragged along by the same silly reasons as everybody else. Thinking they were fighting some wonderful battle. For what? We spoiled that boy, she thought. It wasn't his fault. What could you expect?

'I've just had a phone call from your son, Mrs Annerley. He's bringing the children to see you this afternoon.' Mrs Fransey stood over her with two medicine glasses, one containing water, one the little yellow pill.

'Goodness, I must have dropped off,' Mrs Annerley said. 'The children as well? That is a nice surprise.'

Mrs Fransey seemed not to regard it in that light. 'Yes,' she said, nevertheless. 'Well. We must get on with our decorations.'

The news of a visit and the yellow pill restored, between them, Mrs Annerley's nerve. She made several paper-chains and was trusted to put extra cotton wool on the Father Christmases. It seemed more sensible, after all, to accept the general opinion that Miss Gitting was happier, and a lot less trouble, when left to herself.

After lunch Mrs Fransey told them about Miss Gosling. She'd had a stroke. Only a small one. But of course she needed proper nursing and the hospital was the best possible place for her.

This announcement had quite a tonic effect on the ladies. Even Mrs Annerley was cheered. She was sorry to think of

Miss Gosling in the geriatric ward, especially when Miss Shard had described it to them, but she understood, for the first time, that Bideawhile was not the end of the line. She shook her head and sighed with the best of them. It was so true. You never knew when you were well off. And yet, and yet. This new understanding reintroduced the painful element of hope. The ladies' response to the removal of Miss Gosling, the animated way in which they set about the paper-chains after lunch, now seemed not cosy but desperate. As though they had known all along what she had only just grasped; the ability to manage was what counted here. No, no, I can manage, she heard them say. Their claim to Bideawhile depended upon it.

Opposing currents were causing a certain amount of turbulence in Mrs Annerley's thinking. One moment she would have a little stab at independence. A gesture at least. She would not make that woman's ridiculous paper-chains. She allowed the chain to slip from her lap and looked about her, half-smiling, half-defiant. But when Mrs Fransey stooped to pick it up for her she tore one of the paper links in her anxiety to repossess it.

'I can manage,' she said, and then felt perfect stupid because the tears would keep coming, would blur her vision and splash onto the coloured paper.

'Never mind dear. I expect Miss Gosling's upset you,' Mrs Fransey said kindly. 'Perhaps you'd like to give it a rest. We've nearly got enough anyway.'

Now nothing would persuade Mrs Annerley to stop till the last strip of paper had been joined to her chain.

Something prevented her from remembering that Guy was coming. With the children. She had to keep reminding herself that he was coming and how glad she was. 'The children too,' she said to Miss Kess, feeling that she ought to say something, not quite able to adjust to it. Why should he come, again, so soon after his last visit, so unexpectedly, with so little warning? She couldn't feel at ease with the notion. She hoped he hadn't anything bad to tell her. Well of course he hadn't or he wouldn't be bringing the children.

Again the opposing currents pulled her this way and that. Fancy fussing about a paper-chain. What had she been thinking of? Was she keeping hold of her self-respect or losing it altogether? Whimpering and whining like a peevish old woman. 'Oh I'm a silly old so and so,' she said, laughing, and sighed for her silliness. 'Don't know what my son'll say if he sees me like this.'

Dragged along, she thought, returning in spite of herself and with a growing sadness to the same idea. Following when they thought they'd been leading, joining in without even knowing. She could hear Jim, hear his voice, still with the little touch of Yorkshire after all those years down here. She could see him raising his glass at Christmas time – it must have been Christmas, they didn't keep it in the house, only for Christmas – 'Here's to us, there's damn few like us...' And they're all dead, it went on, but he usually left that bit out because of the boy. I must've been soft, she thought. There were millions. All dragged along feeling different. She allowed herself a moment of weakness. How would it feel, going with the tide, not fighting? Fatigue and the yellow pill were making surrender more desirable by the minute.

'Hello Mother.'

Mrs Annerley looked up in confusion, responding to a longed-for voice, not immediately able to place the source of it.

'It's me darling. I've brought the children. Didn't they tell you I was coming?' he sounded plaintive.

Like the time he made me that thing in woodwork and I couldn't guess what it was, she remembered. 'Of course love,' she said. 'I was only having a nap. Have you brought the children?' She leaned forward in her chair to look for them.

"Here we are Gran,' James said. He sounded aggressively cheerful. He had resisted this visit to the last but was now determined to be the best at it.

Clara hung back.

'Come along lovely,' Mrs Annerley said. 'Let me look at you. Do you know, I think you've grown!'

'I've grown,' James said, like a little chosen seedling happily spreading its roots. 'Half an inch since you went. I've got my own room,' he added, ramming home the message.

Mrs Annerley smiled. 'Have you love? Mind you don't stand in front of the television. Oughtn't we to be in the dining room?' She felt sure that they should. The appearance of her son and her grandchildren before the ladies was causing her to feel quite dizzy with pride and joy and altogether happier than was decent.

'She said we had to come in here,' Clara said, speaking at last.

'Who's she, the cat's mother?' Miss Kess said playfully.

Clara looked as though she might cry.

'Quite right.' Guy frowned at his daughter.

'Well she did,' Clara said.

James sniggered, quietly but audibly.

'That's enough,' Guy said. 'Anyway, never mind you two. It's Gran we've come to see, isn't it?'

It's your mother you've come to see, Mrs Annerley couldn't help thinking. I changed your nappy for you me lad.

The children pressed up against her chair, one on each side. They seemed to be waiting for something. They stared at their well polished shoes, at the television, at each other, at their father. Every now and then they would allow their eyes to flicker briefly at some new corner of this horrible place. There were these horrible old people, wrinkled and powdery, like a horror film when they creak open the ancient tomb and the mummy sits up, James thought. 'We're having Wimpeys and chips afterwards,' he said, hanging on. 'Dad's promised.'

'Goodness, we've only just come.' Guy signalled his disapproval and smiled smoothly. 'Now,' he said. 'Let's get comfortable so we can have a really good talk. I suppose we couldn't go upstairs?'

'I think she wants us in here this afternoon,' Mrs Annerley said. 'They're cleaning one of the rooms onto the landing. Miss Gosling's it was. She was taken very queer in the night.'

'Not…?' Guy said. She looked up and caught the fear, right there in his eyes, looking out at her. He laughed, quickly, but not quickly enough. So that's it, is it? she thought. You'll come to it same as the rest of us, like it or not. For a moment she felt a derisive pleasure in his fear. Only for a moment. Then the aching protective warmth flooded back and she longed to comfort him. Poor love. What a time he'd had of it. Throwing away his health on a treadmill to satisfy that girl. Her longing gave her the strength to take charge, to make a decision.

'We'll go and sit in the dining room like last time,' she said. 'Come on. Help me up. Make yourself useful.'

Miss Shard raised both eyebrows but said nothing.

Miss Kess felt driven to protest. 'Er…I don't think…' she began, and was glad to be ignored.

The party settled itself around a table in the window of the empty dining room, one used for serving, not laid for tea.

'Is there where you eat?' James asked her. They used to stay in places like this. For holidays. Before they went to Spain. She probably likes it if it's a holiday, he reasoned; it was easier to believe without the mummies.

'Guess what I've been doing this morning,' Mrs Annerley said, not hearing him.

The three of them looked at her. What could she do? What was there to do here?

'Making paper-chains,' she said, and lay back against the bent wood chair, laughing at the ridiculous admission.

Guy laughed with her, a little uncomfortably. Did he detect overtones of senility in her cheerful acceptance of such an unsuitable occupation? He must have a word with the matron, alone.

The children seized on the making of paper-chains as a piece of the known world and didn't laugh at all. 'We've got a huge red and gold one that opens out and says Merry Xmas,' James said. 'You don't have to make it.'

'And we're having a tree that reaches the ceiling,' Clara told her. 'When we go to the new house.'

'Shut up you idiot.' James looked hopefully at his father. Now she'd get it. After absolutely promising not to!

'What's that love?' Mrs Annerley said.

Clara's face was crimson with misery.

'Never mind,' Guy said. He knew he shouldn't have brought the children but she would insist. How could you expect them not to mention it? They'd talked of nothing else for weeks. 'I was going to keep it for a surprise, but...' Oh, what the hell, he thought. She's got to know sooner or later. 'Go on. Tell Gran the news.'

She remained quite still and smiled at them, receiving the news with a calm interest, no more. 'Goodness,' she would say from time to time, or 'Well, that will be nice, won't it?', as James, the spokesman, explained about his very own study for homework and how far the kitchen was from the dining room, a feature which somehow impressed him as the extreme of opulence, and how you had to have your own study to do Common Entrance and they didn't do it at his old school but they did at his new one... 'And we're going to have a pony,' Clara almost shouted, wanting her share.

'Won't the food get cold?' she worried, missing the bit about Common Entrance and the pony, while underneath, and all the time, she knew what he had done, and why.

Guy sat there, feeling the pain of it in his stomach. His look begged forgiveness. It's not me, he wanted her to understand. She won't have it and what can I do? Rows and arguments all the time. It's the children who suffer. If it were only me I'd like nothing better than... He heard the whining apology within himself and was sick with anger. Was he supposed to be afraid of his wife or something? Who made the bloody money anyway?

'I've been thinking,' he said suddenly, cutting across the children's competitive babble. He felt his heart thumping and wanted to lie down somewhere cool and quiet. There'd be months, perhaps years of resentment; she'd take it out of him as only she knew how. Cold bitch, he thought, keeping his anger on the boil, afraid that he might not speak, even now. After all he had agreed to this place...

In a perfect panic of weakness he drove himself on to make the offer. 'Look darling.' He leant forward and covered her hands with his own. Soft they were, soft and sweaty; not a bit like Jim's, she thought. 'If you're unhappy here we'll take you back with us now.'

'But Dad,' James and Clara began. Their mother's views had been made clear to them.

'I mean it,' he persisted. His voice warned the children to silence. 'There'll be more than enough room where we're going.'

Mrs Annerley had heard a talk on the wireless once. She had listened to the wireless a lot during the last few weeks before Bideawhile, trying to drown out their quarrels about a room for the boy. Had they assumed that she wouldn't hear or hoped that she would? Anyway, she was not sure if she'd got it right but it impressed her deeply. Leaves, the man said, were supposed to go brown. Leaves that didn't were sick. They clung to their twigs, obstinately green, and died anyway. Healthy leaves grew this little layer of cork between themselves and the branch until they had quite lost touch. Then they died. Heads you win, tails I lose, Mrs Annerley thought, but she could see the sense in it. It was the children who couldn't. They called it guilt these days. She called it pride. They couldn't bear you not to need them. They had to be the most important person in your life. Still. After all these years. She knew who the most important person was in Guy's life. Guy. What made him think she was any different? No, she thought, smiling reassurance at the children. Better to stay. There would be less to leave.

'Thank you dear,' she said. 'But I'm really very comfortable here – I don't think I could face another move.' She glanced away casually, not wanting to see his look of relief.

'But you'll come for Christmas, won't you darling?' he persisted, hating himself for sounding hurt by her refusal.

'Oh yes. I'll come for Christmas. Thank you dear,' she added, doing her best to comfort him in his duplicity. She didn't think Christmas unreasonable. There was, after all, a limit to her strength.

When they had kissed her goodbye and see you at Christmas and he had taken his children to find Wimpeys and chips she sat with the ladies and began, again, to wonder. Was this the little stab at independence, the gesture she had wanted to make? Or had she just been up to her old tricks again, making it easier for Guy?

Chapter XV

Miss Fernihough had decided that the juniors should put on a Nativity play. Miss Byfield privately thought that sort of thing more suitable for infant schools but had been surprised into agreeing. What on earth had come over Fern, she wondered. Still, it didn't do to discourage initiative. Even at this late stage. Couldn't be the change, could it? She decided that parents were not to be invited. A purely domestic affair, staff and seniors only.

The juniors were getting used to surprises. At least it was better than tests, they thought. The memory of Miss Fernihough's reign of terror was still fresh. Those with blue bath towels posed virginally in front of mirrors and Julie O'Connor dreamed about riding up from the back of the audience on a real camel. Top king, with gold. She could scatter a handful or two as she went by. But when the cast list was pinned up on the notice board in the corridor about the lacrosse sticks she was glad enough to be first shepherd. She didn't cry about Margaret Maildon being Mary either, but only because they were all watching her to see if she would.

It seemed to Mss Fernihough an inspired choice. The last shall be first, she thought happily, rendered insensitive to change in the balance of power among her juniors by the absorbing miracle of conception.

Margaret had handled the affair of Miss Fernihough's lover with skill. For one whole week she kept them dangling. Then,

on the evening after the Game, holding court in her box, she had
told them what she now believed to be the truth. The lot. Miss
Fernihough and Harris being secretly married. Gran not being
her gran but Harris's gran. Who looked after the baby for them.
In that big house. Where she'd been to tea.

'She's lying,' Julie said.

'She's been there. You and Fiona saw her. You said so' they
told her. 'Anyway.' Anyway it's more fun believing her than you
they meant, so shut up.

In the glorious weeks which followed, glorious that is for
Miss Fernihough and her Dave, Margaret consolidated her
position. Everyone noticed the difference in Miss Fernihough.
She hardly gave them any homework, she didn't bother with
jokes, she didn't have favourites. You couldn't seem to wind her
up, however hard you tried. It would have been quite annoying
really, if they hadn't known the amazing reason. 'I told you,'
Margaret said. 'I saw them together on the Prom. Kissing. After
that she just started telling me things.'

Ah, but this is what she had waited for. Her own capacity
for belief was irresistible. They sat with her, offered her sweets,
forgot that she was supposed to be their victim. They didn't like
her. She knew that, and she wanted them to like her, but still she
wouldn't join them. It didn't even occur to her to try. Hiding in
the ditch on the afternoon of the Game or sitting in the reading
room with five or six listeners, her plans did not include joining.
Let them join me, she thought, and made sure that they didn't.
She was the ruler of a powerful country, accepting their homage,
despising their foreign ways. The distance between them was
fixed and precious.

'But when did she have the baby?' someone objected. 'She
never even got fat.'

Such doubts merely acted as a stimulant to Margaret's

inventive powers. 'In the summer of course,' she said. 'You should have seen her in the summer. She was fat then all right.'

'You weren't here in the summer.'

'The holiday,' Margaret explained patiently. 'That's when we came to see Miss Byfield to arrange about me coming here and Miss Fernihough was lying on the 'crosse pitch. On a rug. In a swim suit. And she was absolutely enormous. She had a bikini on, a red one, and this huge stomach. Harris was lying next to her, rubbing suntan oil onto it,' she added, fluently and with conviction. 'He hadn't got anything on. Miss Byfield was furious and she made us go back into her study and made us wait there and have tea until they'd gone. They almost wouldn't let me come here, but Miss Byfield said it shan't occur again I assure you.'

'Wish it would,' someone said, and they went giggling off to spread this latest instalment.

Margaret watched them go. She didn't try to stop them. She didn't like them any more when they were friendly than she had when they were unfriendly. They still seemed just as stupid. Not stupid for believing the stories she told them; she believed those herself. Or at least she did while she was telling them. Stupid because they went around in a giggling group and looked at each other all the time to see if it was all right to think what they were thinking or do what they were doing and didn't think it or do it if it wasn't. They're feeble, she decided, and knew herself capable of moving mountains.

Home sickness still gaped in her mind like a black hole, ready to suck her in if she so much as looked in its direction. On the afternoon of the Game, crouching in the green prison, she had failed, just once, to ward off the worst thing in the world. She had thought about her mother and father, blamed them for sending her to this loveless place and hated them for it. Since then she had managed better. Even her compulsory letters home, written each Sunday and collected by the prefect on duty, the same one who handed out the chapel money, were written to strangers. 'You hear so much about this homesickness,' her mother boasted to friends. 'Not Margaret. You'd think she'd been on her own for years.' Privately she thought it unnatural. To be so little missed. Poor Margaret. She always had been an odd child.

As for Sheila Makepeace, Margaret thought her really peculiar. She'd cried for weeks and weeks, almost all the time except for lessons. Then suddenly she stopped. Instead of this boring lump with the red nose and the soggy handkerchief there was somebody different. Much nastier. Making mean jokes, cheeking the teachers, everybody's friend. Except mine, Margaret thought. She didn't want Sheila for a friend. She would really have liked to sleep in one of the corner boxes that the prefects had, even though it would have meant being alone in the dark. Better than Sheila pretending I'm not there when we could lie in bed and hold hands we're so close, she thought. Even now, when the others came into their box at night or crowded round her in the reading room, asking her about Miss Fernihough's baby, Sheila ignored her. Went about with Julie O'Connor and that Fiona as if she was a second-year and made snide remarks about 'some people getting found out sooner or later.'

Margaret didn't care. An audience was enjoyable but not so far indispensable. Whenever she found herself alone she returned, again and again, to this secret child. Wrapped in beautiful soft pink things from Mothercare – it had not occurred to Margaret that Miss Fernihough's baby could be a boy – cherished by the good witches of Bideawhile, protected by Harris (scarred fighting off acid throwing kidnappers), loved by

Miss Fernihough. She had tried saying to herself 'Mrs Harris', but at this, for some reason, her imagination baulked.

When the next extraordinary change came over Miss Fernihough the juniors looked to Margaret. First of all she was supposed to be ill and then she came back in this foul temper and started giving the tests on things they hadn't even learnt. Something awful must have happened, the said, hopefully. Is the baby dead?

'Of course it's not,' Margaret snapped at them. The idea made her angry. 'Of course the baby's not dead. It's ill,' she conceded. 'But it's not dead.'

She sat out the storm with the rest of them, promising to find out about the baby on Sunday. When, half way through the terrible week of Miss Fernihough's anguish, she withdrew into the third stage, the quiet despair experienced by her juniors as relief from persecution, Margaret was able to explain to them that the baby was getting better. Friday's absence was to celebrate its complete recovery.

Mis Fernihough had thought of the Nativity play on that Friday. She walked from the station buffet, in love with each single member of the hurrying crowed on Victoria station; she found herself a corner seat where she would not have to touch any of them, and thought of Christmas. Of annunciation and birth. Of joy and never being alone. Then she thought of the play.

On forms which demanded to know her religion and challenged her to define it in a half-inch box Miss Fernihough had always written C of E. Without a second thought. Now, seeking to prolong and wonder and postpone the decision, she turned to this unexamined area of her mind and found it cosily furnished with the most reassuring images. Life, as she knew it, was about to collapse about her. But not yet. She put aside fear and devoted herself to the manufacture of haloes. When the small amount of money Miss Byfield had allowed her for the production ran out she spent her own. Her room was hung with angel-tunics made from old sheets, sewn sides-to-middle and finally discarded as beyond repair. The gold painted haloes cut from cereal boxes dangled by their elastic from the horse brasses. Every evening of that week a list went up on the notice board and the chosen juniors were allowed to dash across the stable yard in the cold wet night air to try on costumes in Miss Fernihough's room. That Miss Fernihough should have a room and wash tights in it and hang them over the back of a chair at first reduced the juniors to helpless giggling, but they soon got used to the idea.

The amazing thing, when it came to it, was Margaret Maildon. The juniors had hated her, tolerated her, laughed at her weird stories, even half believed her. But on one thing they were all agreed. She was not one of them. She was ugly, and an oik into the bargain. Nevertheless. When she sat in front of the crib, her pale face with the snaky blue vein lit from below by a torch jammed upright in the straw, her thin hair covered by a blue woollen cloth, they adored her. The angels lined the stage, a double row, and hummed the tune of Silent Night; Julie O'Connor, itching in a striped blanket, knelt at her feet and offered a lamb. Margaret, unsmiling, ecstatic, accepted their adoration. The angels divided sweetly into thirds and it seemed to her that she might just be the Virgin Mary.

Miss Byfield was delighted. 'Well done Fern,' she said, shaking her by the hand. 'Come over when you've finished the clearing up dear. We'll celebrate with some sherry. Next year I'll invite the parents.'

The conflict was nearly unbearable. Tears stood in Miss Fernihough's eyes. To offer such praise, such equal intimacy.

Sherry with Miss Byfield – with Clarrie, she corrected herself. But to wait till now. Her cheeks flushed scarlet.

'What shall we do with the haloes Miss Fernihough?' the juniors asked her, clamouring round, glad it was over, hungry for supper. She only stared, so they piled them up on the piano like a stack of plates and made their escape.

Next year, she thought. Next year. She had fallen, she would be driven from the garden. Fear tightened her throat. How would she live? What would she do? She saw again the oak framed picture of the virgin, crouching, terrified. 'One was more than enough for me,' she heard her mother say with a grim smile. There was pain and disgust in that smile. And something more. She wanted me to go through it, Miss Fernihough understood. She was glad I'd have to go through it.

She began to pick up the angel-tunics from the bench at the back of the stage. She'd had one row standing on the bench. So that they could all be seen. They did look lovely, she thought, clinging to her triumph. She had heard the sudden silence as the dusty black curtains were drawn up and sideways by their lead-weighted diagonal cords and the tableau was revealed. It was all her idea, the tableau. Children move so awkwardly when you watch them, she thought. No one was to move. Just the old carols, so that everyone could join in, and the torchlight shining up from the crib. Lovely! That strange little face. Who else would have thought of Margaret Maildon, she asked herself, and for a moment she was safe inside the golden capsule of her success.

Margaret watched her from behind the black drapes on the prompt side. She was not hiding from the others. She wasn't frightened of them any more. But the empty stage was the saddest thing she had ever seen. Where had it all gone? How could it have ended? When the curtains parted in front of her and she felt the audience looking at her, loving her, she thought that she might die of happiness. It seemed quite possible that chariots might descend and draw her up to heaven and as long as they kept on looking at her and loving her she wouldn't have minded. Now there was only this pile of sheets and the cardboard haloes. She decided to pray every day and be so holy that they would have to choose her again next year, and every year. But how to wait till next year? She stroked the black drapes and inhaled the unaccustomed smell of make-up. (The torchlight takes all the colour out of her, Miss Fernihough had said. We'll have to give her just a touch.) Tears began to run down each side of her nose till they trickled into her nostrils and she began to sniff.

'Goodness, Margaret. I didn't see you there. What are you crying about? You were lovely dear. Just lovely. Now. Run along. Run along. The bell will be going soon.'

'Can't I stay and help you Miss?' Margaret said. 'I could carry the haloes. Back to your room.' She picked up the haloes and hugged them to her. On the other side of the curtain Dave Harris began to stack the chairs.

'Come along then. We'll get rid of that make-up. Cold cream, we need. You'll have to be quick though. We don't want to make you late.' Miss Fernihough picked up the pile of angel –tunics and ran down the little flight of steps from the stage. Margaret ran after her. Oh God I am not worthy, she whispered, but please let it happen again.

When she had removed Margaret's make-up and sent her off to join her friends – 'I expect they'll be waiting to congratulate you,' she said – Miss Fernihough went to Miss Byfield's study. It was a pretty room at the front of the main building, full of pale-coloured fabrics and pale water-colours, with down armchairs you could sink into, heavy floor-length curtains double lined against the cold and an open fire. Anyone who met Miss Byfield outside this room felt vaguely guilty when introduced to it, as though they had discovered, by chance, her Achilles' heel, and were intruding upon some undreamed-of sensuality. Her manner was brisk enough to dispel the impression in no time at all but that first moment was disconcerting.

Miss Fernihough had never got used to it. She threw herself down into the chair at one side of the fire and stretched her legs in front of her in simulated ease. 'Well,' she said. Brightly. Smiling with raised eyebrows. 'That was fun.' Oh God Oh God, she thought. What a stupid thing to say. Fun. I ask you.

'It was beautiful,' Miss Byfield said. 'You surprised me.' She nearly filled two large sherry glasses and handed one to Fern. Then she stood with her back to the fire, gazing at her own glass as though inspecting a specimen. A sheepy smell of scorching wool drifted comfortably around the room.

Miss Fernihough sipped at her sherry. Then, unable to think of what to say next, she sipped at it again. She was sure it must be very good sherry, but it made her glands ache and she could only refrain from screwing up her eyes by conscious effort. She didn't know what people saw in the stuff really. She would have preferred something a little sweeter. Or even a nice cup of tea. What with Margaret and the make-up she hadn't had time for one since lunch and she felt absolutely parched. She sipped away, determined nevertheless to enjoy it.

Miss Byfield refilled her glass. 'You're a funny girl Fern,' she said. 'Twenty years you've been here. Twenty Christmases. Then suddenly you get up and organise something like that. In a week. What happened?'

In a desperate attempt to control the angry tears which seemed to be gathering at the back of her throat Miss Fernihough gulped down the rest of her sherry. The result was the reverse of what she had hoped for. Control began to seem not only unattainable but positively undesirable. It was about time Miss Clarrie Byfield heard a few home truths. What does she think I've been doing for twenty years then? Lying on the sofa eating chocolates? 'I thought you enjoyed it,' she said, rather loudly. Goodness, was that me, she thought. This wood fire was making her face burn. Some people did all right for themselves while everyone else did their work for them with no thanks and precious little money.

Miss Byfield laughed. 'No need to go off in a huff,' she said. 'Cheers. Here's to next year.' She sat in the chair opposite Miss Fernihough, pulling up her tweed skirt, not crossing her legs.

'I'm afraid there won't be a next year,' Miss Fernihough heard herself say.

'Good heavens Fern, what are you on about?' Miss Byfield remained irritatingly undisturbed.

'I mean I shan't be here next year.' She could speak perfectly well except when her tongue got in the way. 'I'm handing in my notice.' It was just a matter of concentration. Ignoring the distant buzzing in the ears.

'But why?' Miss Byfield asked her, still smiling.

'Because I am expecting a baby,' Miss Fernihough said. Slowly, with dignity.

My God, it is the change, Miss Byfield thought. Poor old Fern. She had heard of women going like this. 'Now, really, dear….' She said kindly.

'Yes. Really,' Miss Fernihough rose above the sherry. 'I take it you think I couldn't be.' Twenty years' resentment boiled up and over. She struggled out of her armchair, a little unsteadily, and faced Miss Byefield. 'You think I'm incapable of behaving like a real human being,' she shouted.

This was exactly what Miss Byfield had thought. 'No no no,

of course not dear,' she said. 'But. Well. You must admit…'

'I admit I'm pregnant,' Miss Fernihough said more quietly. 'So I'm handing in my notice. I'm sorry it's so short. But in the circumstances…'

'In the circumstances.' Miss Byfield sat forward on the edge of her chair. 'I feel it my duty to tell you that you're behaving like an idiot. Have you given the slightest thought to how you're going to live if you leave here? The two of you,' she added, paying lip-service only to the ludicrous idea of Fern's pregnancy. 'And who's supposed to be the father may I ask?'

'No you may not ask,' Miss Fernihough said. She had never enjoyed anything so much. Not even Dave. Even in their revelatory love-making some little threads, some last connecting links with her parents and their talk of what was naughty and what was decent had held her back, prevented her from abandoning herself completely to the moment. This anger was different. The threads were cut, everything was possible.

'He's not thinking of marrying you then?' Miss Byfield said.

'He's married,' Miss Fernihough told her, with the happy air of one scoring a point. This really was the life.

Miss Byfield's face, set till now in an expression of derisive disbelief, showed signs of shock. 'Well. You're a bigger fool than I thought you were,' she said. 'I told your father…'

It was Miss Fernihough's turn to be shocked. 'You never met my father. He never came to anything. He never would.'

'Of course I met your father.' Miss Byfield drew breath and exhaled sharply. 'Really Fern. As though he'd sit and watch you run off here and never take the trouble to find out what you were letting yourself in for. I might have been everything he thought I was.' She laughed, a harsh unpleasant sound. Though what the hell it was to do with him, the sound meant.

Helen Fernihough looked back and was appalled. They had

cooked it up between them. Her life. The life with which she meant to prove to him that she was right and he was horribly horribly wrong. 'You couldn't have met him, ' she said. 'Not after...' Not after the terrible row on Armistice Day, she wanted to say.

Miss Byfield had regained control. She spoke kindly, with all the venom of her own wasted energy. 'He turned up the day after you arrived,' she said. 'You'd taken the juniors down to the Prom. We had a long talk. I told him it was up to you. The opportunity was there. Take the A levels at your own pace, go off and get a degree with a job here waiting for you. A headship,' she invented. 'A school of your own. I've got no one to leave the place to.' Now you see what you've lost, she wanted Fern to understand.

She leaned back in her chair, exasperated and a little ashamed. It was a bit late to call the doctor now. Better in the morning, when she'd calmed down. Poor old Fern. But a baby! These wretched hormones, she thought. Who'd be a woman? 'You've overdone it, Fern. Overtired, overstrained. I've seen it coming. Go and get a good night's sleep. We'll talk it all over in the morning.'

Miss Fernihough banged down her empty glass and left. She returned to her room and locked the door. She was sick with anger. What did they think she was? Some second best second rate nothing, to be pushed around and planned for? 'It didn't occur to them to ask me I suppose,' she said aloud, heavily sarcastic. And all the while, behind the anger she directed at Miss Byfield, her father, Dave Harris, at any one who might possibly be blamed for her life, there was the creeping certainty that in another moment she would turn it on herself.

'Oh God Oh God,' she moaned. 'How could I?' She pressed both hands against her cheeks, first the palms, then the colder knuckles. 'You've made a fool of yourself,' she said. There was some relief in coming out with it, first, before anyone else did.

She began to walk about the room as though she might be able to find a place in it where the feeling wasn't. After a while, passing the kettle for the fifth or sixth time, she recognised a familiar source of comfort. Once she had filled it and lit the gas it became easier to perform other routine actions. Lighting the fire, talking off her shoes, pulling the red and white check curtains. She even turned on the telly, without thinking, and then snapped it off again. What was flood and famine to her? She had her own disaster. 'What am I going to do?' she asked herself, daring at last to look ahead. 'I've got to decide what to do.'

Tea helped, but not as much as she had hoped. A dragging physical uneasiness seemed to be weighing her down; it was hard to separate it from the pain in her head. Did she really have a pain? She lay on the bed and knew suddenly that the pain was real. Oh damn, she thought, frowning in irritation. The curse.

Then she understood. She would not, after all, have to decide. The decision was being made for her. She sat up and looked wildly about the room. All the films she had ever seen of abortion, miscarriage, birth, of sweating women hanging onto bedposts, ran through her mind like a tape on fast-forward.

'Help,' she said quietly. She had meant to scream but the habit of discretion constricted her throat. Someone might hear. Instead she pulled herself together and began to undress. Good heavens, it was only three weeks late. Anyway, it was out of her hands now.

Miss Fernihough, who had always been better at accepting decisions than making them, began to accept this one, made by her own body without, apparently, consulting her. She tried to see it as the way back. Back to the time before Dave Harris and making a fool of herself...she groaned a little for the pain in her stomach and the awful memory of Helen Fernihough making a fool of herself. With a man half her age to whom she had meant nothing. Well I couldn't be expected to know that, she argued. Yes you could. Better to get it all over with at once. Of course you knew. Right from the start. You knew but you didn't care.

Anyway, it was over now. All over. It's probably just as well, she told herself, and was not consoled. She remembered faces. The women in that office, the young girl at her table in the buffet on Victoria station, the man who had looked at her ticket. When she had seen those faces she had been happy. The faces defended her right to be happy

She summoned up faces for the prosecution. Her mother, condemning. 'Well. You've got away with it this time. Let's hope you've learned some sense.' Her mother's friends, for whom an unmarried mother would always be a most enjoyable scandal. 'What! Helen Fernihough? You're joking!' Miss Byfield, derisive but concerned. 'Have you given the slightest thought to how you're going to live?' she had said. Miss Byfield cared what happened to her.

Slowly, slowly the older women went to work on the pain in her stomach and the pain in her head. She lay on the bed, a thick white towel under her, and watched the decision sliding out between her thighs. Her family. Like bramble jelly, she thought, looking down with interest from somewhere near the ceiling. Was that it? Was that all? Surely that couldn't have amounted to much?

Ashamed, she tried to mourn. Her only chance. Lost. Through no fault of her own, it occurred to her. There was something half-hearted in the lament. A stronger feeling altogether was beginning to lighten her darkness. She folded the towel over any remaining unpleasantness, carried it reverently to the bathroom and flushed it away; then she curled up between the sheets, hugging her shoulders, and sobbed with relief.

Chapter XVI

Nora's physical strength was a source of exasperation to Mrs Fransey. 'Looks like going on for ever,' she said to her sister. Nora could dress and undress herself. She could even be persuaded into a bath. The single room she occupied was wasted on her, but while she could manage the stairs it seemed pointless to risk upsetting the apple cart by putting her in the downstairs dormitory, built on at the back. Apart from hiding under the pier that time and worrying everyone stiff you couldn't really say that she was any trouble. 'She gets on people's nerves,' she told the doctor. Not, according to Dr Walsh, a sufficient reason for packing her off to the geriatric ward. 'Miss Gitting is my cross,' Mrs Fransey put it to admiring friends and watched Nora closely for any sign of a stroke.

The old lady's wanderings she defended as a matter of principle. 'She's at liberty to come and go as she pleases,' she said to Miss Shard. 'I'm not running a prison.' As she explained to her sister, she was the last person to wish the poor old soul any harm. But if harm resulted she was not going to be held responsible.

It was fortunate for Nora that the town had changed so little. She made her way with dream-like certainty through main roads and back streets, to the Prom, the pier, to the bandstand. Sometimes she came up against a block of flats where there should have been an alley; then she stood, surprised in some row with Maureen or a loving interlude with Flick, until her restless memory nudged her onto a different course, or a passer-by asked if she were all right. 'Are you all right?' they said, as if she really might be.

The walking eased the restlessness. While she was walking she still believed in change. That it was over, that she could change nothing was a realisation that plagued her more strongly when she was still. Of course, she couldn't keep walking for ever. And you were never far from a seat or a bench of some kind. The council had seen to that. Nora's favourite was the shelter between the pier and the bandstand. She had sat there with Arthur, with Andrew, with Flick; with Maureen, and later with Betty. Mind you, they'd changed the bench a few times. But it was the same shelter. Layers of paint had simplified its cast-iron decoration, the new concrete floor was littered with can rings and lolly sticks – but the same shelter. How could they all have gone when it was the same shelter?

Autumn had been rained off. It was now generally recognised to be winter. Most of the ladies had given up their walking, some till the nice warm spring weather, some for ever. Mrs Fransey's little breath of fresh air to blow the cobwebs away was thankfully exchanged for the warm used air of the Bideawhile lounge. 'Treacherous, that wind,' Miss Shard said, hugging her stole, and everyone agreed with her. Everyone, that is, except Nora. Nora neither agreed nor disagreed; but she kept walking.

'I don't know why you let her get away with it,' Miss Shard said to Mrs Fransey on Sunday night over tea. Talk of freedom was mere shilly-shallying.

'You try telling Dr Walsh,' Mrs Fransey said.

'Pity they don't all,' Jim Fransey offered battle. 'Stuffy! Cor! That room's like a birdcage.'

'A little cake dear?' Mrs Fransey ignored the challenge. They didn't want any more of that thank you. What on earth was he talking about now, she wondered. A birdcage! No one knew what she had to put up with.

Nora had been out all afternoon. With her knitted hat pulled well down against the treacherous wind, her jumble-sale Burberry and her thick wool stockings, wrinkling round her ankles, she was what Mrs Fransey described as sensibly dressed. Only her shoes were not sensible. Elderly tennis-shoes, split at the bunions. 'Let me fetch those nice lace-ups,' Mrs Fransey pleaded. The hospital had provided the shoes, specially wide to accommodate the bunions. What if they called them in, unused, for repair? How was that going to make her look? She watched Nora flapping away down the wet street towards the Promenade and pressed her lips together. She didn't believe in having words. There was enough trouble in the world without words.

The Promenade was nearly deserted. The tide was out. A few gulls picked about on the shining mud-coloured sand, the rest huddled together on the bowling green. Nora made her way to the empty shelter and sat facing the sea. She wrapped her coat over her knees and leaned back into the corner, out of the wind. Always the same. Depressing, end of season. The place needed seeing to. Painting. Outside front at least. She'd have to manage the inside herself.

An old energy flared in the darkness, flickered for a moment and went out. Poor old Sunnyside, she thought. She had known so well how to make it go. Then, suddenly, she had known nothing. Sat there and let it slip through her fingers. All the work, all the caring. Wasted. I got what I wanted, she thought. But why? Why had she wanted it to stop? Ah, there wasn't much point in it all once Maureen and Betty were gone, she thought. The old Sunnyside, fully booked right through the season, the Sunnyside that came first and made Flick so jealous, had gone long before Maureen and Betty, but for Nora her sister's senseless death marked the beginning of failure. The other failures ran together in a downward spiral to that one disaster. Losing Andrew, losing Flick, losing the baby. 'Losing it,' she said, bitterly, to the seagulls. 'Throwing it away more like it.'

She saw her sister sitting in the little room behind the shop nursing Betty, so pretty and so proud. Maureen was always the pretty one, she thought. Maureen the pretty one, settling for second best. Nora the strong one, out for something better. Had she been aiming high or just plain cowardly? Too fussy by half, I was, she thought, and could find no comfort in any of it.

Arthur. Andrew. Maureen, she remembered. Guilty as charged. She imprisoned herself in the attic bedroom and the days moved on without her. That was Maureen's bit of money, she thought. Couldn't have done it without. There was some kind of justice in that. She wouldn't touch the half she had decided was to be Betty's half. Not at first. But Maureen's little bit of money from the sale of the shop had enabled her to hesitate when she should have made plans, made a move, made a fresh start. What was I supposed to have done, she wondered. She remembered the verdict but not the offence. I didn't take them seriously, she admitted. But then I never could believe in anything or anybody longer than five minutes. As for Flick, he was guilty if anyone was. A smile creased the powdery crevices around her mouth. 'I'm not taking the blame for you me boyo,' she said, suddenly truculent. 'You can look after yourself.'

The warmth was gone from the sun. A cold wind ruffled the shallow rock pools, far out on the mud-coloured sand. A crocodile of uniformed school girls wearing wellingtons crossed the parade and came chattering onto the Promenade. Nora watched them critically. Her mood of uneasy confusion focussed on the little girl left standing alone as the other children scattered. Drat the child. Come pestering her again. That teacher must be soft.

Nora had been many things to Margaret. An ally, however shaky, in a hostile country. A weapon against Miss Fernihough, a cosy children's telly gran, a secret with which to hold off Julie O'Connor and the others, good witch, headmistress, friend and protector to Betty's child. Now all these earlier visions fed the final legend. 'Are you going to find out about the baby today?' the juniors asked her, getting ready for the Sunday walk, and when she told them of course she believed it.

Margaret's place in Nora's mind was less clear. She was never Betty's child. Nora knew that. Nothing but a nuisance with her talk of houses. The old houses were empty. She knew that too. Some of the time she knew it. But the feel of Margaret, sitting beside her in the shelter, badgering, irritable, gave substance to the dream. Children. They're all the same, she thought, and waited for Margaret to join her in an attitude of scornful welcome.

'I'm not allowed to stay for long.' Margaret giggled hopefully. 'We're supposed to be having a quick blow.' She sat up close against Nora for warmth. 'Do you get it? A Quick Blow!' Nora failed to get it. 'We did a play and I was the Virgin Mary,' Margaret said. 'Did you do those in your school? I had this doll in an upside-down stool full of straw and a torch shining right up out of it.' They stared together at the turning tide while Margaret relived her triumph. Where the curtain went up was the best. She played it over several times, felt them looking at her, loving her. 'I'm going to be it every year,' she told Nora in a moment of desperate conviction. 'They said.' She looked up into

Nora's face, trying to catch her eye. 'You never told me about Betty's child,' she complained. 'Not properly.'

Betty's child, Nora heard. These were the memories laid down in middle life. Not the extremes of pain and pleasure seized on in childhood and cherished with a distorting disregard for the boring bits. Not the blurred foreground of Bideawhile. The middle years, their sequence a little disordered, their images sharp, accessible.

Never knew if she had the child, she thought. Fancy not even writing. And I don't suppose she had such an easy time of it that she couldn't have used the money. Perhaps her Pole really was a Count. 'Hmm,' she sniffed. 'Pull the other one.'

Nothing enraged Margaret more thoroughly than not being believed, especially when lying. 'You didn't. You know you didn't. I'm always asking you to and you never tell me. And I am going to be Mary next year. Miss Fernihough said. Because I did it so well.'

For a moment the attack engaged Nora's attention. 'What's that lovey?' she said. But the questions to which she needed answers had all been asked long ago. Maureen and Betty. What a helpless pair. "Lie down and I'll dance for you," her mother used to say. She had performed for their benefit and never guessed it till they left her. What was it I meant to show them, she wondered. They had moved in on her, filled the empty spaces with their needing admiring helplessness. I was a fool to myself, she thought. No good blaming them. She had blamed them though. She felt cheated. She had adjusted her life to the weight of them and their loss unbalanced her. The feckless way Maureen had willed her everything was a cheat. She was to be paid for her help. Account paid, settled in full. As if her little bit of money made up for everything, Nora thought.

She had hovered between guilt and irritation until, day by day, her capacity for living now was eroded.

'You ought to sell it dear. Find somewhere smaller, 'Mrs Piercey said. Up from her daughter's place in the country, visiting old friends after the war, shocked to see the change in Nora.

Nora didn't trouble to reply. Why should she explain to this stranger in navy and white nylon that the last unbroken thread was here; that even necessary excursions into the town for money or food endangered it and were to be avoided as far as possible.

'Or you could let rooms. Fit them with a few plates and saucepans and a Baby Belling. My son-in-law does that. The first floor rooms with their own basins, she remembered, giving the enterprise a shrewd professional sound. 'You can make a packet he says.' How anyone could let themselves go like that! She looks older than I do and she can't be sixty, Mrs Piercey thought. The place didn't smell clean. If there was one thing she couldn't stand it was a cracked cup. She had been fond of Miss Gitting, in spite of being imposed on all those years for a pittance. Her daughter was right; she shouldn't have come.

She transferred the cup of tea that Nora had made to her left hand in order to avoid the crack and remembered what she'd meant to ask. 'I've often wondered,' she said. 'Do you ever hear from your poor sister's daughter nowadays?'

'She's not poor. She's dead,' Nora said, after a long silence. She might have been joking but it was impossible to be sure.

Well, Mrs Piercey thought. Putting me right like that. If that's how she's going to... Anger mottled her neck, reddened the bony line of her jaw. Talking about the woman as if... Her cup rattled in its saucer. She replaced them both on the kitchen table and stood up. Fancy asking me into the kitchen anyway, she thought. What does she think I am?

Mrs Piercey left to join her daughter in the Pier Sun-Lounge and Nora sat on in the kitchen, letting her tea grow cold. She had not been joking. The line between thinking and talking was no longer clear. The habit of releasing a random sentence which now disturbed the ladies of Bideawhile had taken root in Nora's self-imposed isolation. On this occasion it had spared Mrs Piercey a deal of philosophical rambling on the shaky ground of Heaven being a better place; Nora's definition of her sister's present status, deeply offensive to Mrs Piercey, had been merely one possible conclusion to the larger argument.

On the whole Nora preferred being alone. She had never been anxious to please. 'They'll have to take me as they find me,' she said of her boarders. Occasionally a strong minded woman or a man accustomed to being made a fuss off would complain but it seldom came to much. 'I give them value for money and if they don't like it they know what they can do,' she told Maureen. The boarders knew, but very few of them did it. At the height of the season Sunnyside was packed with regulars. Now the effort to adapt, to fall in with some stranger's moods and fancies, seemed hardly worth the making. Mrs Piercey and her kind, full of themselves and their sensible plans. In the swim, going with the tide. They knew how to move with the times all right. Hurrying on to nothing and glad to do it. What was now compared with then, she'd like to know.

Nevertheless, it was soon after Mrs Piercey's visit that Nora decided to let one or two of the rooms. It hardly cost her anything. She had most of the stuff. Old, it was, but then she needn't ask much. The meters were the worst. She bought two small gas-cookers from the 'Houses Cleared' down on the Parade, but the business of getting them installed was nearly unbearable. Forms and letters and the gas-men trampling about. When it was over she put a notice in the sweetshop.

Nora had watched the failure of two greengrocers, a

hairdresser and a second-hand clothes dealer in Maureen's old place. Now, again, it was a sweetshop. Not like in the old days, everything weighed into paper cones. Half of it was ready-packed rubbish. And you paid for it, Nora thought. Still, it had a board in the window and you could put a postcard there for next to nothing. Nora's card went up with the child's bike for sale and the Karri-Kot in excellent condition. Two single rooms, suit business lady or gentleman. Own cooker, share bathroom and toilet.

The first woman to who she showed a room said she'd rather thought of something a bit – well.

'Well?' Nora challenged her.

'Cleaner,' the woman said, shocked into honesty. As she told her friend at the office, 'I don't know what came over me.'

Nora worked off her rage in an assault on both rooms with buckets of hot water, soda and strong pine disinfectant.

The second woman wondered aloud if perhaps there'd been illness in the house but allowed herself to be reassured. She took the front room, and a pale accountant, an acquaintance of the couple who owned Maureen's sweetshop, took the back.

It was the ghost of Sunnyside. The boarders, like Maureen and Betty, had been her audience. The lodgers were an intrusion. Nora had little regard for the present. She watched the business woman and the pale accountant come and go, took their money, paid her way. She keeps herself to herself, they said to each other and privately thought it just as well. Nora was not easy. There's nothing actually wrong with her, they agreed. But she is a bit odd.

Nora herself would have conceded oddness. Never was one for the crowd, she remembered. I can do without that. When, some years later, finally, and in spite of her refusal to answer a straight question – 'That's my affair,' she kept saying – she got her pension, she did without the lodgers too. Not that it felt like doing without. She abandoned them with a will, rejoiced in her privacy and drifted on to Bideawhile.

'Anyway I am doing it next year,' Margaret said. They asked you something and then went to sleep. It must be really boring being old. 'It's a pity we couldn't have had a real baby,' she added; she was rather pleased with this devious line of enquiry. 'But I expect it was too ill.'

Nora looked at her.

'Was it? The baby I mean. Was it too ill?' Margaret persisted. 'You know Gran. The baby.'

Julie O'Connor and Fiona were crouched down by the breakwater, laughing together. Every now and then they glanced towards the shelter and laughed more loudly.

The longing to show them overcame caution. 'Only the others want to see it,' Margaret said. 'And you did promise.' Anyone who asked you a question and fell asleep before you could answer it wasn't going to remember. And she did sort of promise. 'You could bring it next Sunday. For a walk in the pram,' she suggested. I mean, she argued. The baby might be Betty's child. Miss Fernihough's name might be Betty. It might easily. And she promised to tell me about Betty's child. 'You know,' she prompted Nora. 'Betty's child'

Nora struggled to her feet without a word and made off down the Promenade in an easterly direction. She should never have left it. What had possessed her? How long since she had seen the house, boarded up and waiting, a blind beggar of a place. A day? A week? A year? For all she knew Betty might have come and gone. She negotiated the few steps down from the Promenade and the crossing of the Parade. Sunnyside, she thought fondly. That was a laugh for a start. Wong side, facing north, it was. Not the back room, of course. She'd stuck to the attic room, hers and Maureen's, because it was at the back. They used to stand on the dressing table and try to catch a glimpse of the sea through the skylight. Trouble was, by the time they were tall enough she was too heavy and Maureen was too sensible. 'If it wasn't for the houses in between,' they used to sing, before Maureen put her hair up and got sensible. Or stupid, depending how you looked at it.

Why had she let them talk her into it, she wondered. That young girl, call herself a doctor. And the smooth talking little madam that came with her, all papers for this and papers for that, yattering on about houses and homes and annuities till she'd signed to make them stop. It was all down to that nosy bitch in the post office, she was sure of it. 'Leave your pension a week or two they come round and break your door down,' she said, searching the anxious face of a passer-by for some sign that he too deplored the scandal.

Nora took the broad main avenue which led from the sea, passing Maureen's turning on the left. First right, only a few yards further, was the terrace. Sunnyside was the fifth house on the right. She rounded the corner and faced without warning the end of the world. Sunnyside was down. Men balanced on the joists next door and pushed pieces of wall, still papered, into the cellar. They seemed to be enjoying it. A diagonal strip of skirting, stepped along its lower edge, defined the staircase to the attic, but the stairs had gone. A fireplace clung to the wall of a room with no floor.

Nora screwed up her eyes and followed the cream-painted diagonal to the attic landing; there at least she saw, or thought she saw, the familiar flowery stripes. A square of black twill, caught by its wood frame on a sealed off gas mantle, dangled for a moment and then sailed to destruction on the rubble below. She felt the shock of its impact in her stomach and was no longer sure if she were standing on the pavement or lying with the broken bricks.

'You buggers,' she shouted. Her voice, shrill with rage and anguish, was powerful enough. The men paused in their profitable bit of overtime and looked down. 'Buggers,' she screamed, panting. 'You buggers.' They laughed in a friendly derisive way, glad of a diversion, and got on with the job.

The residents of the terrace could hardly be said to fear death; they just didn't believe in it. Not publicly, at any rate. 'Come away from the window,' they called to their children who, drawn by the racket, were peering like young brides from folds of nylon net. 'Come away!' As though time were an unmentionable sickness from which, by cautious isolation, they might hope to escape.

'But Mum,' the children protested, not yet aware of the danger. 'What's she yelling about?'

Most of the locals had seen the old woman at one time or another. Muttering off towards the Promenade in her tennis shoes. Sad really. You'd think the D.H.S.S. would do something. Monopolising the shelter, hour after hour. I wonder the council doesn't do something. Frightening the kids, offending the visitors. Something ought to be done about it. When confrontation was unavoidable, the more gentle, more deadly, don't look it's not kind.

'Nothing,' they snapped. Honestly. You weren't safe in your own front room.

Nora tired of yelling and looked about for a means of entry.

'Piss off,' the workmen shouted kindly. 'Go on home you silly old bat.'

She pushed at the fenceless gate but the short front path was knee deep in debris and it wouldn't budge. She frowned at it for a moment and then walked away, not hearing their laughter.

She had come too late. Hurried to a death-bed and missed the goodbye. There had been things she wanted to explain, to forgive. Never said goodbye, she remembered. Arthur. Andrew. Flick. Maureen. Not even Betty. 'I shouldn't have given her the money,' she said. Lord knows what she'd used it for. I'll have to speak to Maureen about that girl. It's too late, someone said. You shouldn't have given her the money.

Whatever possessed me, she wondered again. Someone had the answer off pat. She thought it might be Nora, sitting in the attic bedroom, staring at the wall. Whatever it was, you must have wanted to do it pretty badly. Sunnyside empty, next to nothing coming in, and there's you throwing it about like the Aga Khan. If you ask me, the voice continued. Nora stood at the junction of the terrace and the broad avenue which led to the sea. These were not the answers she wanted to hear. If you ask me, the voice insisted, it was nothing but common jealousy.

She sat down heavily on the edge of a concrete cylinder planted with evergreens. It was getting difficult to breathe. She wished she was somewhere warm and dark. Jealous, she thought. What did I have to be jealous of? Someone had to help the child. Ah, what was the use? I wanted her to know what it felt like, being alone.

She leaned against the branches and thought that perhaps this was where she would stay; but after a while a stronger impulse persuaded her to stand up, to begin again, one foot in front of the other. Before the ladies were called to tea she was back at Bideawhile.

Chapter XVII

*K*nowledge is Power was the Mount's motto. Embroidered on the pocket of every blazer, enamelled on every prefect's badge. Its simple statement of the facts appealed to Miss Byfield. She thought it a splendid incentive to academic excellence. That the pursuit of power was a proper occupation for her girls she didn't doubt. She had taken on Margaret, accent and all, because she sensed in the child's awkward stance and hostile expression a nature which might end up at the top or the bottom of the pile but which would not be satisfied with the middle.

Margaret herself had never given the motto a second thought. Or a first. She wanted to be top. Didn't everybody? It was not a matter of why, but how. And if the boundaries of knowledge could be a little extended to include more interesting areas like nearly knowing or being practically certain, she was using hers in just the way the blazers advised. In less than a term she had got the juniors where she wanted them.

It seemed that she had only waited to be alone; she had never felt so free to dream. At home with Mum and Dad each action was to be accounted for, each statement double-checked. Not because they thought she was incompetent or a liar. Because they had appointed themselves her loving inquisitors, permitted, here if nowhere else, to know best. When Mr Bury read them the bit about sparrows not falling on the ground without her father she knew just what he meant.

'But the very hairs of your head are all numbered; he warned them. Margaret thought about the faded phrenology chart near the entrance to the pier. She hid the combings from her hair-brush in sweet papers and disposed of them in the lavatory where God, being a man, wouldn't look. It worried her sometimes. If you lost all the numbered hairs, would you end up like the picture on the pier with numbered spaces? They hadn't liked her at Fairmead Juniors. They didn't like her here. Only at Fairmead Juniors you went home.

Margaret was not absolutely certain that home was still there. It was becoming less substantial by the minute. The words 'Mum' and 'Dad' had lost their soft roundness, their smell. They showed her cardboard figures pushed about on wire rods like the ones in the Pollock's theatre she got last Christmas. Marvellous, with lights and everything. But not real. Of course, even when she lived there she never told them about Fairmead Juniors and Marlene Brandon. She meant, they might not have thought she was so marvellous if they found out that no one else did. They liked to be the same as everyone else. She'd noticed that. It was really funny. Margaret hated to be the same as everyone else. They wouldn't have let her anyway but even if they had she didn't want to be. She didn't want to be like anyone. She didn't mind being alone. She never really minded doing Marlene's homework as well as her own; it stopped them asking her all the time if she wasn't going to go out and play with some of her little friends. Or if she wouldn't like to have someone home to tea and was she ashamed of them because if so they would have her know that they were as good as anyone and she was not to forget it.

To Margaret this seemed unambitious. She was not as good. She was better. Still, she loved her parents, home was home, and They couldn't get you once you were in it.

It hadn't taken her long to appreciate, in retrospect, the

advantages of the system. Within hours of arriving at The Mount she had abandoned the dream of something different. Finding places to hide was merely a temporary measure; it was on the second Sunday walk, inspired by misery, that she had hit on the satisfying alternative. Dreaming. Well. Dreaming or lying, depending on where you were standing. She had dreamed at home. But at home she was fixed, unalterably, by adults taking bearings. Where they met, there she was. Here it was different. Between home and The Mount they had lost her. The known Margaret had got on the train at Victoria and someone unknown had arrived at The Mount. At first this new freedom felt too bad to think about. It was not until the second Sunday walk that she had found out what to do with it. That was when it started. Since that Sunday she had fooled Miss Fernihough, got her own back on Julie O'Connor, made them listen to her. It was better than belonging.

Sometimes she became quite worn out with it all. If her dreams were only dreams, the energy devoted to their construction was real enough. She dreamed dreams into living and living into a dull imitation of the real thing. 'Margaret Maildon. What have I just said?' her teachers demanded to know. Even when she could tell them it was as though she heard it for the first time. 'Very well then. But pay attention.' Irritating child. Seemed to think she didn't need to work.

Sometimes she missed chances because of the dreaming. She had hardly noticed the tentative advances of Fiona in the offer of her real leather writing case. She used it, envied it and returned it. Fiona went back to Julie. Margaret no longer wanted friends. Friends were part of the fixing process. 'But you said…' 'but I thought…' 'They couldn't've…' There wouldn't be much left of dreaming once you let friends in. Margaret was more used to manipulating support out of adults than making friends with children. She could have done with some allies. Miss Fernihough was all right, but a bit feeble. Occasionally she resorted to God, prayer being a kind of advanced dreaming. She saw God as yet another unreliable adult, but his very unpredictability made him worth a try. The allies she needed, now turned most frighteningly to cardboard, would love her later. If she thought of them at all – and she never did if she could help it – she saw them as dormant helpless creatures, hedged round with anger. Later she would love them.

Under the benign disruptive influence of Christmas discipline at The Mount was breaking down. Children who had thought that the term would last for ever became silly with relief. Sandra Dawson used up all the red and green chalk drawing holly round the blackboard and everyone boasted about what they were going to get until Fiona said she was getting a pony. There was a softening, too, among the teachers, brought on by exhaustion and the imminent surrender of their prisoners which made them vulnerable, unnaturally friendly, like guards on the losing side. Matron, who was hardly ever seen outside the sick-room or the dispensary, took to interrupting classes with packing lists and questions like 'Joan Simmonds, why haven't I got your navy knickers?' Those who had lost their games kit and borrowed someone else's all term became anxious. Some of them even looked for it.

Margaret counted days with the rest of them and wondered. What had gone wrong? Surely she must want to go home? Mum. And Dad, she reminded herself. Home. Nothing happened. I can't really have forgotten them, she thought. A term of unshared experience separated her from them. It's all right pretending here she argued, but what when I go home? She saw herself greeted, ecstatically, by the cardboard parents. Wold they think she was different? Not just cleverer. Sort of posh. I bet they'll be proud of me, she thought. She meant to give them their money's worth.

In the bootroom Dave Harris was working late at the end of term repairs. Miss Byfield never thought a few knocks did the children any harm but felt it her duty to return their property undamaged. Dave quite enjoyed mending shoes. He'd never done it till he took the job at The Mount, in spite of claims made at his interview. He managed all right. Got by with stick-ons from Woolworths and went to a couple of evening classes. Just till he got the hang of it. As he told his friend at the allotment, nobody had complained yet. He turned up the volume on his pocket-sized transistor radio and started on another repair of brown lace-ups.

The bootroom was not out of bounds, - the children changed their indoor shoes for lacrosse boots there, or fought their way out of wellingtons after the Sunday walk – but it was understood to be Harris's place. A door and one small window opened onto the yard, a steep staircase against the inside wall led up to Miss Fernihough's flat; the two remaining walls were fitted from floor to ceiling with shelves, divided vertically at regular intervals to provide a numbered space for every pupil, large enough to accommodate everything but wellingtons. They stood on the red tiled floor beneath the lowest shelf. A table in the centre of the room was stocked with all the tools of Harris's hastily acquired trade. A fan-heater whirred in the dark below the window; the room smelt of scorched fluff, polish and feet.

Dave stared without seeing at the lace-ups and thought about life. The unfairness of it all. First she leaves and takes the children. His children. She has to have them, doesn't she? She's their mother. Then she says she's got nowhere to live. So she says she'll come back. Make a proper home for the children. But only if he leaves. You're joking, he said, but they weren't, that's how they settled it between them. She had the children and the house. He had the bills. They call that justice, he thought. Daylight robbery more like it. Besides, he missed the kids.

Stupid cow. What did she have to do all that for? 'I'm giving you your freedom,' she said. Corny or what. The way she'd fixed it he'd got the freedom all right and no money to enjoy it. It was coming to him slowly that he had been well and truly done. There were times when the prospect of one more Chinese takeaway in front if the rented telly had him inventing reasons for forgiving her, even though there obviously weren't any. God it was awful though. The loneliness. He'd bored his friends beyond tolerance, at the pub, at the club, up at the allotment even. I'd sell my soul for a Sunday dinner, he thought, and how am I going to get through Christmas?

Then there was all the business about Helen. Standing there in that sexy towelling thing. What the hell, he thought, uneasily defensive; against all the odds, it was not what she had meant. She might not have known it was what she meant, he argued. But it was. So I did her a favour, he assured himself. Oh shit. Anyway. Time I moved on. Drive you to drink, this job. What with Carol banning the bomb and saving whales and Helen pretending she can't see me. I've had it here, he recognised. I'll tell the old girl in the morning.

Helen Fernihough had waited in the staff room until Dave's bike was no longer padlocked to the gatepost. She had sat at the window, correcting books, a position from which she overlooked the stable yard. Through the heavy net curtains she had watched him unlock the bike and wheel it away in the direction of the drive, experiencing such a rage of resentment against him that her nose ached with unshed tears. It was not for leaving her, the rage; it was for ruining the uneventful neatness of things. Years, she had spent, building boundaries, shoring up her defences. He had walked straight through them as though they didn't exist. Come crashing into the neatness, changing everything. She could hardly bear to look at the horse-brasses.

She had taken elaborate precautions to prevent their meeting, staying in the staff room every evening until she was quite sure he had left. Now she sat on her bed above the bootroom, longing to proclaim her independence of him by being there and not caring, to switch on the fire, the kettle, the television, to make her presence plain to him, dare him to explain and then refuse to listen.

Why had he come back? It wasn't just for cigarettes. She could hear him moving about down there, scraping his chair on the red tiles, playing that horrible music. He didn't care that she could hear him. Why should she care? But she did. She sat cold and still till the muscles of her thighs began to shake and she couldn't even bring herself to light the fire.

She had just unlocked her door and turned on the light when she heard him wheeling his bike into the bootroom. He must have seen the light. He knew she was there all right. It simply meant nothing to him. It never had. A flood of shame and hatred swept away the last flimsy props of her self-esteem. Only the certainty of being found out prevented her from killing him. Or at least having a really good try. Something hard and heavy, she felt rather than thought. Cracking open his rotten skull, smashing the smile from his uncaring face. She leapt to her feet, released from niceness, and was caught at once. Her body was on the side of destruction but its convulsive movement woke the gentle soul within. Good heavens, what was she thinking of? She stood for a moment and then flung herself back onto the bed, sobbing without restraint.

Down in the bootroom Dave listened and was not unmoved. Of course it wasn't what she'd meant. But he hadn't been able to resist making sure. He could see that what she needed now was a face-saver but his instinct was to comfort her with more of the same. Just thinking of her up there on the bed, with that amazing body of hers. Like a middle-aged schoolgirl. Amazing. Perhaps he should go up and say something. He certainly ought to say something . As he was leaving at Christmas. The prospect of Christmas with sweet-sour pork and chips and the rented telly nudged him over the edge. After all. His marriage came first. She'd see that. Anyone would. It was the perfect face-saver.

He had not known how close he was to the decision till he found himself making it. I'll go round tonight, he thought. A cold fear gripped his stomach, a feeling unrelated to digestion. Supposing he was too late? Supposing she'd got someone else? Moved in, spoiling the kids. 'I'll break his legs,' he said aloud. He dropped the brown lace-ups onto the table. Everything seemed simple. He felt more cheerful than he had in weeks. I'll go up and tell her, he thought. I'm not pissing about here any longer. I'll tell her and go.

Margaret had been keeping an eye on the table in the back hall, near the kitchen, where the cook sometimes left spare puddings after supper. Persistent hovering had won her a cold yellow slab of thick-skinned custard on pastry, her absolute favourite. Considering where she might eat it in safety she spotted the light in the bootroom. No one went there after dark. There wasn't even a rule about it. Holding the pudding under her blazer she listened to make sure that the corridor was empty and then nipped out into the yard. It was freezing. Her indoorshoes slipped on the cobbles and an icy drizzle stung her face. Why had she never thought of the bootroom before? She could have a nice talk about Harris. She had not so far achieved any kind of talk with Harris but it was bound to be different in the bootroom.

Dave was standing at the top of the stairs when Margaret crept in from the yard, her face arranged for greeting Harris. 'Come on love,' he was saying. He didn't seem to notice her at all.

'Go. Away.' They heard. If it wasn't Miss Fernihough you'd think she'd been crying, Margaret thought. She was almost overcome with the immensity of her good fortune. This was the real thing, grown-ups talking when you weren't there. Like knowing if the light went out when you shut the fridge. First the pudding and now this. Anything could happen.

'I'm not going away,' he said. So you might as well give in now as later, he meant. Margaret recognised the gambit. All grown-ups used it. She began to feel a bit sorry for Miss Fernihough. Not sorry enough to disclose her presence in the bootroom and put a stop to this delightful exchange, but quite sorry.

They waited to see if the gambit would bring her out. It did. The door was dragged open and Miss Fernihough stood there. Margaret could hear her breathing. She could see her feet, placed firmly apart as if to to resist or mount a physical attack. The knees beneath the skirt – Margaret could just see as far up as her knees, and that only by crouching a little and peering beneath the handrail past Harris's jeans – the knees seemed to be wobbling about over the feet. If legs could be angry this was what they would look like. Harris's legs looked more fidgety. One of them began to jiggle up and down, making the wooden stair-case judder.

'I'm not going away,' he repeated, rather boringly, Margaret thought.

'Oh yes you are,' Miss Fernihough shouted suddenly. Margaret took another bite of her yellow slab. This was it. She didn't care if they found her now. She wasn't going to miss this. 'Of course you're going away. There's nothing else here for you, is there? You've had all you came for. Of course you're going away.'

This repetition was a bit disappointing. She knew how difficult it was to think of anything bad enough but she would've thought Miss Fernihough with all her nouns and verbs and adjectives could have come up with something.

'Look,' Harris said. 'It was great. You know it was. Just great.' He sounded sad.

The suggestion that she had enjoyed, perhaps even invited, his love-making pushed Miss Fernihough over the top. 'You're like my father,' she screamed. 'You think there's one way of going on and you've got it. What did you think you were offering me? A quick look at Paradise? Do we all have to be like you?'

Dave thought about it. 'Most of us, love,' he laughed. 'Got to keep it going somehow, haven't we?'

'Well count me out,' Helen said. It came to her, beautifully, like peace after a long war, that she would willingly exchange all such Daves for the chance of communion with Miss Byfield over sherry and biscuits.

There was this long silence. Harris's leg stopped jiggling.

'I suggest that you leave. Now,' Miss Fernihough said. Margaret thought that she had never heard her sound so nasty. Not even to Julie O'Connor. Quiet but horrible; worse than screaming. 'And you can think yourself lucky – I certainly do – that I've lost your child.' She slammed her door on him, triumphantly miscalculating that she had hit him where it hurt.

'Christ,' Harris said, faintly. He sat down on the top step and saw Margaret. Her mouth hung open. Custard trembled on her lower lip.

'Oh fucking hell,' he shouted. He jumped up, ran down the stairs, pocketed his transistor radio and seized the handlebars of his bike, 'Stupid sodding woman,' he yelled back at the staircase. He bumped his bike out onto the cobbles, flung it down and came back for the fan-heater. 'Go on, hoppit,' he said to Margaret, not unkindly. He managed a smile. 'And shut the door.'

Margaret watched in silence while he stuffed the fan-heater into his saddle-bag and wheeled the bike away over the wet cobbles. How could it be lucky to lose your child? She only seemed to lose things she wanted. She supposed it would be lucky if it was something you didn't want. She looked fearfully after him, overtaken by a waking nightmare. Cardboard parents emerged from a dolls' house and tipped their cardboard baby into the bin. They walked back in again, doing a cheerful cardboard hopping. 'That was lucky,' the mother said. Surely they'll notice, she thought, but they didn't.

She began to wish that she hadn't eaten the pudding. Why weren't they all looking for it? She could help. She heard Miss Fernihough striding about overhead, heard her fill something from a tap, a rising rushing sound that ended with a squeak. She heard the man on the television telling Miss Fernihough the news as though nothing had happened, and a really good idea occurred to her. She would find it for them.

The juniors cheered, Miss Fernihough and Harris held hands, even Miss Byfield was smiling. 'They'd completely given up hope,' she said, 'but Margaret Maildon found it.'

The sound of a bell coming faintly through the cheers reminded Margaret that she was still in the bootroom. In another moment the juniors would be crowding up the back stairs to bed. She ran out into the yard, forgetting to shut the door. Wait till I tell them this, she thought. This is better than Christmas.

The juniors were disappointingly unimpressed.

'But I heard them say,' Margaret insisted.

'They didn't mean that. Everybody knows what that means.' Nearly everybody did, but no one was telling Margaret.

'What, then?' she challenged them. There were five children sitting on her bed and six on Sheila's but none of them would risk getting it wrong in public.

'It comes out dead,' Sheila Makepeace said. Her moment had come. 'My aunt lost her baby. In our house. They took her away in an ambulance and she cried for weeks.'

'Where did it come out dead?' they wanted to know. 'What room? Did you see it? What did it look like? Was there blood all over the place?' Who would have thought Sheila Makepeace knew anything interesting.

The spotlight swung away from Margaret. 'I know that,' she said loudly, storing the useful information. 'Everybody knows that. That's not it.' She seemed so sure. They looked at her, trying to guess if she were lying about all of it or some of it. 'I told you. I went over to the bootroom. After supper,' Margaret began to tell them again. Slowly, in a patient chanting manner, with raised eyebrows.

'Whatever for?' one of them interrupted.

'Because I'd got some custard tart and I wanted to eat it where no one'd take it,' Margaret snapped, forgetting to chant.

'When was there custard tart?' Julie O'Connor had refused a corner of bed. She stood at the entrance to Margaret's box, pretending to think that she was still their leader, deceiving no one. 'When was there? I didn't see any.'

'I got the last piece,' Margaret said. 'Anyway, I thought you weren't supposed to have puddings.'

Miss Byfield had dealt the death-blow to Julie's ailing supremacy. She had chosen a fatal moment to notice that Julie had become very fat. Seriously overweight, she told Matron. What were her parents going to think? Julie's habit of exacting tribute from weaker children had become, over the term, an indispensable consolation; a rich deposit of stolen sweets, cakes and pudding distended the pleats of her gymn slip and made it difficult to breath and run at the same time.

Matron was given the two weeks before the end of term in which to work a miracle. Julie was deprived of everything that made life bearable. It wasn't easy to maintain that a diet of undressed salads and grapefruit was a privilege, but she did her best; what destroyed her utterly was the prescription, by Miss Byfield, of remedial gymnastics. Every day at four o'clock, between afternoon school and tea, she was forced to perform to an ecstatic audience. She squeaked up and down the gymn in her plimsolls, galloping, running and jumping till the sweat ran, shouted at by the youngest member of staff (needlework and games) while, behind the black velvet stage curtains, Margaret and a chosen handful of juniors struggled with hysteria.

'Anyway,' Margaret said, defining Julie's altered status in one dismissive word. 'Anyway, I'm going to ask Gran. On Sunday.'

'She's not your Gran, she's...' Julie began.

'Oh shut up,' someone said. Quite a small girl.

Julie returned to her empty box and lay face-down on the bed. Killing people must be lovely, she thought. After she'd invented a few good way of doing it she sat up and wiped her eyes with the sleeve of her pyjamas. She opened Fiona's drawer of the dressing table and felt about under her handkerchiefs. A Mars Bar and some Rolos. I could tell her I saw Margaret Maildon taking them, she thought. She didn't imagine saying it and being believed. It was just something to think while she was unwrapping the Mars Bar. Once she had sunk her teeth into it, cracked through the uneven chocolate and filled her mouth with sweetness she didn't care whether anyone believed her or not. I hate it here, she thought. They're all bitches. She finished the Mars Bar, screwed up the paper and hid the Rolos under her pillow. When Fiona came late to bed, at the very last minute, after the bell, she was relieved to find Julie already asleep. Later Margaret heard her sniff and, since no one had explained to her about being generous in moments of triumph, smiled happily in the darkness.

Chapter XVIII

Miss Gitting had changed. Everybody said so. Goodness, what a change, they said. Miss Shard maintained that she had seen it coming. 'I should mention it to the doctor, dear,' she told Mrs Fransey. 'They go all at once when they get like that.'

On Sunday, after lunch, Nora took her last walk. 'You're surely not going to let her out?' Miss Shard asked. She watched Nora creeping away towards the sea and was loudly glad that she wouldn't be held responsible. 'I don't know what that girl's thinking about,' she told the ladies. She meant Mrs Fransey.

Nora's obstinate physical strength had faltered. Some inner spring had failed; nothing was replenished, nothing replaced. 'I shouldn't think she'll last the week,' Miss Shard said. 'It's just a matter of time.'

Time being in short supply at Bideawhile the ladies felt secretly relieved that Nora wouldn't be using up too much more of it. A week! Their own small store grew most hearteningly by comparison.

'Poor soul. What a change. And so sudden,' Miss Kess said.

Miss Shard sighed. Not sympathetically; with a certain of irritation. She'd already said that. If Miss Kess couldn't think of something to say for herself it was a pity she didn't keep quiet about it. 'She's not the only one,' she said. She raised her eyebrows, pressed her lips together and pulled down the corners of her mouth, directing Miss Kess with a nod to look behind her.

After a struggle with her knitting bag, which tended to slither from her lap at the slightest movement, Miss Kess managed it. 'Oh dear,' she said. She had rather hoped that no one would draw attention to her. Mrs Annerley was sitting against the far wall, next to the window. Her eyes were closed but her lips were not quite still. She might have been sleeping. They couldn't say.

'Won't you come and join us dear?' Miss Kess called to her, but she didn't answer.

'You've got to keep yourself in hand,' Miss Shard said. 'It's no good fight, fight, fight all the time. I've seen it before. They come in here, knowing it all, too good for this place or any other place. Before you can say knife they've got right out of hand. Don't you remember Mrs Beavis?'

They remembered Mrs Beavis.

'You surely don't think…?' Miss Kess was shocked.

'I wouldn't be a bit surprised.'

Miss Kess frowned miserably and touched her pursed lips with one finger.

'She's not listening,' Miss Shard said. 'They never do.'

Mrs Annerley thought about the apricots. Was it last year they made the jam? Fancy. Those apricots. Baskets and bowls and saucepans full of apricots, more than they knew what to do with. Jim getting stung, poor little chap. And Guy remembering vinegar. 'Winegar for wasps,' she used to tell him. 'Bicarb for bees.' Fancy him remembering.

'Mrs Annerley,' Miss Shard said loudly. 'Didn't you want to watch the film?'

They waited for an answer, Miss Kess hoping, Miss Shard with the air of one bringing a scientific experiment to a successful conclusion. 'You see?' she said. 'They're always the first. The awkward ones.'

Miss Kess was reassured. She knew the sort. Straight from

college, full of new ideas, wanting to change everything. The awkward squad, she used to call them. They never lasted long. 'I expect you're right dear,' she said. 'It just seems so…..' she rubbed one papery hand against the other. 'I expect you're right.'

Mrs Annerley smiled. Fancy him remembering, she thought. The layer of cork was growing nicely, to her own and Miss Shard's satisfaction, if to no one else's.

Mrs Fransey came into the lounge. Her brightness seemed to give warning of some careful plan demanding the ladies' unquestioning co-operation. 'Goodness that sun!' she said. 'You wouldn't think it was nearly Christmas!' She twitched the heavy velvet curtains across the right hand window, obscuring the view of the front path, and then, catching Miss Shard's eye, nodded.

'That'll be Miss Gosling's wardrobe,' Miss Shard said, when Mrs Fransey had left the room.

Miss Gosling had treasured her wardrobe. She had wished to leave it to her married niece. 'But Auntie,' the woman had said. 'Why don't we have it now?' 'I'm going to leave it to you,' Miss Gosling insisted. She refused to accept Bideawhile without her wardrobe. Mrs Fransey, reluctantly, took them both. It was in the early days and she needed the money. Now Miss Gosling was dead, the married niece was divorced, and the very last thing she wanted in her bed-sit was a wardrobe. Large, heavy, and not quite old enough. Would Mrs Fransey like it? In appreciation of all that she had done for her aunt. Mrs Fransey had learned to be firm with families. 'No need to give offence but you have to be firm,' she always said. Jack dismantled the wardrobe and she phoned her sister's brother-in-law, Ed.

Ed worked for the council and, to a certain extent, for himself. He was in charge of the crusher. There was almost no limit to what he would crush for a fiver.

'Mr Fransey'll be piling it up by the bins,' Miss Shard said.

Sometimes Miss Kess thought it would be better to be like Miss Shard. So very practical. She mourned the passing of Miss Gosling and her wardrobe until her glasses misted over and she had to take them off. 'It's the sound,' she explained. 'Mrs Fransey's very good about drawing the curtains but I quite dread Monday morning.'

'Don't upset yourself,' Miss Shard said. 'She's had it easier than most. Lived with that niece till she came here. The worst she's ever had to worry about is which bag she put her glasses in.'

Miss Kess stopped polishing her glasses and hid them under her knitting. Well, she thought. Well.

'Hardly any flowers. Mrs Fransey went to the funeral. One spray. From the niece.'

'Perhaps she asked specially. No flowers by request,' Miss Kess suggested. 'Like Mrs Bolton.'

'She only said that so we wouldn't see there weren't any.' Miss Shard's voice, sharp with spite, began to shake.

Miss Kess put her glasses on again. 'I'll never forget your telling me about the flowers that turned up for Dr Stacey,' she said. 'Well. Of course. A man like that who's done so much good in the world. You'd expect him to be appreciated. But they must have been beautiful. Beautiful.' Not so stupid that I can't be useful on occasion, she thought. That remark about glasses was uncalled for. She waited for Miss Shard to pull herself together, pleasantly aware of offering a hardly deserved comfort. You have to make allowances, she told herself. She had been obliged to make several for Miss Shard recently. Goodnesss, she thought. I don't know about Mrs Annerley. She lay back and folded her hands on her knitting bag; if crowns had been in order at Bideawhile Miss Kess would have been trying hers on.

The Sunday film flickered and died. Gunfire was replaced by a soothing burst of palm-court strings and a kindly voice assured them that violence would be resumed as soon as possible.

'Ate like a fighting-cock, my husband,' Mrs Shreeve said. 'Nothing but the best would do for him. I've seen him put away enough steak to feed a family. Think nothing of it. They don't know what a square meal is.'

Miss Shard and Miss Kess remained silent out of respect for this alien experience.

'Like a fighting-cock,' Mrs Shreeve insisted. She looked round at them as though they had tried to deny it.

'Tch,' Miss Kess said. 'When you think of it. But of course he was in the meat trade, wasn't he?' It was hard for her to speak of trade but she smiled as naturally as possible. After all, the poor man couldn't help it.

'They don't know they're born,' Mrs Shreeve said, suddenly scornful; the restoration of gunfire prevented Miss Kess from asking who. Oh no, she thought, frowning. No, no. I shouldn't have liked that. She glanced at Miss Shard to see if she intended to offer any comment on Mrs Shreeve's last remark, but Miss Shard had closed her eyes and was chewing away at her dentures. Goodnesss. If anyone had changed…

Margaret didn't see any change in Nora. Over the long September term she had made her own changes; Nora was cast in Margaret's play, finally and unsuitably, as Harris's gran, the only true protector.

'Hello Gran,' she said, cheerfully confident, to all that was left of Nora Gitting. 'This is the last walk. We go home on Tuesday. Miss Fernihough said you wouldn't be here. Listen. Gran. Have you got the baby? Only they've lost it, so I said I'd ask.' She searched Nora's face for an answer. 'Gra-an. You have got it, haven't you? I could tell them if you like.'

Nora's mouth moved silently.

'Say it Gran. Go on. Say it out loud,' Margaret encouraged her.

The lines around the moving mouth suggested a smile. 'Him and his precious pen,' she mumbled.

'Oh Gran,' Margaret wailed. She had to know. She had promised to tell them at tea.

For Margaret the juniors were always 'them'. Individually they seemed to her dull, lifeless, offering nothing; as a group they had become the indispensable audience. Julie's dream of blaming Margaret for the stolen sweets, while easing the moment, was never intended to convince. Margaret would have considered this feeble; her dreams were built to withstand the assaults of unbelievers. Founded on possibilities, propped and decorated with every kind of misinterpretation, both deliberate and accidental, they became real in the telling. She was at her best when challenged. Some of her most creative lying was achieved in the face of a sceptical audience. Gran could have the baby, she argued. Easily. That was probably it. Round the other side, in the pram.

The Promenade had been reclaimed by the residents. Families with children, pensioners with dogs, hardy young joggers, most of them on nodding terms, smiled their satisfaction at this wintery state of affairs. Miss Fernihough's juniors huddled round her by the bandstand explaining that they'd all die of cold if she made them stay any longer. 'Oh please Miss Fernihough,' they moaned. Julie O'Connor pretended to have frost-bite but no one took any notice.

On the landward side of the shelter a young mother rocked a pram and guarded the pile of white stones collected by her two year old son. Every now and then he would return with another find, place it with the rest and crouch over them, looking up for her approval. 'That's a lovely one,' she said each time.

Through the grimy glass which separated them Margaret watched the ritual. She could see right into the pram. There was the baby all right. Bundled up, asleep. They wouldn't be in Gran's shelter, she thought, unless… She looked towards the bandstand. Miss Fernihough was pushing them into a crocodile, blowing her whistle for silence or something. Any minute now she'd look round. They'd all look round at the shelter.

'Last one,' the young woman shouted. The boy clutched his last white stone as though she's meant to steal it, then flung it from him and lurched off towards the sea. 'Come here at once,' she shouted. He screamed with laughter and kept on running. His mother leaped up and chased after him.

In a minute it would be too late. Margaret ran to the pram and scooped out the baby. 'Here you are Gran.' She pressed it against Nora's chest, wrapped Nora's arms around it. 'Hold it properly,' she said. 'It's Betty's child.'

The crocodile was approaching the shelter. They were looking at her, they were all looking at her and Gran and the baby. She didn't run. She walked towards Miss Fernihough, smiling her most ordinary smile. 'Are we going already?' she said, in her most ordinary voice.

'Who's going to make a three with Margaret?' Miss Fernihough asked her juniors. There were several offers. Goodness, isn't that nice, she thought. It just shows how wrong you can be. She was happy to be wrong in the service of Miss Byfield, to see Miss Byfield's decision to take this awkward child so splendidly justified.

'I'll walk with you Miss,' Margaret said. She grasped Miss Fernihough's hand. Together they led the juniors back to The Mount.

On the Promenade the residents were crowding round the shelter. The young mother was crying, hugging her baby and trying to persuade them, rather incoherently, that no actual harm had been done and the poor thing probably meant to help. The residents were paying her very little attention. They had always known something like this would happen. 'Someone ought to fetch a policeman,' a woman said. 'Don't let her go. Go on. Somebody fetch a policeman.' Those at the back pushed forward for a better view. What of, they couldn't have said. Nora tried to stand but they cornered her, pressed her against the iron side of the shelter. 'Disgusting I call it.' A woman at the front lost her footing, put out a hand to steady herself and fell heavily against Nora, At once the crowd surged forward, leaning and shoving and pushing. In a moment of honest fear they hated her. They hated her unseeing eyes and her smell and her silence and most of all they hated her because she was old, and they would be old, and how could they keep on pretending there wasn't such a thing as death when she sat there like that and showed them that there was?

A jogger, back from West Point, offered to run to the police station. The crowd thinned. 'Well one of you ought to stay. They'll need a witness.' He jumped down the steps to the Parade, looking like someone who actually meant to find a policeman and bring him back to ask questions. The residents sobered up. By the time he returned, with the policeman, Nora was quite alone. The Promenade was deserted. He wasn't even sure he'd got the right shelter till he saw the pile of white stones.

'Come on Granny,' the policeman said. 'Chance of a lifetime. Ride in a car with a strange man. Everything your mum told you not to.' Nora lay back against the dark wooden slats, staring at the sea. She didn't move. He took her arm and hoisted her to her feet. 'Give me a hand down the steps,' he said to the jogger. 'I'll get her to the station. Phone around and see who's lost one.'

It was past tea-time when Nora was brought back to Bideawhile. The velvet curtains were already drawn,

'I knew she shouldn't have gone,' Miss Shard said. 'It's asking for trouble.'

Mrs Fransey had been interviewing a possible replacement for Miss Gosling. A small-boned shrunken little woman who pushed a tubular metal frame in front of her and looked from her son to her daughter-in-law to Mrs Fransey and then at her son again in a birdlike questioning manner, perky but desperate.

'We do have a room on the ground floor, Mrs Fransey was saying, 'but it is shared. Perhaps later, when…'

'Ooh, I can manage,' the woman interrupted her. 'Don't you worry about me.'

'But Mother you know you can't do the stairs,' the daughter-in-law told her. Really. They were only getting her in here because she couldn't do the staris. If she'd explained it once…

'I'll be doing the Palais-Glide once my hip's better,' the woman said. 'Never mind stairs. You see. There'll be no stopping me.'

'Mother,' the daughter-in-law warned, with an irritable emphasis on the second syllable.

The woman went pink and stopped smiling, but was prevented from abandoning her heroic stance and giving the girl a piece of her mind by the arrival of Nora between two policemen. Jack Fransey, who had been sent to answer the door, followed them into the office, grinning unpleasantly. For once he and Miss Shard had seen eye to eye. Fancy letting the old crate out. All on her own. Lucky it wasn't him spending half the night looking for her. He observed his wife's embarrassment with something approaching joy. 'Gave you a proper telling off, didn't they?' He said, when they were alone.

'That's enough of that,' she told him, but it wasn't. Not for Jack. He was still enjoying the joke some hours later when Miss Shard knocked at their sitting-room door.

Miss Shard had been playing Cassandra all afternoon. Every predication of the disaster which would inevitably attend that woman's being let out on her own was innocently parried by Miss Kess.

'Oh surely not,' she kept saying. The remark, intended to reassure, drove Miss Shard to a brooding fury. She even tried to persuade Mrs Shreeve to support her point of view, but succeeded only in convincing her that Nora had left Bideawhile to live with relatives.

'That's nice for her,' Mrs Shreeve said, not without envy.

Miss Shard breathed more heavily. Her silence was not restful.

'She's only gone for a walk dear,' Miss Kess felt bound to explain, as loudly as possible.

'I wouldn't bother.' Miss Shard was rigid with frustration and resentment. I live among fools, her look declared.

When the police car drew up outside the house some instinct informed her that justification was at hand. She was at the window pulling aside the curtain in less time than it took Miss Kess to turn round.

'What did I tell you?' she asked the ladies. Her voice was vibrant. A little vein throbbed at the side of her neck.' That's the second time we've had the police round. It's not what I'm used to.'

They listened to the sound of young male voices in the hall, a rare intrusion.

'They've brought her back,' she said. 'Just listen to that.'

Nora's voice was a little slurred but plainly audible. 'You buggers,' she was yelling, remembering Sunnyside. 'You young buggers.'

Miss Shard returned to her chair, rearranged her mohair stole around her shoulders and sat holding her handbag in front of her. Then she waited in grim repose for her Sunday evening cup of tea with the Franseys.

She had not expected to find an ally in Jack Fransey.

'I told her,' he said, when Miss Shard had delivered her complaint.

'Jack,' Mrs Fransey said, as though the use of his name were an acceptable alternative to swearing.

'Well,' he persisted. 'I did, didn't I?'

Mrs Fransey poured the tea in silence.

'Sending her out like that,' he said, pushing his luck. 'Wonder she wasn't run over.'

The teapot shook, tea splashed into the saucers. 'Go and get a cloth Jack dear, would you?' she asked him, hanging on.

'Proper telling off they gave her the police.'

'Oh get out,' Mrs Fransey screamed suddenly. In all the years of their marriage she had never let go. Never, till now. 'Get out, go on, get away from me, get away.' She banged the teapot onto the tray. 'Go on. Get out and stay out,' she shouted. Tears poured down her face like a blessing. She jumped up and tried to pull him from the sofa.

'She's mad,' he told Miss Shard. 'Look at her. Leave me alone you stupid cow.' Half up, half down, laughing and staggering, he caught the edge of the tray with his knee. Vera Fransey's best china slid to the floor and lay there, largely unbroken; tea streamed over the carpet, darkening spilt sugar as it went.

They watched it, appalled.

'Quick,' Mrs Fransey said. 'Get a bucket. Cold water. I'll stop it spreading.' She dragged out the News of the World from its metal rack beneath the coffee table and soaked up as much tea as she could, burning her fingers, not caring. 'That's it love. Quick. Down here,' she said, when he brought the bucket. Together they tried to save the carpet. 'Whatever will you think?' she asked Miss Shard, still on her knees, intent on salvage.

Miss Shard had finished with thinking. She lay back on the

sofa in an uncharacteristic attitude of abandon. Her legs stuck out awkwardly in front of her. One hand seemed to have dragged at her collar and now rested, as in a sling, on the mohair stole; the other lay limply on the sofa. Her face was the wrong colour.

'She's gone,' Jack said. He nodded as he spoke, and raised his eyebrows, answering his wife's unspoken question.

'Oh Jack,' she whispered.

'It's not your fault. Nothing you can do about that,' he said, answering another. Later he would know how to use the events of the evening. Just now he was being kind. 'You better phone the doctor,' he told her. 'It's all right. She won't bite. Go on. You go and phone. I'll straighten her out.'

The ladies of Bideawhile spent a quiet Christmas. Most enjoyable, but quiet. It was thought, in the circumstances, so very soon after the death of Miss Shard, that this was what everyone would prefer. Miss Kess went to the funeral with the Franseys, and on her return, during the really beautiful tea provided by Miss Shard's nephew – it was generally agreed to be really beautiful – told Mrs Fransey of her intention to stay at Bideawhile for Christmas. In the circumstances. These circumstances included the fact that Miss Gosling's replacement, unaware of the position Miss Shard had occupied at Bideawhile and not wishing to be unkind, as Miss Kess herself said – a little insensitive to the grief occasioned by her passing on, would keep suggesting a sing-song. To keep them all cheerful, she said. 'You've got to keep cheerful, haven't you?' she said. She and Mrs Shreeve had got together from the start. Two of a kind, Miss Kess thought. And once Mrs Shreeve got an idea in her head… It had taken two days to explain to her that poor

Miss Shard had died. 'Where's Miss Shard?' she would keep saying. 'Gone to her nephew I expect.' And then so upset when they had managed to make her understand. Dreadful. Really dreadful. No self-control, that sort of person.

Mrs Annerley had stayed too. The son wanted her to come to them for Christmas but Dr Walsh thought it better not. Since she'd settled down so nicely. Such a sensible woman, Mrs Fransey, Miss Kess thought. A word in time is all that's needed. She would have to mention the little matter of Miss Gitting sooner or later; perhaps over tea on Sunday evening?

On the morning after Nora's last Sunday walk Mrs Fransey had made urgent phone calls to Dr Walsh, the local hospital, the social services, to anyone in fact who might be willing to take Nora away. No one disagreed with her. They did see. She was a bit of a liability. And she would benefit from more specialised care. 'We'll get her assessed, they said. 'Then at least she'll be on the waiting list.'

'What do you mean, at least?' Mrs Fransey asked them. 'You've got to do something. She's upsetting my other ladies. Surely you have some arrangement for emergencies?'

At this point they usually began to define emergencies, with illustrations from case histories, and Mrs Fransey usually rang off.

Nora continued to sit at the window. She had forgotten nothing. She had her life, every minute of it, all muddled in her head like a heap of precious stones fallen from their setting. For a moment she lay in the dark salt triangle where the beach sloped up to meet the pier on the Promenade; then she was there, in the shelter, holding Betty's child, or pulling the blinds on a hot afternoon at the Plage, taking the cool carnation from Flick's button hole.

'Lived round here all her life,' Mrs Shreeve told the new lady.

'Supposed to have kept a boarding house. Never married. No kids. Hardly call it a life, would you? Sad, when you think of it.'

Lightning Source UK Ltd.
Milton Keynes UK
UKOW06f0751251015

261347UK00008B/59/P